**Praise for *New York Times* bestselling author
Lynsay Sands and the Argeneau Vampire series!**

'Sands writes books that keep readers coming
back for more. . . . clever, steamy, with a
deliciously wicked sense of humour
that readers will gobble up'
Katie MacAlister

'Inventive, sexy and fun'
Angela Knight

'Delightful and full of interesting
characters and romance'
Romantic Times

'Vampire lovers will find themselves laughing
throughout. Sands' trademark humour and
genuine characters keep her series fresh
and her readers hooked'
Publishers Weekly

D0812874

C333900159

Also by Lynsay Sands from Gollancz:

Runaway Vampire

LYNSAY SANDS

Copyright © Lynsay Sands 2016
All rights reserved

The right of Lynsay Sands to be identified as the author
of this work has been asserted by him in accordance with
the Copyright, Designs and Patents Act 1988.

First published in Great Britain in 2016
by Gollancz
An imprint of the Orion Publishing Group
Carmelite House, 50 Victoria Embankment,
London EC4Y 0DZ
An Hachette UK Company

This edition published in Great Britain in 2016
by Gollancz

1 3 5 7 9 10 8 6 4 2

A CIP catalogue record for this book
is available from the British Library

ISBN 978 1 473 20504 8

Printed in Great Britain by Clays Ltd, St Ives plc

The Orion Publishing Group's policy is to use papers that
are natural, renewable and recyclable products and made
from wood grown in sustainable forests. The logging and
manufacturing processes are expected to conform to the
environmental regulations of the country of origin.

www.lynsaysands.net
www.orionbooks.co.uk
www.gollancz.co.uk

One

Mary stifled a yawn, and then gave her head a shake, trying to ease the sleepiness closing in around her. Having slept in this morning, she'd started out late and shouldn't be tired yet, but it turned out driving for hours at a stretch was exhausting. It hadn't seemed tiring when she'd had Joe with her on these travels down to Texas from their home in Canada. The two of them had passed the time chatting about this and that and the miles had seemed to fly by. Of course, he'd also helped by plying her with coffee after coffee as well, as she had done for him while he drove. Now, though, it was just endless hours of long roads and nothingness.

Bailey sat up beside her to nudge her arm with a concerned whimper and Mary smiled faintly. Keeping her eyes on the road ahead, she reached down blindly to pet the German shepherd. It was as if the dog had a sixth sense when it came to her moods and was always offering comfort whenever Mary's thoughts turned to her deceased husband.

"It's all right," she assured the dog. "I'm fine. We're almost there. Another hour and we should reach our next stop." She forced a smile and sat up a little straighter in the driver's seat as she returned her hand to the wheel.

In the next moment, a thud startled the smile off her face, and Mary slammed on the brakes as the right wheels of the RV rocked over something in the road. Despite pretty much standing on the brake pedal, the vehicle continued forward a good distance before coming to a shuddering halt that sent drawers and doors flying open, loosing items to tumble out onto the floor.

Jaw tight, Mary glanced into the side mirrors, then the rear camera view as well. She'd hoped to see what she'd hit, but there were no streetlights on this lonely back road and the side mirrors only reflected darkness. As for the rear-view camera screen, despite the camera's night vision capabilities, she couldn't spot what she'd hit. She'd have to get out and look, Mary realized with a sinking heart.

"Probably just someone's trash tossed out and left on the road," she muttered reassuringly to Bailey. Certainly she hadn't seen anything before the thud, just the paved road revealed by her headlights.

Maybe she didn't have to get out and look.

Mary barely had the thought before she was pushing it away. Her eyes weren't as good as they used to be, but she might be more tired than she realized. Had she hit a deer that had lunged out of the trees? It might even have been a pedestrian in dark clothes or something. It was the possibility that she might have hit someone walking on the side of the road that forced her out of her seat.

Pushing the button to ease the driver's seat back several inches, she stood in the space she'd made and then paused, kept in place by Bailey, who had stood up and was now blocking her way.

"Move, girl," she ordered and the shepherd obeyed at once, trotting toward the door behind the passenger chair. Able to move now, Mary shifted to the right a few steps and opened the pull-up doors above the front passenger window to retrieve the large flashlight that was stored there. These doors were among the few that hadn't slammed open in the stop, she noted. A good thing too; she and Bailey would have taken a beating had these opened and allowed their contents to crash down over them.

Flashlight in hand, Mary moved up behind Bailey to reach for the lock on the door. It would have been easier without the dog in the way, but it was a dark lonely road out there and Mary was more than happy to let the shepherd lead the way. Not that she was that worried. Of course, she'd heard the stories of RVers getting jacked on lonely stretches of highway and such, but most RVers wouldn't take this route, they'd stick to the highways. Surely smart criminals wouldn't sit around out here for days or weeks on end waiting for that one idiot RVer who eschewed the highway for the more scenic route?

On the other hand, who said criminals were smart?

Mary asked herself as she pushed the door open. Bailey immediately bound down the steps and disappeared into the darkness.

"Bailey! Wait for me," Mary barked, rushing down the first two steps, only to pause on the last of the inside steps so that she could turn on the flashlight. She then swung the beam over the gravel and grass below, before stepping down onto the metal stairs that had dropped down when she'd opened the door.

Cool damp air slapped her face as she stepped down onto the side of the road, but Mary barely noticed, she was shining her flashlight around in search of her dog. Catching a glimpse of Bailey's tail end disappearing around the back of the RV, Mary muttered a curse under her breath and moved a bit more swiftly, which still wasn't very fast. The side of the road was uneven, littered with stones and weeds. The last thing she needed was to stumble and fall and break something in the middle of nowhere. Help would not come for a while out here, if at all.

"Bailey?" Mary called as she reached the back of the RV and was startled to hear the slight quaver in her voice. She sounded like a scared old woman, and the knowledge annoyed the hell out of her. Irritated now, she snapped, "Bailey! Get back here or I'll get your leash."

A bark sounded to her right, on the driver's side of the RV and she started in that direction, but paused when Bailey appeared before her, tail wagging and excitement in every line of her body. Once Bailey had her attention, the dog barked again.

"What is it?" Mary asked, and in her head heard

Joe's voice finishing the question with "Did Timmy fall down the well?" It was one of his little jokes. He'd had many of them and they'd always made her smile no matter how often he used them.

Pushing the thought away with a little sigh, she turned her flashlight to run it over the road behind the RV. By her guess it must have taken them a good twenty or thirty feet to stop, but it may have been as much as sixty or even a hundred. With 20,000 pounds of weight behind it, the RV wasn't designed for fast braking. Mary often thought that should be written on the front and back of the large vehicles. "Give wide berth, RVs need space to stop." It would certainly help with tail-gaters and those idiot drivers who seemed to like to cut her off on the highways. That was the reason she was on this lonely back road. She hadn't wanted to have to deal with aggressive drivers on the highway today. And perhaps she'd also wanted to avoid the stretch of highway where Joe had suffered his heart attack last year.

Pushing that thought away as well, Mary swung the flashlight from left to right on the road, frowning when the light didn't reveal anything but wet tarmac. It had obviously rained here earlier, the road was soaking and the air was heavy with moisture.

Raising her flashlight to see farther down the lane, Mary started away from the RV, but hadn't gone far before she began to feel unaccountably nervous at leaving the safety of the RV behind. It was silly, she supposed, but the night was so very dark out here. And there was an odd almost waiting quality to the silence around her. The only sound she could hear was the rustle of leaves in the breeze. Shouldn't there have been the chirps and hoots of crickets, frogs, and owls or something? For some reason the lack of those sounds bothered her a great deal.

"Nothing," Mary muttered nervously, and found herself easing backward step after step until she felt the bumper of the RV against the backs of her legs. She almost turned and hurried back inside the vehicle, but her conscience wouldn't let her. She'd hit something. The best scenario was that she'd run over garbage, but if that were the case there would be trash all over the road, and there just wasn't. The next best option was that she'd hit a deer or some other animal but there was nothing on the road. She hadn't just hit something; she'd run *over* it. Mary distinctly recalled the way the RV had bounced over something in the road. She'd think whatever it was might have got caught and been dragged, but there had been two bumps over whatever it was—front tires and back.

Of course, whatever she'd hit could have got caught behind the back tires and been dragged, some part of her brain pointed out, and Mary turned to shine the flashlight under the RV. The double back tires were a good six feet before the end of the RV and she bent at the waist to see more, then straightened abruptly when Bailey began to bark. The dog had moved up the passenger side of the RV and Mary stepped out beside it to find her with the flashlight beam.

Bailey stood next to the door to the RV, she noted, but the dog was staring off into the dark trees along the side of the road, body stiff and growling.

Mary promptly turned the flashlight beam toward the woods where Bailey had focused her attention. She caught a glimpse of something in the trees, but it was gone so quickly. It may have just been a shadow caused by her flashlight, she reassured herself. Still, something had Bailey upset.

Fear suddenly tripping through her, Mary swallowed and began to ease toward Bailey. She did so by shuffling sideways so that her back was to the RV and her flashlight beam and gaze could remain trained on the woods. It seemed to take forever to get to the door, but some instinct was telling her not to turn her back to the dark woods.

She wasted no time in opening the door and the moment she did, Bailey rushed in, galloping up the steps as if the hounds of hell were on her tail. That did not ease her anxiety. Bailey was not a cowardly dog. She was the type to rush into confrontation and stand between any threat and her people. The way she raced into the RV had the hair on Mary's neck standing on end as she scrambled up the steps after her.

Mary pulled the door closed behind her and locked it almost in one motion. Even then she didn't feel safe, though, and found herself eager to get out of there.

Ignoring the doors and drawers that had flown open during her abrupt stop, as well as the items now littering the floor, she tossed the flashlight on the passenger seat and jumped behind the wheel with more speed than grace.

Mary had left the RV engine running and now only had to shift into gear and hit the gas. An immediate clatter arose as the RV lurched forward and more items tumbled out of the open doors she'd neglected to close. There was also a loud thump as if Bailey had tumbled off of, or into, something and Mary glanced around with concern.

It was dark in the back of the RV, but she thought she spotted something moving in front of the closed bedroom door. It should have been open, but it had no doubt closed when she'd stopped abruptly, or perhaps that was the thump she'd heard when she'd hit the gas—the pocket door sliding closed.

"You okay, girl?" Mary asked as she swiveled her head forward again, her eyes shooting to the road, then each side mirror and the camera screen showing the rear-view as well. There was nothing but dark road highlighted by her headlights, and the view behind was all just black nothingness, but she relaxed a little when Bailey barked in answer to her question.

At least she hadn't killed her dog careening off like that, she thought grimly, and immediately glanced to the rear camera view again with dissatisfaction.

Mary was quite sure she'd run over something back there and despite not finding anything, she didn't feel right about driving off. Her search certainly hadn't been a thorough one and she feared she might be leaving someone lying injured on the side of the road. Which didn't make any sense. Whatever she'd hit should have been in the road, easily visible, not at the side or off hidden in the bushes. She'd run *over* whatever it was, not hit and sent it flying.

Her conscience was telling her she should reverse, go

back out and make a proper search, but the idea of getting out of the RV again made the hair on the back of her neck stand on end. Something had spooked Bailey, and yes all right, she'd been spooked too, she acknowledged with a grimace.

Perhaps she could just call the police and have them send someone out to search the area properly. Although, they might demand she turn back and wait for them by the spot, she thought unhappily and didn't even like the idea of waiting in the safety of the RV back there.

Good Lord, she was acting like a teenager left home alone for the first time, Mary thought with self-disgust and clenched her hands on the steering wheel, then released a little impatient hiss and reached for her cell phone, only to find that it was no longer in its holder. A quick glance toward the floor revealed absolutely nothing. She couldn't even see her feet let alone the missing cell phone. Biting her lip, she briefly considered stopping, but then glanced once more to the rear camera screen and quickly changed her mind. She would wait until the first stop sign she reached, Mary decided. At the moment she wasn't sure where exactly she was, other than the name of the road. If she waited until the next stop, she could check the street signs and give the police some idea of the nearest crossroad to the accident.

That thought made her glance down at the mileage gauge. She'd just keep track of how far she drove before she reached the stop sign and then could give the police the exact spot where they should be looking. Surely, that would be more helpful anyway?

Dante groaned and opened his eyes to peer at the edge of the built-in bed's wooden base before him. He wished he had the strength to pull himself up off the floor and back onto the bed's soft comfort, but was quite sure he couldn't even manage that small task at this point. It seemed he'd used every last drop of strength he'd had getting himself into the RV and onto the bed he was now lying beside.

That was a shame. He hadn't exactly landed in a comfortable position when the RV had surged forward and he'd rolled off the bed. His body had twisted and he now lay with his head and shoulders jammed between the base of the bed and one doorjamb, his feet caught between the bed and the other doorjamb, while his butt had fallen through the latched-open door of the bathroom to lie on the cold hard tile.

The discomfort of his position was an added irritation, the final straw that broke the camel's back of the agony his wounds were causing him. Not surprising after being run over by an RV, he supposed, but that was perhaps the wrong description for what had happened. Dante had been racing through the woods when they'd suddenly given way around him. It had taken him a moment to realize he had come upon the side of a road and that he was about to crash into the side of a passing RV. There was no way the driver could have seen him, let alone stopped, and Dante had instinctively tried to stop himself, but instead managed to skid right under the wheels.

His mouth tightened as he recalled the impact of several tons of metal and wood rolling over his stomach and lower chest. He'd actually heard his ribs snapping and the pop as one of his lungs had burst. He hadn't lost consciousness though, and when the first tires had cleared him, he'd instinctively tried to roll out of the way of the back wheels, but dazed and shocked and gasping for breath at that point, he'd merely got turned around under the vehicle so that the back right tires had rolled over one of his ankles. A fortuitous event really, because had he got any farther in the direction he'd been moving, the back left tires would have rolled over his head. Better to have a crushed ankle than a crushed head, he thought dryly, and then let out a short breath and glanced toward where his feet were caught against the wall. He just as quickly looked away again, unwilling to focus too closely on just how badly mangled his one lower leg was.

Damn, he was a mess, he acknowledged. So much so that he had to wonder how he'd managed to even get himself into the RV. The moments after the accident were a bit muddled in his head. He recalled his panic over his pursuers catching up to him. It had been enough to make him drag himself to his feet.

He'd been desperate to reach the driver's door and gain help. Only there had been no driver's door, just a large window high up showing nothing but an empty cab. He'd been considering that with some confusion when he'd heard a door slam closed on the other side of the vehicle. Dante had immediately started to hobble around the front of the RV when a dog had suddenly appeared beside him out of the darkness. Tail wagging and sniffing curiously, the furry fellow had seemed friendly enough as he trailed him around the vehicle, but when the owner had called out, the dog had raced off into the darkness along the RV.

Dante had tried to call out then, hoping for help, but he was barely getting any oxygen into his one remaining lung. He wasn't even sure how he was moving, but shouting was out of the question, so he'd simply continued around the RV. He'd spotted the flashlight moving over the road behind the RV as he came around the front of the vehicle, but it had seemed miles away in his condition. Then he'd spotted the door on this side of the vehicle and it had seemed like the gates of heaven. Dante had opened the door, and dragged himself up the steps. He'd paused then and glanced toward the flashlight by the back of the RV again. The driver had been in view at that point and he'd been surprised to note that it was a woman.

He'd tried to slip into her thoughts and take control of her, hoping to urge her back into the RV and get them moving, but he hadn't been able to either read or control her. Realizing he was too weak to perform what should have been an easy task, Dante had decided discretion was the better part of valor here and had continued on into the RV, easing the door closed just as the German shepherd had rushed back toward him.

It had been dark inside, but his eyes did well in darkness and the moment he'd spotted the bed toward the back of the RV, Dante had headed for it. He'd made his way to the soft berth, relieved to find that there was a door to the small room. He'd managed to find the strength to pull it closed, and then had collapsed on the bed with relief. He must have passed out then, though probably not for long, but the next moment he was tumbling from the bed to the floor as the RV accelerated.

He'd waited stiffly, afraid his pursuers may have overcome the driver and were now in charge of the vehicle, but then he'd heard the woman call the dog to her. Her voice had been a little tense when she spoke, but not the terror stricken type of tense he was sure he would have heard had she found herself in the hands of the captors he'd just escaped. It seemed he'd eluded his pursuers, he'd reassured himself solemnly. Although there was no guarantee they weren't following them even now, waiting for the opportunity to steal him back. He needed to heal and get his strength back so that he could ensure he didn't land in their hands again before he could call Mortimer or Lucian and tell them what was happening. To do that, he needed blood.

His gaze focused on the blanket hanging half off the bed and he almost sighed. He didn't have the strength to pull himself onto the bed, let alone drag himself over it and open the door so that he could see his driver, slip into her thoughts, and make her come to him. It seemed he'd have to wait for her to come to him on her own. He just hoped she didn't wait too long to do so. The woman may not realize it, but she was in danger. Even if his pursuers hadn't shown themselves to her, they must have seen the RV. He had no doubt they would come searching for them. The good news was the men would have to make their way back to the house where they'd been keeping him and Tomasso to fetch their vehicle. It would buy a little time at least, but not much, he feared.

If the woman didn't come to him immediately on stopping, they could both be in trouble.

"Damn," Mary growled as she stared at the broken face of her cell phone. It must have bounced off something as it had tumbled from its holder. Or perhaps she'd stepped on it in her rush to get out or into her seat. Whatever the case, the glass front was shattered and the phone was dead . . . so much for calling the police.

Frowning, Mary set the phone back in its holder and then picked up the pen attached to the tiny memo clipboard she'd affixed on the dashboard, and quickly wrote down the cross street and the miles from it to the accident site. Setting the pen back, she then glanced toward the road, looking both ways before taking her foot off the brake and starting forward again. She'd have to stop at the first store or gas station she came across and use the phone there to call the police with her directions. It meant delaying her arrival at the campgrounds even further, but it had to be done. Her conscience would never rest if she didn't.

The good news was Mary didn't think she would have to go far to find a phone. As she recalled from her perusal of the map that morning, there was at least one truck stop coming up where the 87 met the 10, and this road should take her to the 87 soon, from what she could tell by the quick glance she took at the Garmin GPS. She would have to get gas while she was at the truck stop too, Mary thought, noting where the needle was on the gas gauge.

A whine from Bailey reached her ears, and Mary glanced around but still couldn't make out the dog. A niggling worry that perhaps the shepherd had been injured after all by something falling when she'd accelerated made Mary frown and she coaxed, "Come on up here, sweetie. I know you're tired and we'll be there soon, but come sit with Mama now so I know you're okay."

When that didn't elicit any reaction, Mary eased her foot off the gas and risked leaning quickly to the side to grab the flashlight off the passenger seat. It was quite a stretch and was probably incredibly stupid, but she managed to snag the flashlight and not swerve all over the road while she did it.

Switching the flashlight on, she shone it toward the back of the RV and risked a quick glance over her shoulder, relieved when she spotted Bailey simply lying in front of the bedroom door. She looked fine in the quick glimpse Mary got. Deciding the dog was just tired and complaining of the long journey, she switched off the flashlight and laid it on the huge dashboard.

Bailey liked a certain bedtime and, when tired, would let it be known. Usually she did so by pawing at your arm and giving you the "sad eyes," as Joe had always called her expression when she did that. Fortunately, the dog knew better than to paw at her while she was driving so was apparently making her complaint more vocal. At least, Mary hoped that was the case. But she intended on giving the dog a good look-over when she reached the truck stop anyway, just to be sure a falling object hadn't injured her.

Her mind taken up with this worry as well as what she would say when she called the police, Mary was a little startled when the Garmin announced the approaching turn onto 87. It gave enough warning that she was able to slow down and make the turn without sending anything else clattering to the floor from the cupboards and drawers. Relieved by this, she squinted into the distance, looking for the truck stop despite knowing it was past the I-10 and surely out of sight for now.

Programmed to take her to the campground, the Garmin instructed her to take the ramp onto the I-10 as she approached it, but Mary ignored it and continued on 87. A moment later she spotted the lights and pumps of the truck stop ahead. She slowed almost to a crawl to make the turn, hoping to once again avoid sending anything crashing around in the back that might hit Bailey.

There was a definite sense of relief when she had the RV parked and shut down. At least there was until Mary slid out from behind the wheel and stood to turn and survey the wreckage in the RV aisle. There was enough light from the truck stop coming through the windows that she could see just how large the task ahead of her was to put everything safely back where it belonged. Knowing she'd have to do that before leaving the truck stop, Mary grimaced and then began to make her way toward the back of the RV.

Her purse was safely tucked out of sight in the bedroom closet where she always kept it and she might need change to use the pay phone if the workers in the truck stop refused to let her use their phone. Besides, it was well past suppertime and was going to be even later by the time she cleaned up and tucked everything away. Having dinner here would save her the chore of cooking herself a meal when she did finally reach the campground.

Mary slipped on something slick on the floor, and grabbed for the kitchen counter, then glanced down with a frown at the stain in front of the refrigerator. It was a small dark puddle, one of several she'd half noted. It looked like ketchup, but with a more liquid consistency. The fridge door had obviously also opened and closed during her earlier abrupt stop, but she wasn't sure what had fallen out and spilled over the floor. She couldn't immediately spot a broken jar or anything, although the bowls and towels and other things now scattered across the floor may be hiding it.

Adding washing the floor to the list of chores she needed to perform before getting back on the road, Mary continued toward the back. Bailey stood as she approached, whined excitedly and turned to nose the door to the bedroom, obviously eager to get inside.

"Yes, yes. You can get on the bed and sleep," Mary said with exasperation as she reached to slide open the bedroom pocket door. It was all the permission Bailey needed. The moment Mary had the door open wide enough for her to slide through, the dog was rushing forward to leap on the bed.

Shaking her head, Mary stepped into the small space. She leaned against the edge of the mattress as she turned to open the nearest wardrobe door. It and the drawers below it, which were presently blocked by the bed, had always been hers, while the back half-closet and drawers were her husband's. Mary peered into the dark interior of her closet and felt around briefly, then stepped back to hit the switch to turn on the lights in the small bedroom.

She started to shift her attention to the closet again, but paused as she saw that Bailey had jumped off the opposite side of the bed and stood in the small bathroom, licking—was that a shoulder? Mary squinted and then leaned forward to get a better look at the floor on the opposite side of the bed, her eyes widening as she realized that she was peering at a very large, very naked man lying half in the bedroom and half in the bathroom. His bottom was what was lying in the bathroom and it was his ass, not his shoulder, that Bailey was diligently licking blood off of.

Two

"**B**ailey," Mary breathed, alarm and worry rushing over her as her poor brain tried to sort out how this man had come to be here. He certainly hadn't been there when she'd set out that morning, and there was no way he could have got in while she was driving. The only time she'd left the RV without locking the door was when she'd hit something on the—

Mary stiffened as realization slid over her. This was what she'd hit. She'd run over this man. That was the only thing that made sense. Certainly the blood now covering him suggested he'd been in some sort of accident. But how the hell had he got himself into the RV without her seeing him?

She started to crawl onto the bed, intending to see how she could help him, but immediately paused when he turned his head and opened deep black eyes to stare hard at her. She met his gaze briefly, then backed slowly off the bed. The man was pale as death, coated with blood from top to bottom and there was even more of it soaking into the carpet and pooling on the tile floor around him, but his eyes seemed almost to glow silver with life and she was suddenly afraid of him.

Mary stared at the man briefly, telling herself that she was not going to be able to help him, that this man needed serious medical care, an ambulance and hospital, surgery and gallons of blood. She spun away, calling out, "I'll get help."

She tripped back across the littered floor to the door, then paused and glanced back to call, "Bailey!" When the dog didn't immediately appear, she said more sharply, "Come to Mommy, now!"

This time the dog did listen and came bounding out of the bedroom and toward her. Relieved, Mary unlocked and opened the door, then took the steps to the pavement and waited for Bailey to follow before closing the door again. She automatically reached for her keys, intending to lock the door, only to realize they were still in the ignition. Mary briefly considered going in to get them, but then simply turned to Bailey and ordered, "Sit. Stay."

When Bailey sat next to the stairs and peered at her solemnly, Mary nodded, muttered, "Good girl," and hurried for the truck stop entrance.

There was a gas station/store on one side and a restaurant took up the other. Mary rushed for the door to the restaurant and burst inside, only to pause and take stock of the situation. She noted with some surprise that there were a good dozen people seated at the tables, some in groups of two or three, some alone. It was more than she'd expected at that hour and her gaze slid to the clock on the wall to see that it was after eight. It seemed she wasn't the only one traveling at night.

There were also two waitresses: the younger one stood next to a table, apparently taking an order, while the other, an older lady, stood behind a long counter lined with stools. Since the second one was looking her way, Mary hurried to the counter and blurted, "There's a naked man in my RV bedroom."

Amusement curved the waitress's lips and she said wryly, "Lucky you."

Mary blinked in confusion and then explained, "No. You don't understand. He's injured."

"Got a little rowdy, huh?" The waitress teased lightly.

"Rowdy?" Mary echoed with bewilderment and then flushed as understanding struck. The woman thought she was saying he'd been injured during sex or something. Good Lord! "We weren't—lady, I'm sixty-two years old. The boy is young enough to be my son," she said indignantly.

"Well, double lucky you then," the waitress said dryly. "But it's not nice to brag about a steak meal in front of a gal who's been on a fast for a decade."

Mary clucked with exasperation. "I'm not bragging. He's really hurt. There's blood all over the place. He needs help, but my cell phone is broken. I—"

"Call an ambulance, Joan."

Mary turned sharply at that order and peered at the woman now standing beside her with a man at her back.

They were a young couple, the woman pretty with long brown hair pulled back into a ponytail, while the man had short, fair hair and a solemn expression. Mary had noticed them when she'd entered, but hadn't noticed that they were wearing hospital greens. She did now, and felt relief as the woman smiled at her soothingly.

"Hello, I'm Dr. Jenson and this is my husband, Dr. Jenson. Why don't you take us to your friend and we'll see what we can do until the ambulance gets here."

"Yes," Mary said with relief and turned to lead them out of the restaurant, but as she pushed through the door, she explained, "He's not a friend. I don't know him. I just found him in the bedroom of the RV when I stopped here. I think I may have hit him. He's bleeding badly."

"What did you hit him with?" the man asked, his voice a deep baritone as they crossed the parking lot.

"The RV," Mary answered, noting with relief that Bailey still sat where she'd left her. The dog was good about obeying orders, but the way things had been going—

"I'm not sure I understand," the man said slowly. "You found him naked in the bedroom of the RV . . . and then what? Threw him out and ran him over?"

"What?" She glanced back with amazement. "No, of course not. I think I hit him with the RV and while I was out looking to see what I'd hit, he must have crawled into the RV. I didn't find him until I got here." Pausing at the RV, she opened the door, and hurried inside to lead the way back to the bedroom. She hadn't really needed to, as everything was compact and a straight shot from front to back. In truth, Mary led the way because she wasn't at all sure the man would still be there. She could hardly believe he'd been there to begin with and half suspected he'd been some kind of hallucination brought on by the stress of the trip or something.

However, when she reached the open door of the small bedroom and moved up against the bed to peer over it, he was still there on the floor on the other side, broad shoulders wedged between the bed and wall, and butt hanging out into the bathroom, bare as the day he'd been born.

"Oh dear."

Mary glanced around and realized she was blocking the way. Squeezing into the small cubby space between the bed and wall on this side to get out of the way, Mary glanced from the woman to the man on the floor and back before offering, "Maybe I should open the slide-out."

"It might cause him injury," the woman said, climbing onto the bed on her knees and starting across the surface to the other side.

"Lisa's right," the man said solemnly, taking Mary's arm to urge her out of the cramped room. Even with her squeezed to the side, there wasn't room for him to pass. Really, with the slides in, there wasn't room to turn around in this section of the RV.

"Why don't you go watch for the EMTs and let us see what we can do here first," he suggested gently but firmly as he pulled her back toward the door.

Mary went willingly. In truth, she was happy to go. The sight of the man's twisted body and all that blood was likely to give her nightmares as it was, and she certainly didn't expect he'd survive. She didn't want to bear witness to his death. It was bad enough that she may be the cause of it.

"Send the EMTs in when they get here," the man instructed quietly as he stopped and leaned past her to open the RV door.

Mary merely nodded and descended the steps to the pavement. She heard the door close behind her and glanced back anxiously, then peered down at Bailey when the dog nosed her hand.

"It'll be all right," she murmured and gave the dog a pat, but wasn't at all sure that was true. If the man in her bedroom was what she'd hit with the RV, and he died as she feared—that was vehicular homicide, wasn't it? Or did there have to be intent to be homicide? Perhaps it was manslaughter or something. She had no idea, but it was *something*.

It *had* been an accident, she reminded herself. She'd never even *seen* him, but she had been tired and while she hadn't thought she'd been *that* tired, she should have seen him, shouldn't she? The man was buck naked, not wearing dark clothes that would have helped make him harder to see. She *should* have seen him.

The door opened behind her suddenly and Mary turned to peer anxiously at the pretty brunette as she hurried out of the RV. The woman didn't even glance her way, but slammed the RV door closed and rushed toward the restaurant.

Mary stared after her with a frown, then glanced to the RV door, briefly debating going inside to see what was happening. Had he died? Was he— Her head swiveled again at the sound of the restaurant door opening and she watched wide-eyed as the woman led several patrons to the RV, all of them big, brawny-looking men. By Mary's guess, every last one of them was probably a truck driver . . . or a lumberjack.

"Are you moving him?" Mary asked with concern as the doctor led the men over. It was the only explanation she could think of for the presence of so many big men. Although she had no idea how they thought they would all be able to maneuver through the tight RV carrying the man. And where were they going to put him? Did they plan to just bring him out here and lay him on the pavement, or were they going to take him inside the restaurant? That last thought seemed most likely. The lighting in the RV wasn't great right now. She hadn't turned on the generator when she'd stopped, so the only light was the small LED she'd flicked on to look for her purse.

"Wait here and watch for the ambulance," the brunette said as she opened the door. She gestured for the men to go in ahead of her and then followed, leaving a worried Mary to watch the door close again. The RV rocked slightly as the people inside moved about and Mary bit her lip, wondering how the hell they thought they were going to move the man with so many inside.

She should have put out the slides, Mary thought again unhappily as she peered up the road first one way and then the other, wondering how long it would take for the ambulance to get there and from which direction it would come.

When the door opened behind her again, Mary glanced around expectantly, but only one of the men came out. Mary stepped out of his way as he descended the steps and pushed the door closed. She expected him to make some sort of explanation then, but the man simply walked away back toward the restaurant at an easy gait, a relaxed smile on his face.

Mary stared after him with amazement. She'd almost think he'd been sent to get towels or something else that might be needed, but if so, surely he should be rushing and looking at least a bit concerned?

She watched him enter the restaurant and saw through the large glass windows that he returned to what she presumed was his table and set about eating again as if nothing had happened. She also saw both waitresses move to his side, curiosity evident in their movements and expressions, but whatever he said must have allayed their concerns, since both women moved away moments later, relaxed and smiling as if at some joke.

Mary was frowning over that when the door opened behind her again and another of the men came out. Like the first he looked relaxed and happy as he descended the steps and closed the door. But this time Mary didn't move out of the way, instead stepping in front of him.

"What's happening? Is he—?"

"He'll be fine," the tall, gruff voiced fellow assured her. She noted puncture marks on his neck as he side-stepped her to head toward the restaurant, but got distracted by his words when he added, "The blood was more show than damage."

Mary stared after him with disbelief. The amount of blood she'd seen had been more than show. It had looked like he'd bled out all over her floor. In fact, she hadn't dared looked at his face when she'd led the doctors inside, afraid she'd find herself looking at eyes glazed over with death.

Much to her relief the sound of a siren in the distance distracted her then and Mary turned her head to peer along the road. Spotting the flashing lights, she swallowed and moved forward, ready to flag down the vehicle and wave it over the moment it pulled in. The ambulance was just turning into the lot when movement out of the corner of her eye made Mary glance back toward the RV. Another man had come out of the RV and was returning to the restaurant. Like the others, he looked calm and untroubled, but Mary didn't have time to worry about it, as the ambulance was coming to a halt before her and two men were jumping out.

"Are you the one who called?" the man who had been driving asked as they approached her.

Mary shook her head. "The waitress did for me."

The driver nodded, his gaze sliding over her. "What seems to be the problem? Chest pains? Problems breathing?"

Mary waved the suggestion away and turned to head back toward the RV, explaining, "No. I'm fine. But I hit someone with the RV and he was badly injured. There are doctors with him now, but—"

Mary paused both in speaking and walking. She'd

glanced over her shoulder to see that she'd lost the
EMTs. Both men had rushed back toward the ambulance. She stared after them, relieved when she realized they were just getting their gear. They were quick
about it now that they knew the situation and seconds
later were wheeling a stretcher toward her with several
items stacked on top of it. A strapped spine board was
on the bottom, with a neck collar, an orange bag with
the medical symbol on it, and a defibrillator on top. The
sight of the spine board and collar made her realize
the naked man in her RV probably shouldn't have been
moved until it was determined that he hadn't broken his
neck or back. But she was sure the doctor had seen to
that before she'd called the men in from the restaurant
to move him to the bed. At least that's what she was
assuming they'd been brought out for. She had no idea
why they'd left one at a time rather than all together
after accomplishing the task.

The EMTs were moving quickly now and Mary had
to jog to keep ahead of them.

"Who's the doctor with the victim?" the driver asked
suddenly.

"There are two of them, a husband and wife. I think
she said Jenner or something," Mary muttered, trying
to recall. She'd been in a bit of a state at the time.

"Jenson?" the other EMT asked as Mary paused at
the RV door and started to open it.

"Yes, that might be it," Mary admitted, then glanced
around with surprise as the last of the four men from
the restaurant came out the door she'd just opened and
started down the steps.

She noted a mark and smear of blood on his throat, then glanced distractedly back to the ambulance driver when he said, "Your friend's lucky then. The Jensons are top notch," he announced and then hurried up the steps as the exiting man got out of the way.

"He's right," the second EMT assured her as he followed. He also closed the door behind him, making it obvious they didn't expect her to follow.

Mary let her breath out on a sigh, but didn't really mind being left outside again. There wasn't a lot of room in there, and despite the reassurances from the men who had left the RV, she really didn't think all that blood was just show. Besides, now that she was thinking about what she'd seen in her first glimpse of the man, she was quite sure there had been something odd about his chest. Aside from the muddy tire track across it, it had seemed a bit misshaped or flattened. And she thought one of his legs had been as well.

Muttering worriedly under her breath, Mary moved closer to where Bailey had curled up on the pavement and patted her head when the German shepherd promptly stood at attention beside her.

"It'll be fine," she repeated the mantra reassuringly, and just wished she believed that.

Glancing toward the restaurant, she recalled her intention to eat while she was here, but no longer felt like it. Perhaps afterward . . . if she wasn't immediately arrested and dragged off to the hoosegow, Mary thought with a grimace. The possibility made her wonder where the police were. Surely they should be here by now, taking statements and starting their investigation?

The door opened behind her again and Mary glanced around to see the doctors coming out of the RV. There was blood on their clothes now, Mary noted and it suddenly occurred to her that what she'd thought was ketchup on the floor of the RV was probably blood as well.

"How is he?" Mary asked.

The man paused and turned to close the door behind them. Mary frowned as she noted the marks on his neck, but then glanced to the brunette as she said brightly, "He's fine. The EMTs are with him now."

"But—" Mary paused and glanced toward the RV as the generator came on. They probably needed extra light, or to plug in their defibrillator or something, she thought and then realized they'd left everything but the stretcher and the orange bag out here when they'd gone in to assess the situation.

"What are they . . . ?" Her question trailed away as she swung back to see that while she'd been distracted, the Jensons had taken the opportunity to slip away and were now on the way back into the restaurant.

Letting her breath out on an exasperated hiss, Mary glanced back to the RV and had just started forward when the door suddenly opened and the EMTs started out. She could hear the sound of a shower from inside before the door closed and glanced to the two men with bewilderment as they moved to their rolling stretcher.

"Are you going to be able to get that inside?" she asked when one man moved to the head of the stretcher. "It's kind of tight in there."

"No need," the EMT said lightly, offering her a shiny smile. "He's fine."

"He's not fine," Mary argued quickly. "He was nearly dead. He—you aren't just *leaving* him?" she protested as the man began to drag the rolling stretcher back toward their vehicle. "He needs help."

"He's fine. The blood was all show," the second EMT, the driver, said reassuringly, following the stretcher back toward the ambulance.

"But—" Mary turned to peer at her RV with dismay, wondering what she was supposed to do with the man. Wait for him to come out seemed the most sensible answer. She found it hard to believe he was just fine as everyone kept saying, but if he was, she presently had a huge naked man in her RV. And in her shower from the sounds of it, she thought grimly She'd have to fill up the water tank, and empty the gray tank once she reached the campground, and—who was she kidding, she wasn't going anywhere until the man presently enjoying her shower got his butt out of her RV. Mary wasn't forgetting the shiver of trepidation she'd experienced when her gaze had met his. There had been something about his expression, the concentration, and the deep dark black eyes with silver flecks that almost seemed to glow . . .

No, she wasn't going inside until he came out. If he came out. What if he just drove off with her RV? She'd left her damned keys in there, Mary recalled. And her purse. The man could just drive off with her vehicle and have himself a relaxing holiday in her RV.

She should go in and get her keys while he was in the shower. Not that she was sure he was actually in the shower, she thought. Mary couldn't imagine he was in shape to manage such a task. But everyone kept saying he was just fine, she reminded herself and started to open the RV door, only to pause with it barely cracked as she realized the sound of rushing water was gone.

She'd just wait for him to come out, Mary decided, easing the door closed again as she heard movement inside. The hum of the generator stopped and she shifted nervously, wondering what she should say when he did come out. If he came out. Surely he would come out?

Bailey whined beside her and nosed at the door, suggesting she thought Mary should go in, but Mary shook her head. "We'll wait," she said quietly, turning her back to the door, and watching idly as a speeding black van slowed abruptly on the highway and put on its blinker, indicating its intention to turn into the lot. It would have a bit of a wait, she noted. The oncoming traffic was pretty thick, perhaps from the ramp onto the I-10 just up the road. Then she whirled toward the RV door again with horror as she heard the engine start up.

"Oh, no freaking way," Mary muttered, and dragged the door open to rush in. She had just stepped off the automatically descending metal steps and onto the wooden ones inside when she was nearly knocked off her feet by Bailey as the shepherd raced past her to get inside first.

Grabbing for the counter on her left and the passenger seat on her right to steady herself, Mary scowled at the dog, who had settled in her customary position between the driver's and passenger's seats. The dumb dog didn't seem to realize that the man at the wheel shouldn't be there. In fact, Bailey was staring up at him with something like worship, her tail thumping the floor and tongue hanging out.

She'd have to have a talk with the dog later, Mary decided as she moved away from the door and stepped up onto the RV floor to scowl at the young man in the driver's seat.

Mary's scowl was replaced by shock as she noted the change in him. Gone was the pallid, blood-soaked victim struggling for breath that she'd first spotted in her bedroom. This man was flush with color, his long dark hair wet from the shower and slicked back from his face. He was no longer dragging in raspy, labored breaths, but breathing just fine. He also didn't have a drop of blood on him . . . *any*where. Mary knew that for certain because the one thing that hadn't changed was that he was still buck naked, and his bare ass was presently in her driver's seat.

Three

"**W**hat the hell do you think you're doing?" Mary snapped, moving forward to loom threateningly over the young man. She would do him some serious harm if she had to, but no one was taking her RV from her. "Get your bloody arse out of my seat!"

"I showered the blood off. Sit down." Even as he spoke the calm response, the RV jerked forward, nearly sending her tumbling to the floor. Catching the edge of the dinette table, Mary steadied herself and then grabbed the back of the driver's seat to hold on as she scowled down at the seated man.

"I realize you showered," she said with irritation. "I wasn't being literal. Just get out of my—crap!" she muttered as he jerked the steering wheel right and she lost her hold on the driver's chair and stumbled side-ways, her hip hitting the side of the table. Then he swerved back again and she tumbled to the right this time, toward the steps. He reached out and grabbed her arm, saving her from a nasty tumble, and then steered her toward the passenger chair. Mary dropped into the seat for safety's sake, but immediately turned to scowl at the young man.

"Look," she began, finding it difficult to be stern after he'd just saved her from possible broken bones.

"I apologize for commandeering your vehicle," the man interrupted and Mary narrowed her eyes as she noted his accent. Italian, she thought, as he continued, "I would have just slipped out of the RV and taken flight on foot when I saw that my kidnappers had tracked us. However, I feared they might do you harm in an effort to find out where I had gone. I couldn't just leave you to their less than tender mercies, so until we lose them, I must stay with you."

Mary blinked as his words sank through her brain. He would have fled on foot but had stayed to ensure her safety? Well, that was somewhat reassuring. It made it less likely that she was in any danger from him . . . if it was true.

"Kidnappers?" she asked finally, vaguely aware that he was steering them out of the truck stop.

"The black van behind us," he said grimly.

Mary glanced at the screen showing the rear camera view to see that there was indeed a black van moving up behind them. She was quite sure it was the vehicle that had been waiting to pull into the truck stop when she'd heard the RV start up. Now it was following them out of the truck stop.

"I saw them waiting to turn into the truck stop

through the window when I got out of the shower," her naked guest said quietly as he straightened out on the highway and put his foot down on the gas. The engine revved and then began to whine in complaint as it was forced to a speed it wasn't used to or even really meant to travel at. He eased up slightly on the gas as he explained, "The men in that van kidnapped my twin brother and myself the night before last. I managed to escape and was fleeing them when you ran me over."

Mary winced at the comment. She *had* run over him. She could still recall the way the RV had bumped over something in the road. And he'd had tire tracks on his chest. Yet now he was sitting here, steering her RV around as if he'd suffered little more than a minor bump or bang.

While guilt was trying to lay claim to her for running the man down, bewilderment was quickly nudging it aside. "How can you be okay now?" she asked. "I ran *over* you. You were covered with blood and appeared badly injured. Yet now . . ."

"The blood was mostly show. I'm fine," he assured her and Mary's eyes narrowed. It was exactly what everyone else had said, which seemed somehow suspicious to her. However, he did look fine so she could hardly argue the point. Besides, there were other questions she needed answered.

"All right. So you and your twin brother were kidnapped," she said slowly, trying to imagine two of these young, strapping, gorgeous male specimens in the world. Good Lord, he was huge. It was hard to imagine two of them existed, she thought, her gaze sliding over his big brawny shoulders and barrel chest. Her eyes tried to drop lower, but she forced them back to his face. She didn't need to look further; she'd already seen more than she wanted to and knew the man was big everywhere. "Who are these men and why did they kidnap you?"

He didn't answer right away, his attention focused on the road as he took the ramp to the I-10. She also suspected he was taking the opportunity to try to come up with a way to avoid answering her question, but once he'd merged onto the 10 he said, "Several young . . . men and women have gone missing in the San Antonio area over the past year. Tomasso and I were helping out a task force trying to discover who was taking them and for what purpose."

"Tomasso is your twin?" she asked before he could continue and thinking that the task force would probably be a federal one, maybe FBI if kidnapping was involved. Great, she'd run over a fed. That couldn't be good.

"Yes."

It took Mary a moment to realize he was agreeing that Tomasso was his twin. Sighing, she asked, "And you are?"

His eyes widened slightly and then he offered her a smile of chagrin. "I am Dante Notte. And who are you?"

"Mary Winslow," she said quietly.

"It is a pleasure to meet you, Mary Winslow," he said solemnly.

She nodded, and then stood, stepped over Bailey and

moved carefully back along the aisle until she could reach the folded afghan that had somehow managed to remain on the couch while everything else had gone tumbling to the floor. Snatching it up, she made her way back to her seat. As she climbed back over Bailey, she dropped the afghan in his lap and then plopped back into the passenger seat. If she was going to talk to the young man, she would do so with at least some small semblance of propriety. He was naked, for God's sake.

"Oh . . . er . . . thank you," Dante muttered, and removed one hand from the wheel to quickly spread the blanket over his lap and legs. It was a spider stitch pattern, a very loose spider stitch—which meant it had large holes. It would have been fine had he left it as is, but when he spread it out . . . well, she might as well have saved herself the walk to get it. His legs and groin were now playing peek-a-boo. Not that Dante seemed to notice. He appeared perfectly satisfied that he was now decently covered. But then it hadn't seemed to bother him to be sitting there naked either, so what did she know?

Mary averted her eyes again with a little sigh. "You were saying you and your brother were assisting a task force in discovering how and why people were going missing in San Antonio?"

Dante nodded with a grunt. "Several of us were sent to bars where the missing people had last been seen. Tomasso and I were sent to the same bar, and were taken together as we left at the end of the night."

"How?" Mary asked with a frown. It was hard to imagine this large, muscular young man being forced to go anywhere he didn't want to, but two of him? If his twin was the same size, taking them on must have been like taking on a small army.

"We were shot with drugged darts in the parking lot," he said grimly. "I thought it was a bullet until I glanced down and saw the dart in my chest. I pulled it out, but it was too late. I was already losing consciousness."

"Sunday night?" she asked with a frown, working it out in her head.

Dante glanced to her uncertainly and then back to the road before saying, "I do not understand. What about Sunday?"

"You said you were taken the night before last. That would be Sunday," she explained, and noted the frown that immediately claimed his expression.

"No. It was Friday we were taken," he said and muttered, "I lost more time than I thought. They must have continuously drugged us. Perhaps intravenously," he added and removed his left hand from the steering wheel to turn it over and peer at the unblemished skin as if he was recalling something.

"You would have a mark, possibly even a bruise if they'd put an intravenous in you," she said gently. When he remained silent and merely returned his hand to the steering wheel and his attention to the road, she asked, "How did you get away?"

"I woke up some hours ago, naked and in a cage. Tomasso was in a cage next to mine, also naked."

Mary sat back slightly at this news. Obviously the man had been wearing something when he'd gone to, and left, the bar. So his captors had stripped him. She couldn't imagine waking up one day to find herself naked in a cage. It sounded like a nightmare to her and she was glad when he distracted her from the thought of it and continued his story.

"Whoever had been in my cage before me had obviously made some effort to escape. One of the bars had been loosened. Tomasso's cage was close enough he could help, and together we were able to get the first bar out, and bend another enough to pull it out as well. I managed to squeeze out of my cage and tried to open his, but before I could accomplish the task, we heard our captors coming and he insisted I get away while I could and get help."

Dante paused briefly, and Mary noted the muscles of his throat working, but then he continued, his voice almost flat. "It was a basement with high windows. I climbed out onto dirt and grass and saw the woods surrounding the building we had been held in. I started to run. I had no idea where I was, or if I was headed in the right direction to find help. All I could see were woods and more woods. I had not gone far when I became aware of someone running behind me. Afraid they would shoot me with their dart again, I put on a burst of speed and then the trees were suddenly gone and I was charging toward the road . . . and the side of this RV." He patted the steering wheel with a grimace. "I tried to stop myself, but . . ." He shook his head, and then glanced to her and said, "The truth is you did not run over me, so much as I ran into, or under, your vehicle."

Mary stared at him silently. She was glad she wasn't at fault for the accident. The knowledge relieved a good deal of the guilt that had apparently been clouding her good sense, because now she was thinking more clearly. Voice firm, she said, "You need to turn around and head back to the truck stop."

He glanced at her with surprise, then turned his gaze forward again and shook his head. "We have to lose our pursuers to ensure your safety when I leave you."

"You're not going to do that in an RV," she said dryly. "These things are like me, built for comfort, not speed. That van—" she glanced to the vehicle revealed in the rear camera view to see that it was still stuck on their tail like a burr on Bailey's butt "—is not going to lose us. And if what you say is true, the minute we stop, the men in that van will attack. But the waitress at the truck stop called 911. By now the police should be there. If they aren't there yet, at least there are others there to help. Right now we're on our own. Those men could force us off the road and take you again at any minute. In fact, I'm surprised they haven't tried already."

"They have not tried because the highway is busy and they do not want witnesses. So long as we stay on it we should be safe," he said solemnly. "And if we lead them back to the truck stop, someone there could get hurt. It is important to avoid that. It is why I led them away to begin with," he argued.

"I thought it was to keep me safe?" she reminded him tightly.

"Yes. That too," he agreed. "I wish to avoid any mort—innocents coming to harm."

"Any more innocents?" she questioned with a frown. "You mean besides your brother?"

"*Si*," he agreed quickly, but kept his gaze on the road ahead.

Mary frowned, suspecting he hadn't meant that at all, but unsure why she thought so. Leaving it for now, she asked, "Well then, what's your plan? Are you intending to lead them to the police station in Kerrville in the hopes they can catch these men and go rescue your brother?" She paused and frowned, wondering if it wouldn't actually be the sheriff's office. In Canada and some of the northern states it was the police, but it seemed to her it might be sheriff here. She wasn't sure though. She'd never had cause to call the authorities here before. Realizing that didn't matter, she waved a hand and said; "Anyway, I seriously doubt your friends will hold off on stopping us until we reach the police station or sheriff's department. Once we're off the highway, there's no guarantee there won't be a stretch of road without anyone to stop them driving us off the road."

Dante scowled, apparently not pleased by what she'd said. "I need to find out where they were holding us so I can send help for Tomasso."

"It's written on that notepad next to my phone," she informed him quietly. "At least the spot where I hit you is. Surely you couldn't have run that far before getting there?"

Dante glanced sharply to the tiny memo pad attached to the clipboard on the dash, and then turned questioning eyes to her. "This is where I ran into you? You wrote it down?"

"Yes." She grimaced and admitted. "I knew I'd hit

something, but I got spooked out there and drove off without making a proper search. I wrote down the distance it was from the first stop sign I came to, intending to send the police there when I got to the truck stop."

A slow relieved smile lit up his face and he said, "Mary Winslow, if I was not driving I would kiss you. You are brilliant."

Mary smiled faintly and just shook her head. He had a very nice smile and she was happy to help the fellow.

"May I use your phone?"

She glanced to the phone in its holder and shook her head. "I'm sorry. It fell out of its holder and broke when I hit you. That's why I stopped at the truck stop, to use their phone."

His smile slipped at once and he glanced to the item in question, asking, "Are you sure it is broken?"

"Well, the glass face is smashed and it had gone dead," she said. "That seems broke enough to me."

He nodded, but asked, "Did you try turning it on?"

"Well, no. But I never turned it off," she pointed out, glancing at the phone now as well.

Dante pursed his lips, then took one hand from the wheel and picked up the phone. He pushed the button to turn it on and Mary almost groaned aloud when the damned thing lit up like a storefront at Christmas. She was such an idiot when it came to modern technology. Honestly, how could she be so stupid as to not even try to turn it on?

Dante smiled at her widely. "It is working."

"I see that," she said dryly.

"May I use it?" he asked.

Mary nodded and then watched as he began punching in numbers, his gaze shifting between the road and the phone.

"That's kind of dangerous," she pointed out. "Why don't you let me put the number in for you?"

"Thank you," Dante murmured, passing the phone over.

Mary took the phone and then glanced to him expectantly. "What's the number?"

"4 . . . 1 . . . 6," he began, and then paused.

"Okay," Mary said, thinking he was waiting to give her the chance to punch in the numbers, but they were still there from his attempt.

Dante frowned. "416 . . ." He released an impatient sound, and then admitted, "I need to be looking at the phone screen to remember."

Mary smiled faintly, completely understanding. For some reason it was always easier for her to remember numbers with the number pad in front of her too.

"You must drive," Dante announced now. "I have to call the Enforcer House."

"Who?" she asked with confusion.

He waved away her question. "The authorities. Come, you must drive."

Mary instinctively glanced to the rear camera view. The van was still tight on their tail. She shook her head. "They'll attack the minute you pull over for us to switch places."

"Si. So we cannot stop. You sit in my lap and I will slip out and leave the seat to you," he said as if that was the most reasonable suggestion in the world.

Mary pursed her lips and shook her head. "Sonny, I wouldn't sit in your lap even if you were wearing a Santa suit."

Dante frowned with confusion. "Santa?"

Mary raised her eyebrows. "Don't you have Santa in Italy? A big bearded guy in a red suit? Comes down the chimney and fills kids' stockings with candies and toys?"

"Oh," he smiled. "For us it is Befana."

"Befana?" she echoed, trying to emulate his pronunciation.

"*Si.*" He smiled faintly. "She is the old woman who comes down the chimney and delivers gifts to the children of Italy who have been good that year. However, she comes on January fifth, Epiphany Eve, not Christmas Eve."

"Hmm," Mary murmured, her gaze sliding between the rear camera view and the steering wheel. She really did want to drive. It was her RV after all, and while Dante wasn't doing too bad a job, it was obvious he'd never driven an RV before. He kept trying to make the vehicle go faster than it was able too, causing the engine to whine. If he kept it up, they could blow the engine and she didn't want that. There was no way she was sitting in his naked lap though.

"What if I just hold the wheel while you get up, then slip onto the seat and take over?" she suggested. It shouldn't be too tricky a maneuver. She just had to keep the wheel straight as she sat down, and even if she moved it a little they should be all right. There were no cars directly beside or in front of them at the moment.

He shook his head. "We will slow down the minute I take my foot off the gas," he pointed out. "And that might be all the encouragement they need to force us off the road, witnesses or no."

Mary scowled at this argument and glanced toward the back of the RV, trying to think of some way to avoid his suggestion. There was a broom in one of the cupboards, as well as a mop. Perhaps she could push down on the gas pedal with that while he vacated the seat and . . . She stood up, intending to go fetch either the mop or broom, and then gasped in surprise when Dante suddenly reached out to snake one arm around her and drag her into his lap. She landed sideways with a squawk and immediately tried to struggle up off of him, then froze as the RV swerved slightly.

"Sit still," Dante commanded firmly as if she hadn't already caught on to the fact that she would have to unless she wanted yet another accident that night. After straightening out the vehicle, Dante released a breath, then glanced to her face and offered a charming smile. "All is well. Just turn in my lap to face front and place your foot over mine on the gas pedal."

"I don't think . . ." Mary began weakly, only to fall silent as he removed his left hand from the steering wheel to rub her back in what she supposed was meant to be a soothing manner, but really did not have a soothing effect on her.

"It is all right. We are halfway there," he cooed, his voice coaxing. "Just turn to face forward for me, yes?"

Mary closed her eyes briefly, but then released a small sigh, firmed her mouth and carefully shifted in his lap until she sat facing forward. She was immediately sorry she had. This new position left her completely enveloped by the man, his arms on either side of her, his body behind and beneath her and his clean, wholesome scent encasing her like a sausage in a bun.

Speaking of sausage, what the hell was that poking her in the bottom? Surely it wasn't—Good Lord, it was!

"This is good, yes?" Dante asked, his words a breathy whisper that stirred the hair by her ear and Mary swallowed against the response her body was having and gave her head a firm shake. This was not good. Although she didn't get the chance to say so before he added, "We are almost there."

She nearly asked, almost *where*? But managed to bite back the question.

"Now. You put your foot on the gas pedal and I will slip my foot out from beneath yours."

Relieved to have something to think about other than what she was quite sure was poking her in the bottom, and the fact that young men were such a horny mess of hormones they could be turned on by tired old women like her, Mary tried to put her foot on the gas pedal and found she couldn't. The boy had long legs and had pushed the seat back. She couldn't reach it.

"Scoot forward," Dante instructed.

Mary didn't have to be told twice. She shifted forward on his lap so swiftly one would have been forgiven for thinking he'd lit a lighter under her butt. Once she was perched on the very tip of his knees with as little of her behind touching him as possible and the steering wheel digging into her belly, she was able to reach the pedal. She pressed her foot down hard, half on his foot and half on the pedal itself and heard Dante suck in a quick pained breath behind her.

"Sorry," she muttered, unable to infuse even the slightest bit of apology into her voice. Poke her in the bottom with his body parts, would he? Hmmph. Take that, horny boy.

"Now grasp the steering wheel," Dante instructed.

Mary raised her hands and grasped the wheel above his hands, careful to avoid touching him.

"Good," Dante praised. "Now, all you need do is concentrate on keeping your foot on the pedal and steering straight, I will do all the work."

"That's what she said," Mary heard her husband's old line in her head and smiled weakly, wishing something fierce that he was there right now. He would be the one sitting in Dante's lap if he was, or no one would be. Joe had been a brilliant man. He would have come up with a way to handle all of this without so much—

"Who said what?" Dante's confused question interrupted her thoughts and Mary glanced over her shoulder to see that he looked as confused as he sounded.

"What?" she asked uncertainly.

"You said, 'That's what she said,'" he explained. "To whom were you referring? And what did she say?"

Mary's eyes widened as she realized she'd spoken the words aloud, and then she just shook her head and turned to face forward again. "Never mind. It was nothing. I was just muttering to myself." Scowling at the stretch of highway ahead, she added, "I thought you were getting up to make your call?"

A moment of silence followed, as if he wanted to question her further, but then he agreed on a small sigh, "*Si*. Keep the RV going this speed and steering straight. I will be as quick and careful as I can."

Mary merely nodded and waited. But when his hands released the steering wheel and suddenly dropped to her bottom, she stiffened and jerked the steering wheel again.

"Steady," Dante admonished. "I am going to lift your bottom and slip out from under you."

"I can probably—" She'd been about to say she could probably lift her own bottom by standing on the gas pedal, but swallowed the words as he slid his hands under her butt cheeks. It was probably done quickly, but to Mary what followed seemed to take forever as he lifted her up off his lap, his fingers squeezing her butt cheeks with more than necessary familiarity, and then his body seemed to slide forward before sliding sideways under hers, the pokey part rubbing across her bottom toward the right before it was out from under her.

"Steady," Dante repeated by her ear and Mary shifted her attention back to the steering wheel that had somehow started to turn to the right as well. Straightening it out, she tried to ignore the fact that he seemed really slow about setting her down on the edge of the seat. Letting her breath out on relief, she glanced toward him and cursed. "You—"

"*Uno momento*," Dante breathed, interrupting her complaint that he'd lost his afghan and was now completely naked again.

Mary almost swallowed her tongue then when he practically laid his head in her lap as he felt around under her seat for something. At first she thought it was the afghan he was trying to reclaim, but when she realized it was lying on the floor next to the seat, she snapped, "What the hell are you doing?"

"Trying to find the lever to adjust your seat," Dante explained and then jerked upright just in time to avoid getting his head crushed by the steering wheel when she hit the button on her armrest to adjust the seat herself.

"It's automatic," she said shortly.

"Ah. Good," he murmured, and stood. Much to her relief, he recalled the afghan and arranged it around himself as he straightened. At least, Mary was relieved until she glanced to the side and saw that she'd been right about what she'd thought had been poking her in the bottom. The man had a boner, and it was presently poking through one of the holes in the spider-stitched afghan. He might as well not be wearing the damned thing at all. Good Lord!

Mary turned her eyes quickly forward again, wishing she could burn the sight she'd just seen from her memory. But she couldn't even remove it from her gaze, the damned thing seemed burned into her retina and there was now a big dancing penis bouncing around in the middle of her view of the road ahead.

"So not cool," Mary muttered to herself.

"What was that? Did you say you are cold?" Dante asked with apparent concern and Mary instinctively started to turn to him to answer, caught a glimpse of his penis poking out of the colorful afghan, and jerked her head forward again.

"No," she said firmly. "Go make your call."

Dante hesitated, but then said, "I will be quick," and finally snatched up the phone, ripped off the top paper from the memo pad, and moved away.

"Take your time," Mary muttered under her breath, and meant it. She needed a little breathing space from the man. He wasn't her type—too big, too young, and just too damned sexy—but he hadn't been the only one affected by the past few minutes. If women could have boners, she'd be sporting one too and that was just pitiful. Dante was young enough to be her son . . . maybe even her grandson. She had no business responding to him at all.

And she wasn't, Mary assured herself. She was just reacting to the night's excitement: the accident, and then the danger and excitement of finding herself with a man whose kidnappers were now hunting them. No doubt she was experiencing an adrenaline rush and was simply mistaking that for a response to the man— the only man—with her. She'd heard, or perhaps read somewhere, that high-risk adventures could lead to swift bonding and sexual attraction and that's all this was, Mary assured herself. She just needed to keep her head on straight until this was all over and everything would be fine.

Four

Dante moved to the back of the RV and sat on the edge of the bed to punch in the number to the Enforcer House. Something cold and wet pressing against his leg drew his attention to the fact that the dog had followed him, and now sat on the floor at his feet, her head on his knee. Petting the beast absently, Dante glanced toward the woman in the driver's seat. As he listened to the phone ring at the other end of the line, his mind was chasing itself around inside his skull like a dog chasing its tail. He needed to keep Mary safe from their pursuers, needed to save Tomasso, needed to pass on the information they'd learned, needed to . . . claim his life mate.

Christ, who would have thought he'd find her now in the middle of all of this madness? It hadn't even occurred to Dante that Mary might be his life mate when he first hadn't been able to read her. He'd just assumed it was a result of his injuries and lack of blood. But he'd had no problem at all slipping into the thoughts of the doctors and the others and taking control of them. In fact, he'd controlled several of them at a time and with ease, and yet when she'd stormed back into the RV after he'd fed and got his strength back, he still hadn't been able to even peek into her thoughts, let alone control her.

His body's reaction to her nearness was another rather telling point that suggested she was his life mate. Those brief moments when he'd held her on his lap, her intoxicating scent wafting into his nose and her warmth imprinting on his groin . . . He still had a damned erection from the encounter, and he was quite sure she'd felt something too. He'd heard her heartbeat accelerate and her swift, shallow breathing. Oh yes, he was quite certain Mary Winslow was his life mate. He just didn't know what, if anything, he should do about it at the moment. There were so many things that needed tending just now.

"Yes."

Dante glanced down at the phone in his hands with surprise at that abrupt word. It wasn't the usual way Lucian answered his calls to him. Usually he answered with "Speak, Dante." But then, Dante usually called from his own phone. This was Mary's phone and Lucian wouldn't recognize this number, he realized and cleared his throat.

"It's Dante."

"Thank Christ," Lucian growled. "Where the hell have you been? And where is Tomasso? When the two of you went missing—"

"We were taken from the bar you sent us to," Dante interrupted. "Both Tomasso and I were kidnapped. They used drugged darts. I was apparently out for two days and nights," he added grimly, and wasn't surprised by the silence that followed his announcement. No doubt, Lucian was as taken aback at this news, as Dante had been when he'd realized what had happened. Mortal drugs did not work on their kind. They were flushed from the system too quickly to do more than make them woozy or a little faint. They'd had to develop their own drugs to use on rogue immortals and even those only worked temporarily and had to be re-administered too quickly to be viable as more than a temporary stop-gap measure to get the rogue bound up. Yet he'd apparently been unconscious for two days. It suggested that an immortal was behind the kidnappings, or a mortal with information about them that they should not have . . . as well as access to their specialized drugs.

"You got away, obviously," Lucian said finally. "Are you both all right?"

"They still have Tomasso," Dante said quietly, and quickly related how he'd got free and why Tomasso hadn't, finishing with, "We have to get him back."

"Where is he?" Lucian asked at once.

"Do you have a pen?" Dante asked, glancing down at the piece of paper in his hand. Mary had lovely handwriting, he noted. When Lucian said he was ready, Dante read off the instructions Mary had written down. Once Lucian read it back to him, he added, "That is where I came out of the woods onto the road. The house was perhaps a five minute run east from there through the trees."

Lucian grunted and then asked, "Where are you now?"

"In an RV, heading northwest on Interstate 10. The kidnappers are following us. I am hoping that means Tomasso is safe for now. But you need to get someone to him as quickly as possible. I can't guarantee the kidnappers will continue to just follow us, and with the drugged darts they have—"

"Who is this *us*?" Lucian interrupted. "You took control of a family traveling in an RV to help with your escape?"

"No." Dante glanced toward Mary, and then cleared his throat and said, "I had a little accident with an RV when I was escaping. The woman who was driving it is now helping me."

"A lone woman in an RV?" Lucian asked sounding suspicious.

"She has a dog with her," Dante said with amusement, peering down at Bailey as he petted her again. The shepherd immediately twisted her head to give his hand a swipe with her tongue.

"Still, women do not generally travel in RVs by themselves, even with dogs," Lucian said thoughtfully. "Are you sure she is not one of them and letting you think you are escaping while she delivers you back into the hands of your captors?"

"I'm sure," Dante said at once, his voice firm, but his gaze was now on the back of Mary's head as he tried to slip into her thoughts once more.

"No, of course she's not one of them," Lucian muttered. "You would have read that from her mind were it the case."

Dante grimaced and gave up on trying to read Mary. It was impossible for him to do so. He didn't, however, tell Lucian that, but simply allowed him to think what he would.

"If they have drugged darts that are that effective on us, it would be dangerous for you to try to take on your kidnappers on your own," Lucian muttered.

"Yes," Dante agreed wryly. He'd said, or started to say that just moments ago. It was why he'd done as Tomasso had insisted and fled when they'd heard their captors clattering down the hall outside the room where their cages were. His first instinct had been to stand and fight, but that would have done them little good when their adversaries had the drugged darts. He would have ended up unconscious and back in a cage, probably one that had no loose bars too, and then they simply would have been two more immortals who had gone missing from the bar scene in San Antonio. Escaping to get help had been more sensible. Still, it had been a terrible wrench to leave his brother behind.

"Can you keep ahead of your hunters for a while? Long enough for me to send men to find Tomasso and arrange a trap to catch your kidnappers?"

"I can try," Dante said determinedly.

"Good. Stay on your present course. I'll call you back," Lucian announced and then the phone went silent.

Dante lowered it to peer at its face. Through the

cracked glass he saw that the call had been ended. Breathing out a little sigh, he stood and caught at the edges of his afghan as it tried to slip away to the floor. His gaze then moved over the mess he'd traipsed through to get to the bed. Plastic dishes, utensils, and foodstuffs littered the floor, obviously escapees from the open doors and drawers throughout the RV.

He considered the mess, and then his gaze settled on a bag of chips and his stomach rumbled with interest, reminding him that it had been four days since he'd fed it. Glancing to the back of Mary's head, he asked, "Do you want something to eat or drink?"

Shifting her gaze from the rear camera view to the road ahead, Mary frowned at that question from Dante. She hadn't gotten her supper at the truck stop and was hungry, but that wasn't why she was frowning. His question made her realize that, if he'd been unconscious since Friday, Dante couldn't have eaten since some time that day. The poor man must be starved, she realized and quickly reviewed what she had available to feed him. She'd shopped yesterday to stock up for the trip home. She'd picked up hamburgers and sausages to grill, but she'd also bought fresh bread, wraps, lettuce, tomatoes, onions, and lunchmeats for sandwiches, as well as chips and pop.

"There is stuff in the fridge to make sandwiches if you like," she said now. "And bread in a Rubbermaid container in the cupboard over the television. Chips, too, should be up there. Go ahead and make yourself some sandwiches if you like."

Her attention divided between the slowly thinning traffic on the highway and the rear camera view of the van following them, Mary listened idly to the activity behind her as Dante presumably made himself a sandwich. Doors and drawers opened and closed, accompanied by a lot of crinkling and rustling sounds.

"The coffee machine does not work," Dante announced after several moments had passed. "What do you want instead of coffee?"

Mary's brows knit briefly at the news about the coffee machine, but then she realized what the problem was and said, "Flick the switch on the side of the lower cupboard it's sitting on. The switch is for an inverter."

"Inverter?" he echoed with interest.

"The coffee machine works on one hundred twenty volts, and the RV battery only gives twelve volts or something." She explained, then frowned. "I don't know if I'm getting this right. Joe explained it to me at the time, but . . ." She shrugged. "Basically to use the coffee machine either the generator has to be on when we're stopped, or you turn on the inverter while we're driving. Just remember to turn it off after you're done."

"Okay," he muttered and then she heard the click of the switch being thrown.

Sighing, she concentrated on her breathing and the road ahead, refusing to allow the image of him to rise up in her mind again. Also refusing to glance around for another peek at him. You're much older than him, she reminded herself firmly. It is inappropriate to be drooling over such a young man. Behave.

"How do you take your coffee?"

Mary almost glanced around at the question, but caught herself and said, "Black, please."

The words had barely left her lips when he appeared at her side to set a travel mug in the cup holder next to her empty phone holder.

"Thank you," Mary murmured, catching a glimpse of the colorful afghan out of the corner of her eye before he was gone. Several more minutes passed with sounds coming from the back. It was long enough that Mary began to think he'd sat down at the table to eat, but then he suddenly appeared next to her and settled in the passenger seat. Bailey followed and immediately settled in her usual spot between the two seats. It was only then that Mary realized the dog had abandoned her in favor of their guest. She didn't know whether to be insulted, or be glad Bailey approved of the man. Bailey didn't like many people. If Bailey thought Dante was okay, then Mary's own judgment was being supported. It was nice to have that backup.

"I made you a sandwich too," Dante announced, and then glanced from her to the road and asked, "Do you want me to feed you?"

Mary's eyes widened at the offer, but she quickly shook her head, shaking away the images that question brought to mind: Dante kneeling on the floor beside her, holding a sandwich in front of her mouth for her to bite from. Good Lord, how could that seem erotic? she wondered with dismay.

"No. I can manage," she said and then paused to clear her throat when she heard how croaky she sounded. Good Lord.

Dante set a plate with a sandwich and chips on the dashboard next to the GPS, then settled in his own seat properly and set his own plate on his lap as he did up his seat belt.

Mary chanced a glance at her plate, her eyes widening incredulously at the size of the sandwich. Dear God, the man had stacked it so full of meat and vegetables that she'd have to have an expanding jaw like a snake to eat the darned thing. She switched her gaze to him to say as much, only to pause and stare wide-eyed at the four sandwiches he'd made himself, all even bigger than her own. Dante had one hell of an appetite.

"Eyes on the road," he said and Mary automatically turned forward, but had to wonder how he'd known she was looking. Dante had been concentrating on his plate as he lifted one of the sandwiches to his mouth and couldn't have seen her looking.

Leaving the sandwich for now, she picked up her coffee instead and took a cautious sip. As expected, it was hot, but it was also darned good and exactly what she needed just then.

"Why are you traveling alone?"

Mary glanced to him with surprise, but quickly turned her gaze back to the road. She was slow to answer the question, however, and after a moment, asked, "What do you mean?"

"Most women would not travel alone in an RV, yet you are," he pointed out and then asked simply, "Why?"

Mary sighed and set her coffee back in its holder, before saying dryly, "Good question. That's one I've asked myself several times this trip."

"I do not understand," Dante said and she could hear the frown in his voice.

Grimacing, she switched mental gears and pointed out, "I'm not completely alone. I have Bailey. Besides, there are lots of women who travel alone in their RVs."

Mary wasn't sure if that was true, but she'd met one or two women traveling alone on this trip and had been assured that there were many more than you'd expect. Personally, Mary wasn't sure that was true. She didn't see the attraction herself. This trip had been terribly depressing for her and had pretty much convinced her that she should sell the RV when she got home. But perhaps that was just because of the memories it stirred to life in her. She had found herself constantly reminded of past trips with her dear departed husband during this outing, and missing him horribly. She'd even left early because of it, heading home a week earlier than planned just to bring it to an end.

"How long have you been doing this?" Dante asked curiously.

Mary was silent for a minute and then said, "My husband and I have been driving south for the winter ever since he retired six years ago." She frowned and added,

"Well, I guess we both retired then. At least I stopped seeing clients. Although I still sit on several boards that I am involved with. I attend the meetings when home and skype with members while travelling."

"You are married?"

Startled by the strangled tone to his voice, Mary glanced to Dante with surprise. The horror on his face made her eyebrows rise slightly, but she shifted her attention back to the road and said quietly, "I was. I am widowed now. Joe had a major heart attack and died on our return journey last year." Hearing the beginning of huskiness in her voice, she cleared her throat, before adding, "This was my first trip alone. And my last," she added dryly.

Silence stretched out between them briefly and then Dante murmured a quiet, "My sympathies for your loss."

Mary nodded stiffly, suddenly having to battle back tears. She'd managed to get the information out without losing it, but he offered her his sympathies and she was hard put not to cry like a baby. Damn, this grief business was a tricky bitch, sneaking up on her at the most inopportune times.

Swallowing the sudden lump in her throat, Mary quickly dashed the back of one wrist over her eyes to remove the few tears that had escaped. Apparently her upset didn't escape Dante, because he suddenly murmured, "Perhaps I should take over driving."

"No!" Mary barked, her mind filling with a sudden image of his sitting in her lap with nothing but the ridiculous afghan covering, or not covering, his bits while she tried to slip out from under him. Good God! Trying for a calmer tone of voice, she said, "No, but thank you. I'll be fine."

Dante was silent for a minute, and then murmured, "If you are sure . . . ?"

"I'm sure," she said solemnly, and then changed the subject, asking, "How did you end up working for the Feds?"

"The Feds?" Dante queried uncertainly.

Mary glanced to him with surprise, but then turned her gaze back to the road and said, "I assumed since this was a kidnapping case, that the task force you were helping out was federal. Isn't it?"

"Oh, yes, I see," he murmured and then cleared his throat and said, "My brother and I volunteered."

"Really?" she asked with surprise. "So you aren't a fed yourself?"

"No," he murmured.

"What do you do then?" she asked curiously.

Dante hesitated and then shrugged. "Some protection work, some other things. Whatever is needed."

"I see," she said slowly, and thought the translation of that was probably that he was mostly unemployed. There seemed to be a lot of that today. When she'd been young, most people had graduated from high school to go on to further education, work, or sometimes—for the girls like her—marriage. There had been perhaps a handful of kids who hadn't graduated and had fallen by the wayside, but for the most part they were the exception to the rule. Nowadays, it seemed like there were a lot more exceptions to the rule. More of the young seemed to be not settling into work or a career, but wandering through life, mostly unemployed and unsettled, couch surfing their way through life.

Mary grimaced to herself and acknowledged that she was sounding like her own grandmother. She couldn't recall how many times the woman had started a rant by saying, "when I was young."

"Tell me about your husband," Dante said suddenly.

Mary glanced around with surprise at the request and then turned forward again. She opened her mouth to say no, and instead found herself saying, "He was a good man."

When she didn't continue, Dante asked, "How did you meet?"

"We were high school sweethearts," she answered solemnly. "My first kiss, my first date, my first everything."

He seemed to consider that and then asked, "Do you ever feel like you missed out? Not getting to date other men or experience—?"

"No," Mary interrupted. She'd been asked the question before. Usually by younger people who seemed horrified that she hadn't kissed and slept with loads of men before settling down with Joe. "I was very lucky. Some women go their whole life searching for, but never finding their perfect life mate. I was lucky enough to find mine before I was even looking."

"Life mate?" Dante asked and something about his tone of voice made her glance curiously his way.

"Yes," she murmured, noting his odd expression before glancing back to the road. "Mate for life. I could have said *husband*, I suppose, or *dream man*, but *dream man* sounds stupid, and husband just doesn't cover all that Joe was to me." She paused briefly, and then said, "I suppose life partner is the better description. He was my partner in every sense, my best friend, my lover, my husband, my cohort in crime," she ended with a grin.

"Crime?" Dante sounded shocked and she chuckled at his tone of voice.

"Not criminal type crime," she assured him. "We weren't Bonnie and Clyde or anything. I just meant, if there was a prank to be pulled, or a gag joke . . ." She shrugged. "We had the same sense of humor and laughed a lot over the years."

"It sounds . . . perfect," Dante said, and she noted that he sounded less than pleased to say so.

"No," she said solemnly. "Nothing is perfect. Not even my Joe. But after a couple of bumps in the beginning we had a good life."

"What kind of bumps?" Dante asked at once, sounding almost eager.

Mary hesitated, very old, very painful memories welling up inside her, but then she merely shook her head. "It doesn't matter now. No one is perfect, Dante."

They were both silent for a moment. Dante was eating and Mary was shifting her attention between the road and her own sandwich, trying to figure out how the hell she was going to eat it. She hadn't come up with anything by the time Dante finished his sandwiches and headed back to set the plate in the sink. At least, she hoped he put it in the sink. It would go flying at the first turn or stop if he didn't, she thought, and risked a glance over her shoulder. Her attention was caught then as she noted the RV had been cleaned up. There were no more items littering the floor. Everything had been stowed away and all the doors and drawers were now closed once more.

"Eyes on the road," Dante said mildly, catching her looking when he turned to head back toward the front seats.

Mary turned forward again, but said, "Thank you for cleaning up."

"It was my fault," Dante said simply as he reached her side. He didn't immediately take his seat again, however, but scooted Bailey out of the way, and knelt where the dog had been lying.

Mary glanced warily toward him to see that he was eyeing her solemnly.

"You are tired," he announced. "And no doubt hungry."

"I'm fine," Mary said quietly.

"I can either feed you, or I will take over driving. Your choice."

"I'm fine," Mary repeated, swallowing nervously as she considered both options.

"You are afraid because you are attracted to me," Dante announced with amusement and Mary scowled at the road.

"Someone has an ego on them," she growled. "I am not attracted to you. You're a child. I'm an older woman. I like big boys."

"I am a big boy," Dante said easily, managing not to sound like a braggart as he stated the obvious. And it *was* obvious. The man stood at least six feet eight, and his shoulder breadth was breathtaking. He was like a wall beside her, even on his knees.

"I meant a grown-up," she said irritably.

"I am older than I look," he assured her mildly. "And I know you are attracted to me. Your heart rate and breathing pick up every time I am near you."

Mary glanced at him sharply at that comment, and froze when she noted that the silver flecks in his black eyes appeared to have at least doubled in number. It almost seemed like they were glowing too, she noted faintly.

"The road," he reminded her and Mary tore her gaze from him to concentrate on the road again, but she couldn't get his eyes out of her mind. She'd never seen eyes like his before. So deep and dark and beautiful at first, and now glowing with silver like fine jewels.

"You must eat," Dante announced and her sandwich suddenly appeared in front of her face.

Mary peered at it reluctantly, but shook her head.

"Come," he coaxed, pressing it against her lips. "If you will not let me feed you, I will take your place at the wheel. I will lift you up, slip under you and take over driving."

Mary actually felt the way her heart jumped at the suggestion. It then began to beat away at an accelerated rate that was almost scary. She had an old ticker. It shouldn't be this active.

"See?" There was no mistaking the satisfaction in Dante's voice. "Your heartbeat is racing at the thought of my hands on you."

"My heart is racing with anger at your insolence," she countered shortly. "Did no one ever teach you to respect your elders?"

"Mary, you must—"

"Your friends are dropping back," Mary interrupted and Dante immediately lowered the sandwich and turned his gaze to the rear camera view. They both watched silently as the van behind them grew smaller on the screen. It had grown to about half size when a pickup pulled in front of it and between them.

"Do you think they're giving up on you?" she asked.

"I am not sure. I must call Lucian to see if they got Tomasso out," he muttered and set her sandwich back on the dashboard before standing to move to the back of the RV.

Mary relaxed a little the moment he wasn't hovering at her side. Honestly, the man was just overwhelming. His size, his scent, and his sexy deep voice with its charming accent . . . everything about him was distracting and overwhelming. So much so that she was hoping that his followers were giving up and letting him go. If so, it meant she could soon be rid of him. A good thing, she assured herself, ignoring the disappointment that the thought of his leaving brought up in her.

Her gaze slid to the rear camera view and she squinted as she noted that someone seemed to be leaning out of the passenger window of the pickup behind them. The image was all different shades of gray and she couldn't be sure, but it almost looked like the person was aiming a gun at the RV. Not a gun, she thought in the next moment, more like a crossbow or something maybe.

"Dante," she said with alarm, afraid they were perhaps with the van and were about to shoot out the tires on the RV or something.

"What is it?" Dante asked, his voice growing nearer.

Mary opened her mouth to answer, but then paused uncertainly. The person had slid back into the pickup and it was now dropping back too. The RV tires were all still intact as far as she could tell, so she gathered they hadn't been shot out.

"Mary, the road!" Dante cried suddenly and she switched her gaze back to the road to see that in her distraction she'd been steering to the right, toward the shoulder of the road. In fact she was already on the white line. Heart jumping in alarm, she quickly steered back to the left. Once she had it straightened out in the center of the lane, she let her breath out on a slow sigh.

Dante relaxed beside her and then leaned past her to set her phone back in the holder.

"Did they get your brother out?" she asked quietly.

"I do not know. Lucian did not answer," Dante said unhappily. "I left a message for him to call me."

"What are you doing?" Mary asked with alarm when he dropped to his knees next to her again.

"I am going to feed you," he said firmly.

"Dante—" she began in a warning tone.

"You need to eat," he interrupted sternly, picking up one half of her sandwich and turning toward her.

"I will eat," she said quickly. "You can take over driving at the next gas station."

"Mary, we cannot stop," he said solemnly. "It is too risky."

"Your friends have dropped back so far I can't even see their lights anymore," she countered, and then added, "We have to stop, Dante. We're almost out of gas."

"What?" he asked with alarm and glanced to the gas gauge to see that it was nearly on empty.

"Why is it so low?" he asked, sounding shocked that she would let that happen.

"Because I didn't get gas before leaving the truck stop as I intended," Mary said dryly. "I didn't get the chance. I wasn't driving."

When he merely stared at her, worry on his face, she said, "They've dropped back. I think they've given up on us. For all we know they've pulled off the highway and turned back to head to the house where you were kept," she pointed out.

"But what if they are just feigning giving up?" he asked with a frown. "They could just be letting us think they have given up in hopes that we'll stop somewhere and they can catch us unawares."

Mary's mouth tightened at the suggestion, and she glanced to the rear camera view, wishing it had telescoping abilities so that she could see if they were still back there or not. It didn't, however, and after a moment she sighed and said, "We'll have to take the risk. We need gas."

Cursing, Dante stood and set her sandwich back on her plate, then glanced around as if for a spare gas tank they might use.

"According to the Garmin there's a gas station not too far ahead. We should make it there," she added hopefully and couldn't believe she hadn't noticed until now that they were so seriously low on gas. She usually kept an eye on it. Of course, this wasn't your usual day, she excused herself. Besides, she wasn't lying; she had intended to get gas at the truck stop. At least she had before she'd found Dante naked in her bedroom bleeding all over the place. After that she hadn't thought of it once.

"You have no back windows," Dante announced suddenly, as if that might have escaped her notice. "If you had back windows I could—"

"You could what?" she asked curiously when he paused. When he didn't respond at once, she glanced around to see that he was poking at the air vent in the ceiling next to the dinette table. It looked like he was considering it as an escape route or something. She had no idea why. The man couldn't possibly fit through it. Besides, where did he think he was escaping to?

"No good," he muttered and moved back between the seats.

A glance showed her that he was now eyeing the passenger side window with interest. Even as she noted that, he settled in the passenger seat and then opened his window. The screen followed, sliding smoothly to the side.

Mary considered the hole it left and thought that he might very well fit through it. She just had no idea why he'd want to. Where did he want to go? He was safer inside than out . . . at least until his kidnappers broke in and shot them full of darts.

"How far until the gas station?" Dante asked suddenly.

Mary glanced to the GPS and frowned. "Maybe five minutes."

Dante nodded and then turned to lean out the window and peer up.

"What are you thinking?" she asked with concern.

Dante settled back in his seat and glanced around to explain, "If they *are* feigning their lack of interest and do suddenly appear when we stop for gas, they could shoot me with their darts as soon as I opened the door," he pointed out. "We would not have a chance."

Mary bit her lip at his words, knowing he was probably right.

"However, they would not expect me to be on the roof of the RV," he pointed out.

"The roof?" she squawked with amazement.

"*Si*. If I slip up on the roof now, I can watch for them while you get the gas. Then if they do suddenly appear, I can—"

"You are not getting up on the damned roof," Mary interrupted with dismay.

"Mary," he said solemnly. "We need to stop for gas, and for us to do so, I must get up on the roof."

"How the hell is your being on the roof going to help us get gas?" she asked with disbelief.

He hesitated, but then sighed and explained, "If I can see them, I can take control of their minds and make them keep their distance or perhaps even capture them. But I must do so without their seeing me, else they will shoot me with one of their darts and all will be lost." He glanced to the side mirror again and added, "It should be all right. They cannot possibly see me in the dark from as far back as they are now, and they will not be expecting this so I should have the time I need to slip into their minds and take control before they spot me and shoot."

Mary tore her gaze from him and back to the road ahead, her mind filled with disbelief. After a moment, she heaved a sad sigh and shook her head. Of course, she'd run over the crazy guy. Gorgeous, but completely bonkers was her diagnosis. Such a shame.

Clearing her throat, she finally spoke in soothing tones. "Dante, I think maybe you hit your head when I ran you over. Why don't we— Dante!" Mary gasped as she looked over to see his head and bare chest disappearing out of the window. The rest of his nakedness was following.

Mary reached instinctively toward him, but stopped and straightened the wheel when the RV swerved with her. Cursing, she shifted her gaze from the road, to each of the mirrors and then the rear camera view, but of course, none of them showed a view of the roof of the RV. Fortunately, none of them showed a naked-ass man rolling away from the RV after tumbling from the roof either, she thought and tossed a scowl toward the colorful afghan that was now pooled on the floor in front of the passenger seat.

"Down Bailey," she ordered firmly when the dog jumped up onto the seat to peer curiously out the window after their absent guest. The dog jumped down at once to sit on the afghan and Mary shook her head, thinking with irritation that she really should have made him put on some damned clothes. He was ob-

viously crazy and incapable of looking after himself.
Why hadn't she insisted he go to the bedroom and get
some of her husband's clothes and put them on, she
asked herself grimly. But knew the answer was that
she'd been reluctant to see anyone in her Joe's clothes.
She hadn't even been ready to remove them from the
RV and give them to charity, as she should have. It had
been a year, and she still hadn't removed a single item
of his from either their home or the RV. She'd clung on
to them as if keeping them meant he wasn't really gone
and that he would walk through the door one day with
hugs and kisses and flowers.

Her gaze lifted to the ceiling of the RV as the sounds
of movement overhead reached her ears. Dante was
moving along the roof of the RV. Dear God, she had a
naked-ass man on her roof! That thought kept screaming through her head as her gaze continually shot from
road, to mirror, to mirror, to camera screen, but it went
suddenly silent when she spotted the lights of the gas
station ahead.

Five

"Damn," Mary breathed, knowing there was nothing else but for her to pull into the damned station. She couldn't afford not to unless she wanted to be stuck on the side of the highway, as helpless as Jonah in—what in this case would be—a beached whale. So she *had* to stop, and with a naked-ass man on her roof.

Mary muttered under her breath and slowed the RV to turn in. She was more than relieved when she saw that there were presently no other vehicles in the station. She would only have a shocked and probably hysterical attendant to deal with then, she thought with a grimace.

"My apologies, Mary. You will have to pump the gas. I must remain up here to watch for our hunters so that I may control them if they pull in after us."

Mary rolled her eyes as that announcement floated through her open window. Not because she had to pump gas. She'd pumped her own gas all the way south and had intended to all the way back. What caused the eye rolling was his claim that he had to control their hunters. Really? Did he believe he could? Or that she'd believe he could? Dante was pretty but crazy and that was just sad, she decided, maneuvering the RV as close to the pumps as she could get. It seemed a terrible shame that God had made such a perfect specimen and forgotten to ensure his brain worked properly as well.

"Dear God, I have a naked-ass man on my roof," Mary muttered the thought aloud this time as she put the RV in park and turned it off. Saying it aloud did not help. Shaking her head, she slid out of her seat and moved to the door. Bailey immediately tried to follow, but Mary gave her a firm, "Stay," and managed to slide out without the dog escaping.

Closing the door with a firm snap, she glanced toward the gas station, expecting to see the attendant either plastered to the plate glass window, gaping like a fish out of water, or on the phone to the police. But the young man inside the building was looking down at something on the counter and didn't seem to have even noticed their arrival.

Grateful for small mercies, Mary walked hopefully to the pump, but of course it was prepay. The pumps were prepay in Canada too. You either paid at the pump with a credit or debit card, or you prepaid. At home she would have just used her credit card, but Mary never used them in the States. She'd get soaked when it came to charges and exchange by her credit card company.

Despite that, she almost used her credit card anyway this time, but in the end, headed for the building.

Mary glanced toward the highway as she walked, searching for the van. But it hadn't made an appearance. Yet. Her gaze then slid to the RV and she saw that Dante was lying on the roof at the rear end of the vehicle, his bare ass shining under the glare of the station lights like some kind of beacon. Closing her eyes, she shook her head and then turned and slid into the station to pay for the gas. It didn't take more than a moment. The attendant was busy reading an auto magazine and barely glanced up to ring up her request and take her money. He wasn't even interested enough to look out the window to see what kind of vehicle might need so much gas.

Beginning to think they might make it out of there without causing the scene she'd feared, Mary headed back out to the RV, her gaze steadfastly avoiding Dante on her roof and shifting to the passing vehicles. If anyone was taking note of a naked man lying on his belly on the roof of an RV, you couldn't tell. The cars were just cruising by, none of them with any sign that he'd even been noticed.

Marveling over that, Mary set about the business of pumping gas into her vehicle, her attention shifting between the pump and the oncoming traffic.

"There is no need to fret. I will control them if they come."

Mary glanced up at that announcement to see Dante peering over the back of the roof at her. Nodding, she said wryly, "Good to know."

His eyes narrowed, but Dante didn't comment and merely ducked back out of sight, presumably to continue watching for the kidnappers, so he could *control* them. She shook her head at the thought. As if anyone could control another human being with his or her thoughts.

Muttering under her breath, she glanced from the spinning numbers on the pump to the passing traffic and back. The van had dropped back in traffic, which when she thought about it was weird. It wasn't like the RV had been speeding down the highway. It simply wasn't capable of speeding. She'd been driving the speed limit, maybe even a little under it, yet the van had backed off, going under the speed limit to do so. What were they up to? she wondered with a little concern and then glanced to the pump with surprise when it clicked and stopped pumping. She'd reached the amount for which she'd prepaid, which should just about fill it up, by her guess.

Removing the handle, she set it back in the pump, then quickly screwed the gas cap back on and closed the cover.

"Go ahead and start out."

Mary glanced up at that instruction. Dante was peering down at her again.

"I'll climb in once we're on the road again," he said and then pulled back out of sight before she could comment. Mary glanced to the building, and then shook her head and walked around the RV to the door.

Bailey was waiting by the door when she opened it and Mary had to urge the dog back to get in. Locking the door, she then sat in the driver's seat, started the engine and pulled away from the pumps. She eased up to the road and paused to wait for traffic to clear. It wasn't as busy as earlier in the day, but there were still a good number of cars passing . . . and then a pickup passed with a dark van behind it.

Mary narrowed her eyes on the two vehicles, but they flew past without slowing and didn't pull over farther down the highway that she could see. Once they were out of sight in the distance, she started to turn her gaze back to the oncoming traffic, only to whip her head around in surprise as Dante came swinging in through the passenger window. Her timing could not have been worse; she got an eyeful of the man's junk as his hips were framed in the opening before he dropped into the seat.

"They've driven past," he announced. "But they went by too fast for me to take control."

Mary simply gaped at him.

"They may be planning to ambush us further up the highway. Maybe I should drive now," he suggested. Dante had landed sideways in the seat with his knees pointed her way and his lap fully exposed.

He shifted forward on the seat now to get up and Mary snapped, "No, you're not driving. You're going to sit there and cover up that dangler you keep waving in my face before I cut it off."

Dante's eyebrows rose, and then he calmly leaned to the side to pull the afghan out from under Bailey who had again settled on it. He pulled it across his lap, started to spread it out as he had before, then seemed to realize how ineffective that made it and left it in a pile over his groin.

"Seat belt," she said more calmly now.

Dante hesitated and she suspected he was considering insisting on driving, but then he simply turned in the seat to face front and did up his seat belt.

Satisfied, Mary glanced out to see that there was an opening in traffic, and hit the gas harder than she should have, sending the RV careening out onto the highway at a speedy 10 mph. Apparently the opening wasn't as big as she'd thought, that or the approaching car was far exceeding the speed limit. Whatever the case, the driver laid on the horn in protest.

Mary sighed to herself and ignored it to concentrate on driving. That was difficult to do with Dante seated beside her. Honestly, she'd never seen a man so comfortable being naked. She'd always considered her husband a confident man, but even Joe hadn't wandered around and swung through windows with his Johnson out. Hell, he wouldn't have stepped out the door of the RV naked, let alone climb around on the roof like some hairless monkey . . . a very buff and handsome hairless monkey.

"You should let me drive," Dante said quietly. "They may be planning to ambush us further up the highway."

Mary opened her mouth, closed it, and then sighed to herself as she looked at her sandwich. She really should have let him drive, then she could be eating her sandwich, which really looked delicious. Fortunately they'd nearly reached her planned destination, and she did intend to stop. The question was, what she was going to do about Dante once she did? Mary didn't have an easy answer to that. The man thought he could control people. It might be a result of his head injury, but she wasn't sure head injuries could lead to delusions. She'd have to research that once they'd stopped, she decided. In the meantime, she needed to see how deep his delusions ran.

"Dante, if you can control your kidnappers, how did they kidnap you?" she asked in a conversational tone.

He hesitated beside her and she suspected he wanted to continue to pester her about driving, but then he sighed and said, "We were taken by surprise. They must have been waiting. The first we knew of their presence was when the darts hit us."

"Right," she murmured, staring at the red rear lights of the cars ahead on the road. After a moment, she pointed out, "But when you woke up in the cage, you couldn't have been taken by surprise. Why didn't you just wait for them to enter the room and take control of them then?"

She felt him look her way, but kept her gaze on the road and after a moment he patiently explained, "There was a square panel in the metal door to the room at about eye level. We feared they might open it and shoot us without our getting a look at them and being able to control them."

"I see," she murmured. Mary considered that briefly, than commented, "So you have to see them to control them."

"Of course," he said as if that should be obvious.

Mary didn't comment, but her thoughts were now

spinning through her head as quickly as the numbers had spun on the gas pump. Dante had seemed so sane at first. Well, mostly, she thought with a frown as it occurred to her that perhaps the whole "I'm being chased by kidnappers" maybe sounded a little farfetched now, but it had seemed plausible at the time. The man had been running around naked, for heaven's sake. And that black van had seemed to be following them. Now though, she was beginning to wonder if anything he'd told her had been true. Had he really been kidnapped?

And what about that claim that he and his brother had volunteered to help an FBI task force? Mary had never heard of that before. Surely the agency wouldn't send civilians into such a dangerous situation?

The truth was, now that he was claiming to be able to control people, everything he'd told her was suspect. It could all be a lie, or some sort of delusion his mind had created. He could be an escapee from a mental ward or something. That was certainly more plausible than his being an escaped kidnap victim, volunteer for the FBI, and able to control people with his mind.

Biting her lip, she glanced to the GPS and was relieved to see that they were approaching the turn for the campground. There she could stop dividing her attention between driving and what to do about Dante. She'd also have help in dealing with him. She and Joe had used this campground every year since they'd started driving south for the winter, stopping on their way down and on the return journey. She knew the owners, Dave and Carol Bigelow, very well. They were originally from Winnipeg and had been friends to her and Joe since long before the couple had retired, bought the campground, and moved here to Texas. Carol and Dave would help her if she needed it. Although, Mary wasn't that concerned that Dante might be dangerous. He might be a little deluded maybe, but she didn't think he was dangerous.

"Mary," Dante said tentatively. "You seem a little agitated, and I hate to keep harping on this, but we need to be prepared in case they are planning to ambush us."

"It won't be a problem," she assured him.

"But— What are you doing?" he asked with surprise when she slowed.

"I'm turning, Dante," she answered patiently.

"Why?"

"Because we're stopping for the night. I booked a spot at a campground just up this road."

"But Lucian said to keep them chasing us," he protested.

"Look in the rear camera view, Dante. Do you see anyone following us?" She shook her head. "That ship has sailed, and I'm tired. We're stopping. At least I am. You, of course, are free to get out any time." Turning to glance at him, she added, "Now, please go into the bedroom and find some clothes to wear. The last thing I want is for my friends to see me pull in with a naked giant in the passenger seat. I'm going to have enough trouble explaining you as it is."

Dante considered her solemnly for a moment, and then stood up, gathering the afghan in a ball in front of his groin. Before moving away he asked politely, "May I use your phone again?"

"Yes," she said quietly, and he picked it up out of the holder and moved toward the back of the RV.

The moment she heard the door to the bedroom area slide closed, Mary felt herself relax. It was only then she realized how tense he made her. And it wasn't just his nudity that caused that tension, although that hadn't helped. She really should have sent him to put on clothes much sooner than this, she acknowledged and wondered what he would put on. Joe's jeans and dress pants probably wouldn't fit him. They'd probably be too big in the waist, although she supposed a belt would handle that issue. But there were joggers too. As for shirts, again Joe's dress shirts probably wouldn't fit, this time being too small, but there were T-shirts that might be a bit tight but should do.

Spotting the sign for Dave and Carol's campground, Mary pushed thoughts of Dante's fashion choices aside and concentrated on slowing for the turn. She pulled into the driveway, passing the stone columns with the sign overhead and stopped beside the office, then threw the RV into park and was about to shut her down, when a shout drew her attention out the window to see Carol rushing to the RV, waving.

"We saved your usual spot, Mary. Go ahead and park. Dave is getting the golf cart. He'll bring you back to register and have a drink," she called through the window once she got close enough.

Mary nodded. "Thanks, Carol."

"Our pleasure. See you in a minute," she called with a big grin and turned to head back to the building. Mary watched her go, then shifted back to drive and started forward. Carol and Dave had been saving "their spot" for them for years now. A pull-thru spot on the end, surrounded by trees, it had a lovely view of the river. They'd always parked with the door and awning side facing the other RVs, welcoming friends they'd made over the years. This year, Mary wasn't sure how she was going to explain Dante, so she pulled in with the door and awning facing the woods and the river. Basically, putting her back to the others.

Feeling guilty for it even as she parked that way, Mary glanced around, but not seeing Dave approaching yet on his golf cart, she pushed the auto button on the automatic leveling system and listened to the hum of the jacks lowering to the ground. The RV bounced a little one way, then another, then up in the front and then the back and then stopped moving and the green light came on indicating it was level. Releasing the breath she always held during this process, she turned off the engine and got up, then paused, looking for Bailey. The dog was nowhere to be seen.

Frowning, she moved to the back of the RV and knocked on the door. "Dante, is Bailey in there with you? She'll need walking, and she hasn't eaten yet, but Dave is coming to collect me to go register and—" She paused as the door started to open, and then she merely gaped at the man.

He had gone for joggers and a T-shirt as she'd expected and yet not what she'd expected at all. He was wearing *her* joggers and T-shirt. The man had donned her favorite pair of pink jogging pants that were so tight on him they were like a second skin. They also only reached halfway down his calves. The T-shirt fit no better. It was a white one with tiny pink and red roses all over it and the damned thing stretched tight across his shoulders and encased his chest like a stocking, a pink and white flowered stocking.

Dante should have looked ridiculous in the getup, and she was sure he probably did, but the clothes also drew the gaze to the breadth of his beautiful chest. At least it did if you could tear your eyes away from the way the tight joggers emphasized the huge bulge between his legs.

Mary closed her eyes on the sight he made, but once again found that the image appeared to be burned into her retinas and continued to dance on her eyelids.

"I shall feed and walk Bailey," Dante offered quietly and Mary blinked her eyes open and merely shook her head. Not expecting her dead husband's clothes to still be in the RV, he'd obviously just grabbed what he thought he might squeeze into from her closet and hadn't even thought to check the closet on the other side of the bed. Mary was about to tell him that there were men's clothes there when a knock sounded at the RV door.

"Dave," she muttered, glancing to the door in a bit of a panic. She started toward it, then paused and whirled back. "My purse . . ."

Dante must have seen it when he'd found the clothes he was wearing because he immediately turned and pulled the door open to retrieve it. Handing it to her, he patted her arm. "Relax. All is well, I will see to Bailey."

"Right," she muttered, rushing toward the door, and then as she opened the door, thought to call out, "Her leash is hanging on a hook in my closet."

"Talking to the dog now, Mary?" Dave teased curiously as she started down the steps.

Mary forced a laugh and shook her head, then said, "My nephew is driving back with me."

The lie came out so smoothly you would have thought she'd planned it out. She hadn't though; it just came to her on the spot, but she was grateful for it.

"That's nice," Dave said, smiling as he led her to the golf cart he'd driven from the office. "I could tell you found it a bit much driving down on your own when you stopped here in the fall."

"Yes," Mary said quietly as she got in next to him. "It was a bit more than I expected. It's much nicer when you have someone to share the driving."

"I can imagine," Dave assured her as he headed the golf cart back the way he'd come. "I sure wouldn't want to run this place without Carol helping."

Mary smiled, and then found herself glancing over her shoulder back toward the RV. She hadn't turned on the lights or let the sides out or anything. She should have done that, she supposed. It would make things easier for Dante. While there were hookups for water, sewer, and 50 amp power supplies, there were no night-lights around the RVs to give him light. He'd be feeling his way around inside.

Clucking her tongue with irritation at her thoughtlessness, she turned to face forward again and listened to Dave's cheerful chatter about how busy the winter had been for them with all the snowbirds coming and going.

"But when you called last week and asked if you could move your booking forward, Carol worked her magic and managed to rearrange our other bookings for you," Dave informed her.

"I appreciate that," Mary said quietly. "But I told her I'd take anything you had available. I didn't want to put you out."

"You didn't. She was happy to do it. You know Carol," he added affectionately.

"Yes," Mary said with a smile. It would be hard to find a woman with a bigger heart than Carol had. She'd become a dear friend over the years. They both had. Which was why Mary had booked two nights here this time. She'd already decided she wasn't doing this again. The trip just wasn't the same alone. Knowing this would be the last time she made the trek back and forth, she'd wanted to have a nice last visit with this couple who had been so good to her and Joe over the years. But with Dante to worry about, Mary now wasn't sure she should stay the extra night.

"Good God, woman, what did you do? Drive thirty all the way from Padre Island?"

Mary smiled at that greeting from Carol as the petite bottle blonde pulled her into a hug the moment Dave ushered her inside the office.

"I'm sorry," Mary said as she hugged her back. "I know it's late. You probably wanted to close shop and go relax hours ago."

"Nonsense. We keep the store open late," Carol said

at once, stepping back to scowl at her. "We were worried about you is all. Started thinking we maybe should call the sheriff's department and see if there was an accident on the highway or something."

Mary grimaced at the word *accident*, but just shook her head. "I'm fine. Just slow."

"Hmm, well you come sign in and we'll get you a nice drink to soothe your nerves from driving," Carol said, leading her to the registration counter. "Dave, fetch her a rum and coke on ice."

"Oh, no," Mary protested at once. "Thank you, but I still have to hook up and put out the slide-outs and stuff."

"Let your nephew take care of that. That's what he's here for," Dave said lightly, moving into the office to fetch glasses.

"He doesn't know how to do any of that . . . yet," she added when both Carol and Dave turned to peer at her in surprise. "This is his first day in the RV."

"Oh," Dave smiled wryly. "How's he liking it so far?"

Mary merely shrugged helplessly and turned her attention to the clipboard waiting on the countertop. It was her registration, already mostly filled out by Carol for her. Mary merely had to sign it. She did so, then pulled out her credit card and offered it, but Carol waved it away.

"You can do that when you leave, Mary. We trust you."

Mary hesitated, but then decided it might be best to pay up front. She wasn't sure what would happen in the morning and didn't want to have to make explanations if they did leave early. This way, she was covered. Smiling, she shook her head and held the card out insistently, saying lightly, "I'm used to doing it at the start and I'm not getting any younger, my memory isn't as good as it used to be. Best do it now."

Shrugging, Carol took the credit card and rang it up.

"Well, if you won't have a drink with us now, promise you'll come by for breakfast in the morning," Dave demanded, then added, "On the house."

"That would be nice," Mary said and meant it. At least that way if anything happened to force her to leave early she'd have gotten in a bit of a visit with them first.

"Good," Carol said firmly as she handed her back her credit card. "We'll hold you to that. Dave will come fetch you and your nephew if you aren't both here by eight."

"Understood," Mary said with a tired smile.

"Ah, honey, you're exhausted," Carol said with concern, then glanced to her husband. "Dave, maybe you better take her back to her RV and help her hook up. She looks ready to fall over."

Nodding, Dave grabbed a large flashlight off the counter and walked back around the counter to usher her to the door.

"See you tomorrow morning," Carol called as they left.

Dave kept up a steady chatter about people at the campground that she knew from previous stays as he drove her back to the RV, but she noted that he kept sending worried glances her way. It made her wonder just how bad she must look. Pretty bad, she decided when he stopped at the RV and turned to her to ask, "How's your health, sweetheart? Everything okay?"

"I'm fine," she assured him on a weak laugh. "I'm just tired. I'll be right as rain after a good night's sleep."

"Good, good," Dave said, but didn't look like he believed her.

With his help, hooking up to the power, water, and sewer was quick work. Mary thanked him for his help, hugged him and promised she'd be by for breakfast in the morning, and then waved him off, before turning to peer at the door to the RV. There were no lights inside, but she wasn't terribly surprised. Dante probably didn't know where the switches were.

Sighing, Mary walked to the door, opened it and started inside, hitting the switch on the counter next to the steps as she ascended them. Letting the door close behind her, she then paused and glanced around. Dante and Bailey weren't there.

Still out for their walk, she thought. After being cooped up in the RV all day, Bailey would probably drag Dante all over the campgrounds. She just hoped Dante didn't let her chase the deer or any of the other wildlife.

Shrugging that worry away, Mary moved to the panel on the wall before the bedroom door and pushed the button for the living area slide out. The front half of the RV's left wall immediately began to slide outward, taking the dinette and couch with it. Once it was all the way out, there was a good three or four foot span of open space between the furnishings and the kitchen counter along the opposite wall. Mary then turned to peer into the bedroom as she pressed the button for the second slide-out and watched as the wall at the head of the bed began to move out, taking the bed with it. When it stopped there was room enough to walk around the end of the bed, open the drawers, and whatnot. The cramped RV was now a more spacious little house on wheels.

Relaxing a little, Mary turned on the water heater, and flipped on some lights, then moved to the coffee machine to make herself a cup. She set out a Keurig cup and a mug for Dante as well, but didn't make it. She doubted he'd appreciate cold coffee. He might even prefer a cold drink.

After setting her coffee on the table, Mary retrieved her sandwich from the front dashboard where it still sat. She had just picked up the plate, and had started to turn back toward the table when she spotted her phone. Dante had obviously put it back in its holder before taking Bailey out, she thought and snatched that up as well. She carried both items to the table and slid onto one of the dinette's booth seats to eat.

Even after having sat out for half an hour or so, the sandwich was as good as it had first looked and Mary found herself gobbling it down. It seemed like no time before she finished the first half, and that's about the time that she began to realize how much she'd needed to eat. It was almost nine now, which meant it had been almost nine hours since lunch. Her brain had obviously needed the nutrients, because it was suddenly thinking more clearly than it had since she'd run over Dante. The day's events ran through her head like a film and she began to get more and more uncomfortable as it went. She had a complete stranger traveling with her, one who was slightly delusional and possibly dangerous.

Where was he going to sleep tonight?

And how well was she going to sleep with him in the RV with her?

Mary sat back at the table with a frown, and then her gaze dropped to the phone and she recalled the calls he'd made. Three of them in all, she thought. Picking up the phone, she opened it to the recent calls page and peered at the number he'd called.

The area code was 416. It had seemed familiar when he'd first spoken it to her, but now it suddenly clicked in. Toronto, she thought. Her daughter lived there and had that area code. FBI based in Canada? Mary's mouth tightened and she tapped the number, making the phone redial it.

Six

Mary pressed the phone to her ear and listened to it ring, then stilled when a ring was prematurely silenced and a male voice snapped, "Speak Dante."

Biting her lip, she glanced toward the open window and then cleared her throat and asked, "Who am I speaking to?"

When silence came to her through the phone, she recalled what Dante had said earlier and asked, "Is this Lucian?"

"Yes," he said finally, his voice wary but edged with concern. He asked sharply, "Did Dante's kidnappers recapture him?"

Mary's eyes widened slightly. When she'd realized it was a Toronto area code, she'd thought for sure everything Dante had said was lies or delusions, but it seemed that part, at least, was true.

"Hello?" the man snapped after a moment.

Realizing she hadn't answered him, Mary cleared her throat and said, "No."

"He's hurt then?" the man asked next, his voice sharp.

Mary hesitated, and then sighed and said, "I think so."

"You *think* so? What the hell do you mean you think—?"

"I ran over him with my RV," Mary rushed out, interrupting his caustic words. "And I think he may have taken some damage to his head."

Silence came down the line at her in response and Mary frowned and continued, "Look, he told me he's working for a task force looking into a case where several young people have been disappearing from bars in the San Antonio area."

"Yes," came the calm response this time when she paused and Mary frowned uncertainly.

"That's true?"

"Yes," Lucian said again.

Mary sat back in her seat. So that hadn't been some sort of delusion of Dante's. He really had been kidnapped while trying to find out who was kidnapping these unknown people in San Antonio, she thought, then frowned with confusion and said, "But you're in Canada. Why would a task force looking into kidnappings in Texas be based in Canada?"

There was a pause and then he said simply, "It's an international case."

Mary waited for further explanations. For him to tell her that both the Feds and the Canadians were working the case together, that perhaps Canadians were amongst those who had gone missing, but he didn't say anything.

Sighing her frustration, she shook her head, and then said, "Okay, so he really is helping out this task force, and he really was kidnapped and escaped his kidnappers. But the kid thinks he can control minds."

"He told you that?" Lucian snapped, his voice so sharp and hard, Mary actually pulled the phone away from her face a bit.

She peered at the broken glass of the phone face, her eyebrows rising slightly. That had certainly got a reaction. Putting the phone back to her ear, she said, "Yes, he told me that. Crazy huh?"

There was another silence and then the man cursed on the other end of the phone and muttered, "He shouldn't have told you that . . . and he wouldn't have told you that unless . . ." Despite the fact that he'd spoken aloud, Mary suspected he'd been talking to himself. She doubted he even realized she'd heard what he said, but then his voice grew louder and he suddenly asked, "What else did he tell you?"

Mary tilted her head, her gaze on the second half of the sandwich the fingers of her free hand were picking at.

"Nothing. What else should he have told me?" she asked quietly.

The question was met with silence again.

Sitting up a little straighter, Mary tightened her grip on the phone and said, "Surely you aren't suggesting that Dante really can read and control people's minds?"

Rather than answer the man asked, "Why are you helping him?"

Mary paused, nonplussed by the question, but after a moment, said, "Because I ran him over."

"So, out of guilt," he suggested.

"No," she said quickly and then grimaced. "Well, maybe a little because of guilt. But also because he just needs help. I mean he's being chased by kidnappers and he was bare arsed, and I could hardly leave him at the truck stop naked like that. Not that I actually wanted to help him to begin with," she admitted honestly, aware that she was babbling, "but it was that or let him steal my RV, and no one is stealing my RV."

"Commandeering."

"What?" she asked with bewilderment.

"Dante would not have stolen your RV. He would have commandeered it for the purposes of aiding in the investigation. We would have seen to it that it was returned with compensation for its use."

"Right," she said dryly. Taking it was taking it no matter whether you called it stealing or commandeering. It still would have left her high and dry in the middle of Texas with no way home.

"So," Lucian said slowly, "You haven't felt any sort of . . . er . . . compulsion to help? It was just out of the goodness of your heart?"

"Compulsion?" Mary asked, eyes narrowing. "You mean like mind control?"

Silence was again her answer.

"Surely you aren't suggesting he really can control minds?" she asked with a nervous laugh.

"Apparently not yours or we would not be having this conversation," he said dryly.

"*What?*" she squawked.

A sigh slid through the phone and he said, "He should not have revealed his special skills. This is all highly top secret and not for public knowledge. Where is he? Not there I presume or he would not have let you make this call."

"Let me?" she growled. "Mister, this is my phone. And I'm an adult. Nobody gets to tell me what I can or can't do anymore."

"Sadly, I have to tell you that is not true and inform you that should you repeat anything Dante has revealed to you to anyone, anyone at all, the ramifications for you would be rather unpleasant."

Mary stilled and pulled the phone back to peer at it again. Was that a threat? Putting the phone back to her face, she snapped, "Did you just threaten me?"

"I do not threaten," he assured her. "I am merely making you aware of your precarious position. The knowledge you have is dangerous and I will do whatever is necessary to ensure it spreads no further."

His voice was so cold and matter of fact it was hard not to believe every word he said, and Mary began to worry what that "whatever is necessary" might extend to. Arrest? Her disappearing? Death?

"Judging from the change in your breathing, I gather you understand me. Good. Have Dante call when he returns from whatever task he is performing."

It took Mary a moment to realize that the silence that followed this time was because he'd ended the call without bothering to say good-bye or otherwise indicate he was done with the conversation. Lowering the phone, she stared at it briefly, noting that her hand was shaking, and then tossed it onto the table as if it were a snake she'd suddenly found in her hand.

Mary watched it slide across the table's smooth surface, but did nothing to stop it when it slid off the opposite edge onto the bench seat across from her. In fact, she felt a little better once it was out of sight.

Shifting her gaze to her sandwich, she stared at it briefly, then stood and carried the plate over to dump the uneaten half of her supper into the garbage under the sink. Mary then set the plate in the sink and turned to survey the RV. Her gaze slid around, but then settled on the couch. It was a long couch, presently with an arm across the first of the three sections of the couch. Mary moved to it, grabbed the arm and pulled it toward her. A lower section of couch immediately slid out to turn the couch into an L shape. Mary then shifted in front of this new section and caught the canvas handle sticking out of the top. She tugged it up and back, lifting the seat out of the base and up into position. She then slid the front of the remaining two panels out and set the pillows in place, turning it into a bed that was actually a little bigger than the one in the bedroom.

Mary wasn't sure it would be long enough for Dante to sleep in without curling up a bit, but it was the best she could do for him, and it was bigger than the actual bed she slept in, so she turned and went into the bedroom to fetch sheets, pillows and a blanket. They were stored in the base of the built-in bed. Mary bent, caught the wooden top of the bed base and lifted it. It rose like the lid of a chest, mattress and all. A handy feature she'd always appreciated.

She quickly collected what she needed, then set them on the side of the couch-bed before turning back to push the mattress back down into place, closing the chest-like storage space. Aware that Dante should return soon, Mary was quick about making up the bed. She'd just finished putting the last pillow in place when the RV door opened.

Bailey was the first to enter, bounding in, practically vibrating with excitement. The dog immediately leapt up on the couch-bed to cross to her and lick her face.

"Yes, yes, I'm happy to see you too," Mary murmured, catching the dog's head between her hands and massaging her behind the ears as she pressed a kiss between her eyes. "Now," she said, releasing her, "get off Dante's bed. He doesn't want to be sleeping in dog fur."

Bailey gave Mary's arm a swipe with her tongue, then bounded to the floor and jumped immediately up onto the bed in the bedroom where she curled into a ball and lay down, apparently all ready to go to sleep.

Mary raised her eyebrows. "What? You don't want supper?"

"I fed her before we went for a walk," Dante said quietly.

Mary turned back to the room to peer at Dante and noted that while the RV usually seemed large with the slide-outs open, his presence seemed to fill all that extra space now and make it smaller. Honestly, he was a mountain of a man, a big pink and white mountain.

It wasn't just that he was six feet eight, but he was as wide as a football player with padding on. Realizing she was staring, Mary dropped her gaze, and found herself looking at her phone on the dinette booth seat. Eyes widening, she blurted, "You're supposed to call Lucian."

"He called?" Dante asked with obvious relief, turning toward the driver's seat behind him, no doubt looking for the phone he'd placed back in its holder.

"It's on the dinette seat," she told him, and then admitted, "And no, he didn't call. I called him."

Dante had turned to grab the phone off the seat beside him. Straightening with it in hand, he raised his eyebrows. "You called him?"

Mary nodded apologetically.

"Why?" he asked softly.

Mary grimaced, her gaze shifting away from him, but then drawn irresistibly back. Sighing, she shrugged helplessly and admitted, "Because I thought you were a crackpot."

His mouth dropped open at her honesty and she smiled wryly.

"Well, you were claiming you could read and control minds," she said as if that should explain her reasoning, but realizing that since he apparently could read and control minds, that wasn't as convincing a reason as she'd first thought. Grimacing, she said, "I've never heard of anyone being able to do that in real life. It made me start to doubt everything else you'd told me."

"So you called Lucian?" he asked solemnly. "Why did you not call the mortal police?"

Mary blinked at the term. Mortal police? Who the hell called the police mortal police?

"Mary?" he asked. "Why did you not just dial 911?"

She hesitated and then shrugged helplessly. "I didn't want to get you in trouble, so I thought I'd just see who you called and find out what I could and go from there."

"I see," he murmured, and then added softly, "Thank you for that."

Mary shifted uncomfortably and then straightened her shoulders and gestured to the phone. "You should call him back."

"Yes," Dante glanced down at the phone. "I need to find out if they got Tomasso out. Excuse me."

Turning, he stepped down to the door, opened it and slipped outside.

The RV suddenly seemed to have a lot more room again, and a lot more air too. Mary took in a deep breath, feeling like it was the first she'd drawn in since he'd entered, then turned to slip into the bedroom and close the door. She'd had a long day, and quite enough of her guest for now. She needed her own space and sleep.

She moved around the end of the bed, petting Bailey in passing, and then slipped into the bathroom. Her robe and the old T-shirt she wore as a nightgown hung from a hook beside the door. Mary left them there for now and unlatched the lock on the shower door that was to prevent it sliding around while the RV was in motion. Leaning in then, she turned on the taps to start the shower, then turned to collect a towel, shampoo, soap and a washcloth from the cupboard. The water was already warm by the time she accomplished that, and Mary stripped and stepped into the shower. She was usually quick about showers in the RV, but not tonight. Tonight she stood under the warm, soothing spray until it had washed all her tension away.

When she finally got out, Mary dried herself and pulled on the T-shirt she'd been wearing to bed. It was one of her husband's old T-shirts. While not as big as Dante, he'd been a good-sized man, six feet with nice shoulders. His T-shirt was big enough on her that it reached almost to her knees. She brushed her teeth and hair, and then turned to open the door. It was as she flicked off the bathroom light that her gaze landed on her husband's closet. Mary peered at it silently, then glanced to the bedroom door.

She doubted very much if her clothes were comfortable for Dante. He didn't seem to mind their femininity, but surely with their being so tight he'd have trouble sleeping? Besides, while he didn't seem to mind wearing pink pants and flowered T-shirts, she really didn't want to explain it to her friends. One look would be enough for them to know they were hers.

Hopefully it had been too dark out for anyone to really see what he was wearing when he took Bailey for her walk, she thought with a frown, and then opened her husband's closet door to consider the items inside. She then opened the top drawer beneath it to check out its contents as well.

Mary ended up pulling out a pair of dark blue cotton pajama bottoms, a pair of faded jeans she wasn't sure would fit him, a pair of grey joggers that definitely would fit better than hers, and both a black T-shirt and a white one. Mary headed for the door then, but paused as she remembered she was wearing only the T-shirt. Muttering under her breath, she set the clothes on the bed, opened her own closet to retrieve her robe and pulled it on. After quickly tying the sash of the robe, she collected the clothes again and opened the bedroom door.

Mary wasn't surprised to find that Dante was finished with his phone call. She was a bit surprised, however, to find him seated on the side of the bed, face in his hands and shoulders slumped.

Setting the clothes on the corner of the couch-bed, she moved up beside him and placed a tentative hand on his shoulder. "Dante? What's wrong?"

When he didn't answer right away, or even raise his head, she bit her lip, and then ventured, "Your brother?"

He sucked in a deep breath at that and straightened where he sat. "The house was empty when they got there."

"So your kidnappers managed to leave us and get back to the house before your people could get there?" she asked with a frown.

Dante shook his head. "No. What with the investigation and everything, most of the team is in the area. Lucian says there was someone at the spot on the road within ten minutes of my giving him your directions, and it only took them moments to find the house. There must have been more kidnappers at the house. They must have moved him while the others came after me. Probably to make sure that nothing would be found there if I got to authorities before they could catch up to me."

"I see," Mary said quietly, then sat down on the couch-bed beside him and rubbed his shoulder gently. "I'm sorry." It was all she could say. She wasn't stupid enough to think there was anything that was going to make him feel better just now. Tomasso was his twin . . . and he'd left him behind and escaped alone. He had been right to do so, but it wasn't likely to make him feel better or lessen his guilt at getting away while his brother didn't.

"Lucian is collecting a group to fly down to Venezuela to see what they can find," he muttered unhappily.

"Venezuela?" Mary asked with surprise and he glanced at her with surprise of his own.

"Did I not tell you that Tomasso had been awake longer than me and had overheard them talking above stairs about our being transported to Venezuela?" he asked, and then muttered, "I thought I had."

"You might have," Mary allowed quietly. "My memory isn't as good as it used to be." Smiling wryly, she added, "And, I was a bit stressed out when we were first talking. I maybe didn't take in everything."

"Oh." Dante nodded and bowed his head again, muttering, "My apologies. I did not mean to distress you."

Mary frowned. The last thing he should be worrying about right now was any stress all of this had caused her. Besides, he sounded so defeated. Taking a deep breath, she stood abruptly and clapped her hands together. "All right then. I guess we'd best get moving."

"What?" he asked, lifting bewildered eyes to her.

"Well, if your boss, this Lucian fellow, is arranging a rescue party to go down to Venezuela and hunt up your brother, you'll want to go too. So . . ." She paused and frowned uncertainly. They'd hardly wait for her to drive Dante back north before launching their rescue attempt. At least she hoped they wouldn't. They probably expected him to fly, she thought and said, "I'll take you to the airport, then you can fly to Canada to meet up with your group. Or, are you supposed to fly straight to Venezuela and meet them there?"

"No." He caught her hand and drew her back onto the bed beside him. "I am not going."

"You aren't?" she asked with surprise.

Dante shook his head and stared down at her hand, trapped in his own. "Lucian said I was too close to the situation and might jeopardize Tomasso's life by doing something stupid," he said grimly, and then cleared his throat and added, "He also agreed I must stay and look after you in case the kidnappers who followed us are still in the area looking for your RV."

"Oh, that's just silly," Mary muttered impatiently. "They dropped back and then drove right past us when we were getting gas. Obviously they decided you weren't worth the effort."

"I'm not sure that is true," Dante said quietly. "They were talking when Tomasso and I heard them approaching the room where our cages were. One of them was saying that someone they called 'the Doc' would be extremely pleased with them for catching twins for his experiments, and would no doubt give them a bonus for it," he explained quietly and then added, "That is why I suspected they had driven ahead to try to ambush us. None of the others taken were twins. They would want me back."

Mary frowned at this news. She knew that twins were considered useful when it came to experiments. Certainly Josef Mengele had preferred them and she'd recently read that NASA was performing some sort of experiment involving twins. And this certainly did explain why he'd kept harping on the possibility of the van waiting ahead to ambush them.

"We are to wait here. Lucian is sending hun—" He paused abruptly, and then said, "He's sending officers to trail us in the hopes of capturing the kidnappers when they do make their attempt. That is the other reason he does not wish me to go to Venezuela."

"Because he wants you to be bait," she said solemnly.

He nodded, and pointed out, "Catching them is the fastest way to learn where Tomasso is, as well as find the rest of the kidnap victims."

"Yes, I suppose it would be," she agreed quietly.

"That and the need to protect you are the only reason I am not already headed for the airport."

"I see," Mary murmured, and found she was surprisingly concerned about this bait business. Not for herself, but for Dante. She'd thought that worry was over when the van had dropped back then driven past them, but this put a new light on things. They may have simply been preparing an ambush as he'd suggested which made her very glad she'd turned off the highway when she had. They should be safe enough here. It wasn't like this was the only campground in the area. So if they had set up an ambush and then realized they'd turned off when they didn't appear, his kidnappers would spend the night driving around in search of them. Even if they came to search here they'd run into difficulties. The campground gate had been open when they'd arrived because she'd been expected, but she was quite sure Dave would have closed the gate on his return to the office if all the booked people had arrived.

Sighing, Mary glanced to Dante and then followed his gaze to where he still held her hand. Swallowing, she watched his thumb slide gently across the top of her fingers in a gentle caress and was startled at the heat the light touch raised in her. And then she noticed that her fingers looked like her mother's did in her memory: old and lined compared to his smooth, youthful skin.

When had that happened? she wondered, and then tugged her hand away and stood abruptly. Heading for the bedroom door, she announced, "I brought you more clothes. They should fit better than what you're wearing. If you don't like them, the back bedroom closet is full of Joe's clothes and you're welcome to try them."

"Mary," Dante said as she paused inside the bedroom and turned to shut the door.

She stopped with the door half open and risked glancing at him in question. The damned man should not have been attractive in the ridiculous clothes he was wearing, but he was. Like a diamond in an ugly setting, he sparkled and shone despite the feminine apparel.

"I will keep you safe," he vowed.

Her eyes widened slightly and she didn't know what

to say to that. She hadn't really considered herself in any danger. Her concern had all been for him.

"In the meantime, we need to talk," he added. "There are things I need to tell you."

Mary hesitated. She did have some questions she'd like to ask him. Questions like, what else could he do besides read and control minds? And had he controlled her at all? She didn't think so. At least, she didn't feel like she'd done anything she hadn't chosen herself to do. Even if she'd been compelled by guilt or pity at the time, she was quite sure every step of the way had been her choice.

Narrowing her eyes on him, she asked, "Have you controlled me at all since meeting me?"

"No," Dante assured her solemnly. "I was unable to."

Her eyes widened. "You mean you *tried* to control me?"

He nodded. "But I could not. That is why we need to talk."

Mary stared at him, unsure whether she believed him or not, and too tired to care. It had been a very long day for her, full of various stressors, and she was obviously exhausted or she wouldn't be reacting to him the way she was. She needed sleep and some time to herself.

"Right now, I'm fighting to keep my eyes open," she said finally. "We can talk in the morning."

Dante looked as if he were about to protest, but then suddenly relented and even smiled a little as he nodded. "Very well. Sweet dreams."

Something about the tone of his voice and his smile made Mary hesitate and narrow her eyes. But when

Dante turned toward the couch-bed and began to strip off her much too small T-shirt, she quickly closed the door between the rooms and then locked it. The clicking noise it made as she did so had her wincing with displeasure. While Mary had wanted it locked, she hadn't really wanted him to know she was locking it. After all, it suggested she suspected he might come creeping in the middle of the night, and how egotistical was that?

Shaking her head, Mary quickly unlocked it again. She then shrugged out of her robe, laid it across the foot of the bed, and crawled under the covers. The moment she'd situated herself on her side facing the wall, Bailey scooted up behind her to curl against her, back to back. Mary smiled faintly at the familiar heat of the dog's body along her spine. Joe used to insist the dogs they'd had over the years sleep on the floor, but Mary wasn't Joe, and Bailey had been sleeping on the bed since his passing. She liked it that way. At least she did when Bailey wasn't hogging the whole bed, she thought with amusement. Many was the morning she'd woken up to find herself curled up on a corner of the bed, feet hanging off the side while Bailey lay spread out next to her. Bailey liked the bed much better than the floor.

Shaking her head at the thought, Mary reached back to give the dog an affectionate pat, then closed her eyes and quickly drifted off to sleep.

Seven

Dante finished stripping, and then picked up the clothes Mary had set on the corner of the couch-bed and shifted them to the table before climbing between the sheets. He preferred sleeping nude. The only time he wore clothing of any kind to bed was when he was on one of those protection gigs he'd mentioned to her. The possibility of having to wake up and jump directly into action was enough to make him wear his leathers to bed in those instances.

He was pretty sure that wouldn't happen tonight, however. They had lost his kidnappers today when she'd turned off the highway onto the road where this campground was situated. Dante had no doubt that his kidnappers were searching for them by now, but he'd walked the grounds while out with Bailey and the camp was situated in the curve of the river with just the front facing the road as a possible approach.

However, that was lined with a high, barred fence with the entry gate in the center and the owners had apparently closed and locked the gate after their arrival. At least, it had been closed by the time he'd led Bailey that way. And it was a good sturdy gate that had to be opened from inside. There were also cameras trained on the gate to discourage anyone trying to force it open. Dante was quite sure that his kidnappers wouldn't want that kind of attention, especially when they couldn't be certain he was in here. They'd probably go check out the other camps first if they were easier to enter, and then simply come back to wait for them to leave. At least, that's what he was hoping for. Dante was sincerely hoping they hadn't given up on him completely. He needed them to tell him where Tomasso was.

Frowning, he shifted to his side and slid one arm under the pillow his head rested on. Today had been a roller coaster ride for him. Waking up in the cage, escaping, having to leave Tomasso behind, getting run over, and then realizing that the woman who had run him over was most likely his life mate. His emotions had been up and down like a yo-yo.

Blinking his eyes open, he glanced toward the door to the bedroom. His life mate. He'd never expected to find her so early in his life. Many immortals waited centuries or even millennia to find their mate and yet here he was with Mary. Dante had found in life that God often gave even as He took, but sincerely hoped this was an exception. Finding Mary was the best thing to happen in his life, but at the same time, losing To-masso would be the worst and there was no way one could balance out the other in his mind.

Sighing, he closed his eyes, trying not to feel guilty for doing so. He felt like he should be out driving around trying to find his kidnappers to draw their attention. However, Lucian had said it would take until dawn for the hunters he was sending to reach them, and that they should remain at the RV camp for the night. A fortuitous order in a way, since Dante couldn't control Mary and make her leave the campground, as he would otherwise have done. He suspected he'd have had a battle on his hand had he tried to force the issue. Mary had been amazingly accepting of everything so far, and hadn't even pestered him with questions about his abilities as he'd expected. But he knew she was exhausted and suspected that was the reason why. He'd put her through a lot tonight, and that after she'd spent the day driving the monster presently housing them.

Actually, Dante was rather impressed with how she was handling everything so far. She was obviously a strong woman not given to hysterics and that could only be a good thing. He suspected they'd both be grateful for that before this was all over.

Grimacing, he rolled onto his back and closed his eyes, trying not to think of all the things that could go wrong when they left this campground tomorrow. The worst scenario was one where Mary was hurt and he was taken out by another drugged dart and unable to help her. The very thought of that was enough to scare the crap out of him and Dante began to wonder if he shouldn't convince Mary to wait here while he drove out alone, promising to return for her.

He was contemplating how to convince her to let him do that when he felt sleep overtaking him. Dante drifted off to sleep with a little sigh, then was startled awake by the sound of the bedroom door sliding open. Opening his eyes, he rose up on one elbow, and peered at Mary uncertainly as she stepped into the room. The RV was dark as could be, but his eyes were made for darkness and he could see her clearly in the overlarge T-shirt he'd caught glimpses of earlier when her robe had parted slightly. It looked surprisingly sexy for a man's shirt, clinging to her breasts and hips and stopping halfway down her thighs, leaving her shapely legs on display.

Forcing his gaze back to her face, he asked with concern, "Is everything all right?"

"Yes, I'm sorry," Mary said softly. "I just wanted to be sure you were all right. I know you're worried about your brother."

Dante let his breath out on a sigh, his body releasing the tension that had suddenly claimed it.

"Yes. Thank you," he added softly. "I am worried about him, of course, but we will find him."

"Of course we will," she said, but her voice sounded distracted now. Noticing that her eyes had dropped, he glanced down to see that the sheet had slipped down, leaving his bare chest on show. Resisting the urge to flex his muscles to try to impress her, he instead held out his hand and said her name softly.

Mary gave a start at the sound of her name and glanced to the hand he held out. After a hesitation, she took the couple of steps necessary and took his hand lightly in her own.

When Dante smiled and squeezed her hand, then tugged gently, urging her to sit, she didn't fight, but sank slowly to sit on the side of the couch-bed. Trying not to rush her and scare her off, he toyed with her hand briefly, then glanced up to her face and said, "I would like to kiss you."

"Yes, please," she murmured, and that's when Dante realized he was dreaming. He was quite sure that in reality, Mary Winslow would not come out to check on him in nothing but an overlarge T-shirt, would not cross willingly to the bed to take his hand, and would not agree to his kissing her. This was one of the infamous shared dreams immortals and their mates enjoyed when they found each other. Mary wouldn't realize what it was, that he was here with her. She would think it was just a normal dream, the result of her desires, which meant she wouldn't be held back by fears or anxieties. She would do as she truly wished without being held back by all the morals and societal pressures that normally affected behavior. But this dream was also an opportunity for him to show her what she could have with him.

Nodding to himself, Dante released her hands and sat up, noting the way Mary's eyes followed his sheet as it dropped to pool around his waist. Smiling, he slid his hand around her head and pulled her forward to claim her lips. She went still at first, but when he slid his tongue out to urge her lips apart, she opened to him and the moment he deepened the kiss a moan sounded deep in her throat and she melted against him like butter on a warm muffin. The moment she did, Dante slipped his arm around her waist and twisted his upper body on the bed, dragging her across his lower body to lay her on her back on the inside of the bed.

Mary gasped in surprise at the action, her arms instinctively closing around him and holding tight. Once her back touched the cool sheets, though, she began to kiss him back. She also eased her panicked grip and began to run her hands over his shoulders and then up into his hair.

Dante moaned his pleasure as her nails scraped across his scalp. He was leaning on one arm to keep from crushing her, but let his other hand begin to move then, following the curve of her side and hip, and then following that curve back up, before allowing it to slide over to cover one breast.

Mary moaned and arched into the caress, her hands tightening in his hair. But in the next moment, she released that tight grip to begin moving her hands over the skin of his back again. Mary alternately massaged the muscles of his back and pulled at him, her body shifting and arching as he kneaded and squeezed first one breast then the other through the cloth of her overlarge T-shirt.

It wasn't long before that wasn't enough, and Dante wanted the T-shirt gone. His kiss growing more demanding, he slanted his mouth over her one way and then the other as his hand dropped away to find the bottom of the T-shirt. He started out thinking to slip his hand under and snake his way back up to her breast so that he could touch her without the cloth between his fingers and her flesh, but when his fingers brushed between her legs as he started to move his hand up and he realized she wasn't wearing panties . . . well, that, combined with the way Mary cried out into his mouth, her hips bucking in response, immediately changed his plans. Instead of continuing upward, his hand paused and then he cupped her there.

Mary tore her mouth away on a gasp and twisted her head from side to side. Her gasps quickly turned into mewls of sound as he began to caress her. Dante watched her thrash beneath him, fascinated. She was incredibly beautiful to him, glowing with passion and need and . . . suddenly gone. He didn't know if it was her sudden disappearance from the dream or the sound of her voice that startled him awake, but he opened his eyes to the dark RV and sat up, listening to the sound of her murmured attempts to soothe her dog.

"It's okay Bailey. Mommy's fine. She was just dreaming. It's okay. Stop licking my face, sweetie. Mommy's fine."

Dante let his breath out on a sound that was half amused and half frustrated, and then sank back on the bed. Mary must have been moaning and perhaps even thrashing in her sleep as they'd had their shared dream. It had obviously alarmed the dog to the point she'd woken up her mistress . . . bringing an end to the lovely dream.

He listened to Mary as she continued to soothe the

dog, but when the dog apparently settled and she fell silent, he closed his eyes, eager to return to sleep and the dream they'd been sharing.

Mary moaned and pushed Bailey wearily away for about the hundredth time since she'd gone to bed. The dog had repeatedly wakened her from sleep through the night, licking her cheek and pawing at her arm to pull her from sleep and the dreams that had apparently made her restless and disturbed Bailey's sleep.

Sighing her relief when Bailey gave up licking at her face and merely dropped her head to rest it on Mary's belly, she wiped her eyes tiredly. She was exhausted, and extremely frustrated after a night of wet dreams that had constantly been interrupted before they could reach their happy ending.

Each one of those dreams had been about her and Dante, and Mary supposed she should be embarrassed, but hell, they were just dreams and they weren't the first inappropriate ones she'd had in her life. Besides, what they amounted to was her subconscious telling her that she was attracted to Dante. Not surprising. He was a good-looking young man and built like a damned Adonis.

Actually, Adonis probably would have envied him, she thought. But the point was that of course she'd lust after him. Who wouldn't? It didn't mean anything. It wasn't like she was going to try to drag those dreams into reality with her. She'd just enjoyed them for the private fantasy they were. Well, as much as she could enjoy them with Bailey taking on the coitus-interruptus cape. Honestly, Mary loved the dog, but sometimes she could just smack her.

Bailey shifted her head a little higher on Mary's stomach and whined piteously, a sure sign she wanted to go outside and relieve herself. Mary pulled her hands from her face and scowled at the dog.

"Really?" she asked in a hissed whisper. "Keep me up half the night with your nonsense and then expect me to crawl out of bed to let you out?"

Bailey blinked at her innocently, eyes wide, and Mary sighed and sat up, forcing the dog off of her. She muttered, "Fine. But I have to dress first, so you'll just have to wait a couple minutes."

Bailey whimpered and sat up to give her "the sad eyes," and Mary shook her head and grimaced in response. She supposed, to be fair about it, she had obviously kept the dog awake with her thrashing about and moaning in her sleep. In fact, Mary supposed she should be grateful Bailey had woken her repeatedly, otherwise she might have disturbed Dante's sleep . . . and wouldn't that have been embarrassing? It probably would have been obvious that her dreams were sexual in nature. Bailey had woken her up at one point as she was gasping, "oh, oh, oh," over and over again. In her dream, Dante was— Well, point being, she'd still been crying out when she'd woken up. Had she got much louder, her guest would have heard and had no doubt about the kind of dreams she was enjoying.

Which is perfectly normal and healthy, Mary told

herself as she crawled to the end of the bed and stood to tug the closet door open to find clothes. Hell, she was surprised she could still have wet dreams.

Sunlight was pouring in through the open blinds at the head of the bed, making it easy to see and pick out clothes. Mary moved quickly into the bathroom with shorts and a T-shirt and closed the door so Bailey wouldn't try to follow. The bathroom, while spacious for an RV, was tiny enough that the two of them in there would have made it as crowded as the subway at rush hour.

Very aware that Bailey needed to relieve herself too, Mary started out trying to be quick about getting herself ready to face the day, but then as it occurred to her that they would no doubt wake up poor Dante as they traipsed through the living area, she frowned and slowed a bit. It was times like this that she realized how inconvenient an RV could be. Of course, with just her and Joe in it, having only one door had never been a problem, but the few times they'd had guests with them, she'd thought that a second exit in the back of the RV might have been nice. Of course, there was nowhere to put one back here, unless she wanted to walk through the shower to a door, but . . .

Grimacing, she grabbed the brush and ran it quickly through her hair. There was nothing for it; she'd have to take the risk of disturbing Dante. It would be cruel to make Bailey wait until they heard Dante stirring out there. He was young and might sleep for hours yet. Sighing, she set down the brush, then turned and slid the bathroom door open, only to pause when she saw that the bedroom door was cracked open and Bailey was gone.

Frowning, Mary crossed to open the pocket door all the way and peered out into a pristine living area. The couch was back to its L shape, the sheets and blanket removed, folded neatly and resting on the last seat with the pillows on top and Bailey and Dante were nowhere to be seen.

Moving to the window over the sink, she shifted the blinds aside and peered out, a small smile claiming her face when she saw Dante walking Bailey toward the river. He was wearing a pair of Joe's jeans and the black T-shirt from the small stack of clothes she'd given him. Both items were tight on him, the jeans hugging him in all the right places, but at least reaching to the tops of his feet, which sort of surprised her. Joe had been six feet, but this man was a good eight inches taller. Of course, he was wearing them low on the hips whereas Joe had worn them at the waist, and he appeared to have a longer torso than Joe, who had been all legs. As for the T-shirt, well, it had certainly never looked that good on Joe. Where Joe had preferred loose T-shirts, this one was tight on Dante, at least across the chest and on his upper arms where it hugged him like a woman in love. It was loose at the waist though. The man had a smaller waist than most women she knew, Mary noted with appreciation.

Damn, he was a fine-looking man, she thought. His long hair was tied back in a ponytail low on his neck. She'd never thought much of long hair on men, but he could convert her. It was a shame she wasn't thirty or forty years younger, she thought with a sigh and then made herself stop ogling the poor man and turn to the chore of making coffee.

Mary made a cup for herself, then prepared one for Dante and set them on the counter by the door before filling a dog dish with food and water. She carried the double-bowled dog dish outside first, and set it on the picnic table to protect it from visiting neighbor dogs. Mary then returned to the RV and grabbed both coffees and carried them to the picnic table as well. She'd barely settled on the seat and taken her first sip of coffee when Dante appeared, walking up the path with a well-behaved Bailey leading the way.

The perfect dog performance Bailey was giving ended the moment she spotted Mary seated at the picnic table. The German shepherd immediately jerked at her leash, trying to charge forward. But one word from Dante and she settled back to a walk, if a much faster one.

"I made you coffee," Mary said, pushing his cup across the table as he sat down across from her. She then moved Bailey's double dog dish to the ground, smiling faintly when the dog attacked the food as if she hadn't eaten in days. Bailey always acted like she had to gobble it all up or someone might take it away. Perhaps a remnant of the first eight weeks of her life, where she'd been part of a litter and probably had had to eat quickly or her siblings would eat it all.

"You look tired," Dante said quietly.

Mary stiffened and then continued to stare at Bailey, aware that she was blushing. Hoping he hadn't noticed, she shrugged. "Didn't sleep well. Probably just all the excitement of the day," she added, although that was a blatant lie. It had been the excitement of her dreams and their disturbing Bailey that had caused her lack of sleep.

"Neither did I," Dante murmured and then suggested, "Perhaps we should nap after Bailey has finished her meal. She could stay in the front of the RV with me so that she does not disturb you."

Mary glanced at him sharply, but his expression was innocent. Still, he'd obviously heard something last night to know that Bailey had woken her repeatedly. Clearing her throat, she shook her head. "Dave and Carol are expecting us at the Round Up for breakfast at eight."

"The Round Up?" Dante asked uncertainly.

"The restaurant here," she explained. "It's just a little shack, really, with outdoor tables, but they make the best food, and Carol and Dave invited us to join them for breakfast."

"Ah," he nodded and picked up his coffee. "Then we will have to leave soon. It must be almost eight now, it was ten to eight when I put Bailey's leash on her."

Mary automatically looked at her wrist, but hadn't put her watch on yet. She glanced to Bailey to see that she was half done with her food already, and said, "As soon as she's done then," and picked up her coffee to take a drink.

She was only half done with hers when Bailey finished eating. Not wanting to have Dave drive down after them, Mary left Bailey to drink her water and took her and Dante's cups and carried them quickly into the RV to set in the sink. She grabbed her keys then, locked the door of the RV and took Bailey's leash as she joined Dante to walk to the main building, where the office, restaurant, store, and entertainment room were situated.

"I told them you were my nephew," she murmured as they walked.

"I see," he said slowly, and then asked, "Why?"

Mary felt the blood rush to her face at the question, and grimaced, but said, "It seemed easier than . . ." She shrugged. "I figured you didn't want me telling anyone about your circumstances; the kidnapping and everything."

"No, but you could have said I was your lover."

Mary almost stumbled over her own feet at the suggestion and turned to scald him with a look. "The hell I could. You aren't my lover, and I'll be damned if I'm having them all looking at me like I'm some sort of cradle-robbing cougar. Good Lord, they'd think I'd gone off my rocker."

"Who'd think you'd gone off your rocker?"

Mary turned her head sharply to see Dave standing a few feet ahead on the end of a path leading off the lane they were on.

"And more importantly, why would anyone think that?" he continued when she stared at him wide-eyed. "You're one of the sanest women I know. You never get hysterical like Carol does."

"Oh," Mary blinked, uncomfortable at the more favorable rating he was giving her than his wife. Then she forced a smile and waved the question away. "No reason, we were just—" She waved again vaguely and then changed the subject. "Sorry if we're a couple minutes late, but you didn't have to come looking for us."

"I wasn't," he assured her easily, falling into step on her other side as they reached him. "I was just coming back from a walk around to check on everything. Someone tried to break into the campground last night. The dogs chased them off," he added quickly when Mary glanced at him with alarm. "But I wanted to make sure they hadn't found another way in and caused trouble."

"Who was it?" Dante asked, tension in his voice.

"I don't know. A couple of tough-looking characters from what I could tell. But I didn't get a good look. Brutus, Little Mo, and Tiger scared them off."

"They're Dave and Carol's Dobermans," Mary explained. "Beautiful dogs. Good guard dogs too."

"Yeah. Troublemakers think twice when those three come running. They were out for their nightly constitutional when it happened and scared them off. So we decided to leave them out all night after those yahoos tried to force the gate. Didn't hear another peep from the dogs so it isn't likely they tried again, but I just wanted to be sure."

Mary nodded, but glanced to Dante. He met her gaze and she could tell he was thinking the same thing she was, that it might have been his kidnappers trying to ascertain whether they were there or not, and perhaps even hoping to steal him back.

"Thank goodness for Brutus, Little Mo, and Tiger then," she murmured.

"Yes," Dante and Dave said together.

They'd neared the office by then and Mary found herself glancing toward the gate and the road beyond, her eyes searching for a black van. There were no vehicles on the road though, that she could see. If it had been his kidnappers, they'd obviously moved on to check out other campgrounds. There were several around the area. She just had to hope they didn't return. The gates were open again now, and would remain so all day. Which meant they had to worry about what the kidnappers would do if they got inside and found the RV and Dante.

Eight

The Round Up was busy when they got there, every picnic table on the deck around it seeming occupied, but Carol had saved one for them and stood to smile and wave them over when they approached. The men dropped back to let Mary lead the way with Bailey, and she smiled and greeted several regulars she'd met on past stops as they made their way through the tables. Carol had chosen an outer table, probably because she expected Mary to bring Bailey as usual, and Mary quickly attached Bailey's leash to one of the legs on the outside, then greeted Carol with a hug.

"How did you sleep?" Carol asked as they settled at the table. "You look tired. I hope the dogs barking didn't disturb you when those men tried to break in?"

"No. We're back far enough we didn't hear a thing," Mary assured her and it was true, at least for her. She didn't tell Carol that she hadn't slept well anyway though. She didn't want the questions that would follow.

"You must be the nephew," Carol said, turning her attention to Dante as he stepped over the picnic table's bench seat to settle next to Mary. Carol's eyes widened slightly as she took him in and then she murmured, "My, you're a big fella."

"Dante, this is Carol and Dave Bigelow," Mary said, trying to look at him without actually looking at him. A tricky business, but she suspected if she did look at him properly her less than aunt-like appreciation might show. "We've been friends for years. Since before they even bought the campground."

"Yes." Carol grinned and then leaned across the table to brush a hand over Dante's arm and explained, "We lived in Winnipeg just around the corner from your aunt and uncle. We've been friends for decades."

"You are Canadian as well?" Dante asked with surprise.

Carol nodded. "We used to be snowbirds too, driving the RV down here like Mary and Joe, but about eight years ago the four of us booked in here as usual, and during our stay the owners mentioned they were looking to sell and move to California to be closer to their kids. We decided we'd buy it and stay year round."

"The best decision we ever made," Dave announced with a smile.

The waitress appeared at their table then and Carol smiled at the girl and said, "Oh, Andrea. You remember Mrs. Winslow? And this is her nephew, Dante."

Mary smiled at the young woman. Carol and Dave

hired a lot of locals to help out at the campground in the busy season, but Andrea was one of the year-round workers who had been with them since they'd bought the campgrounds. As Mary recalled, Andrea had started here fresh out of school at eighteen, which put her at about twenty-six, Dante's age or a little older, she thought. Mary had always liked the girl, but noting the way she was eyeing Dante like he was a tasty treat, she found herself cooling toward her.

"So, what does everybody want?" Carol asked cheerfully. Twisting in her seat, she gestured toward the blackboards on the wall of the cookhouse. "Everything we make is there on the boards, Dante."

"Yes." Andrea beamed at him. "Have whatever you want."

Mary's eyebrows rose at the suggestive offer and she asked sweetly, "How are you finding married life, Andrea? When I stopped here in the fall it was just a week or so until the wedding, wasn't it?"

"Oh," Andrea flushed, and then glanced quickly to Dante and back before mumbling, "Yes. It's fine."

"The wedding was beautiful," Carol put in when Andrea didn't say anything else. Smiling at Dante, she added, "They held it here along the river. The pictures turned out really nice."

Mary nodded as if she cared, and then glanced to the blackboards and quickly gave her order. The others followed and Andrea slipped away to take their order to the cook.

"I think our Andrea is a little taken with you, Dante," Dave said with amusement once the girl was out of earshot.

"Any red-blooded female would be," Carol said on a laugh and then teased, "If I were thirty or so years younger, Dave would have something to worry about with you here."

"You flatter me," Dante said with a smile and leaned to the side to pet Bailey as she moved to sit on the ground behind him and Mary.

Carol frowned and then glanced to Mary and asked, "I don't remember any of your or Dave's siblings moving to Italy."

Mary's eyes widened with confusion. "None of them did."

"But Dante has an Italian accent," she pointed out and then said, "Oh, is this one of Joe's chil—" She broke off sharply as she realized what she was saying. Eyes wide with alarm, Carol turned to her husband for help.

Rolling his eyes with disgust at her gaff, he changed the subject abruptly by announcing, "Carol thinks we should sell up and move back to Winnipeg."

Mary had frozen at Carol's words. She now glanced quickly to Dante, noting that he was staring at Carol with the same concentration he'd had in his eyes as he'd looked back at her the first time she'd seen him lying on her RV floor. Had he been trying to read her mind then? she wondered. And was he now reading Carol's thoughts to find out what she'd been talking about? The possibility was a humiliating one for Mary. Forcing a smile to her face, she said quietly, "You mentioned that when I stopped in the fall. But you didn't seem interested."

"He isn't," Carol said unhappily.

"Of course not," Dave said with a grimace. "It's damned cold in Winnipeg in the winter, and I'm too old to be shoveling snow."

"We could get an apartment," Carol argued at once. "Besides, I miss the kids, and the grandbabies are growing up so fast."

"They visit," Dave pointed out with irritation.

"Once a year," Carol countered. "I want to see them more than that."

"You could always visit them up there," Dave pointed out. "I told you. You should go this summer and stay a couple months, then come back for the winter. We'd be driving an RV down here for the winter anyway if we didn't own this place. In fact," he continued, "If you want you could get a small apartment and stay there for the summers, we could afford that. Then you could come back in the fall for the busy season."

Carol frowned at the suggestion. "And leave you here alone all summer?"

"I'd have help running the place," he pointed out dryly. "I'd be fine."

Her mouth tightened. "Don't you want to see your grandchildren too?"

"I see them when they visit," he pointed out with a shrug. "Hell, I probably wouldn't see them any more than that if we lived in Winnipeg. Their lives are so busy, they wouldn't have time for us old fogies. Look, here comes Andrea with the drinks."

Carol opened her mouth as if to continue the argument, but then just sat back with a sigh and shook her head wearily as Andrea arrived at the table and began to set out the coffees and juices they'd ordered.

Mary murmured a thank-you as the girl set an orange juice and cup of coffee in front of her, and then glanced from Dave to Carol with concern. It was obvious that Carol wasn't happy, and it seemed equally obvious that Dave didn't care. He was happy with their life the way it was and was unwilling to bend. She had noticed that Dave had suggested Carol go north alone if she wanted, not even mentioning the possibility of his joining her for part of the time. It seemed after forty years of marriage, there was trouble between the Bigelows.

Once Andrea had left, Dave turned the conversation to attractions in the area that Dante might like to see. Mary noticed that Dante murmured politely in response to each suggestion, but didn't encourage him much, and then the food arrived and the conversation dwindled as they tucked into their meal.

Dave often claimed they had the best cook in Texas working for them, and Mary couldn't argue the point. Every meal she'd ever had at the Round Up had been excellent, and this breakfast was no exception. She would have enjoyed it more, however, had the mood at the table been less tense. Where she usually enjoyed visiting with Dave and Carol, this time she was actually glad when one of the workers hurried to the table as they finished their meal and dragged Carol and Dave away to deal with an unhappy camper.

"I'm sorry, we'll visit more later," Carol said apologetically as they rushed away.

Mary murmured in agreement, but was kind of

hoping that later never came. She knew if Carol got her alone she'd have more questions about Dante that she just had no idea how to answer. And Mary really didn't want to get in the middle of the argument Carol and Dave were having about moving or not moving. Her advice to Carol would be to do whatever the hell she wanted. If she wanted to move back to Winnipeg to be close to her kids, then do it. Life was too damned short to constantly push your own desires down and always do what others wanted. On her deathbed, Mary's mother had told her to follow her dreams, that on her own deathbed she wouldn't lie there patting herself on the back for all the times she was so good and kind-hearted and did what others wanted, she'd be regretting all the things she'd wanted to do and hadn't.

Mary hadn't always followed that advice, but the older she got, the more she recognized the sense behind the words. Her mother hadn't been suggesting she act without considering others. She'd just been saying to be kind to herself as well as to others. Her own wants and needs should be at least as important as those of the others in her life. Because, frankly, if you didn't care about yourself, no one would, and you'd spend your life living for others.

"Your husband was unfaithful," Dante said bluntly once they'd left the restaurant and started the return walk to the RV.

Mary's hand tightened on Bailey's leash at that comment. He obviously *had* read Carol's thoughts. Either that or he'd realized the significance of what Carol had stopped herself saying. "Oh, is this one of Joe's chil—"

Joe's children was what she'd started to say. One of his biological children, not with her, but with one of the many women he'd had affairs with over a fifteen-year period during the first part of their marriage.

"I told you he wasn't perfect," she muttered with a shrug.

"Yes. But you neglected to tell me he was repeatedly unfaithful to you during your marriage," he said grimly, sounding angry on her behalf. "That is a little less than imperfect."

"It was during the early years of our marriage," she said quietly. "But he made up for it during the last half of our marriage. He was the best husband a woman could ask for then."

"He was not," Dante assured her. "He simply got better at hiding his indiscretions."

"What?" Mary asked sharply, her steps halting. Then she scowled at him. "You don't know that."

"I read both Carol and Dave," he said quietly.

Her eyes widened with alarm. "He and Carol didn't . . . ?"

"No. Carol, like you, is a faithful wife," he assured her solemnly.

Mary let her breath out on a sigh. She and Carol had been good friends for a long, long time. The thought that she could have betrayed her like that would have been crushing. Which was ironic, she supposed. She should have been more distressed at Joe's betrayal had they had an affair. Instead, it was Carol's betrayal that would have hurt more. She supposed it was because she'd long ago given up any hope of being able to trust her husband in that regard. At least back then.

"Dave is how I know your husband continued his infidelities," Dante continued, "He and your husband were made from the same mold. The pair often trolled the bars together, knew each other's girlfriends, and covered for each other with "the wifey" as he put it in his thoughts."

Mary sighed at this news and continued walking. She wasn't terribly surprised by the information, but also wasn't sure what she was supposed to do with it. Should she be furious and confront Dave? Why? What did it matter? Joe was dead.

"He continues to philander here in Texas," Dante said grimly. "And Carol is aware of it. That is part of the reason she wants to move back to Winnipeg. Dave uses the campground as his own personal hunting grounds. He has affairs with many of the women who camp here, married or not. He also has had the occasional fling with workers."

Mary's mouth tightened and her heart went out to Carol, but again, she didn't know what to do about it. If, as he said, Carol knew . . . well, she wouldn't want to add to her humiliation and bring up the subject with her. They'd only discussed the subject of Joe's infidelities once, years ago, after the car accident that had led to her not being able to have children. Mary had almost left Joe then, but . . .

"Carol believes you stayed with Joe because you could not have children," Dante said quietly. "She believes you felt no other man would want a woman who couldn't give him children."

"Children are important to most men," she said quietly. "But that wasn't the only reason. He made a mistake, but no one is perfect."

He was silent for a minute and then said uncertainly, "Are the pictures in the RV of your husband's children with other women?"

Mary's mouth tightened. She hated being reminded of the children he'd had with other women. She knew they existed, but not how many. "No. They're our adopted children. We adopted a boy and a girl. Both grown now with children of their own."

"I see. But Joe had children of his own without you?" he asked, not letting the subject go.

Mary opened her mouth to tell him she didn't want to talk about that subject, but then sighed and said, "He traveled a lot for work when we were younger. It was at a time when we were having marital problems. Sometimes he was away for months in foreign countries negotiating this deal or that one. He was lonely and took up with other women."

"I would never be unfaithful to you Mary," he said solemnly. "No matter how long we were apart."

The words surprised a short laugh from her and she shook her head. "Dante, you're far too young for me. Save proclamations like that for someone your own age."

"I am older than I look," he said solemnly.

Relieved to see that they'd reached the end of the lane and were approaching the RV, Mary smiled at him and said dryly, "So you've said. But, sweetheart, if you're over twenty-five or twenty-six I'll eat my hat."

"I am well over twenty-five but would never make you eat anything you did not want to, especially a hat."

Mary raised her eyebrows, then just shook her head and led Bailey to the picnic table to collect her double dish. She carried it to the RV and quickly unlocked and opened the door. Bailey immediately tried to rush up the stairs, but Mary stopped her with a sharp, "Stay."

Bailey sat then and waited for Mary to mount the stairs before following her into the RV. Mary wasn't very good at consistency, but according to the dog training books she'd resorted to lately, she should have made the dog wait for Dante to enter as well, but the leash made that difficult. Pausing next to the table, Mary set the dish on it, then bent to undo Bailey's leash as Dante followed them in.

"I am serious, Mary. I am much older than I look," he insisted, pulling the RV door closed behind them.

Something about the tone of his voice made Mary glance warily his way as she finished removing Bailey's leash and straightened. He had sounded determined. He looked determined too. She wasn't sure what that determination was about, but it made her nervous, so she simply slipped past him to hang the leash from the hook next to the door and waited for him to continue.

"Come, sit," Dante suggested when she turned back.

Mary watched him take a seat at the dinette booth, but grabbed Bailey's dish, rinsed it out at the sink and filled both sides with water. She set it on the floor by the table for the dog, then settled at the dinette across from Dante, sliding further in and petting Bailey when the shepherd jumped up to lie on the bench seat next to her. "Okay, I'm sitting."

Dante nodded, and then paused briefly as if considering how to start, before saying, "Mary, my people are different."

"Your people?" she queried uncertainly, her gaze sliding over his dark hair and olive skin. That and his accent had made her assume that he was Italian. But Indians had darker skin and black hair, they also had sharp cheekbones as he did and often referred to their tribe as their people. Tilting her head, she asked, "Are you Indian?"

"No. Atlantean."

"Huh?" Mary peered at him blankly. "You mean from Atlanta, Georgia?"

"No," he said with a small smile, and then reached across to take her hands gently in his. "You've heard of Atlantis?"

"Atlantis?" she repeated slowly. "That place that supposedly existed and sank into the ocean or something like forever ago. That Atlantis?"

"Yes." Dante smiled as if pleased she knew that much. "That Atlantis. My ancestors were from there."

"Riiiiight," she said slowly. "And who told you that?"

"My grandfather Nicodemus told me."

Mary nodded slowly, and then shook her head. Grandparents told their grandkids all sorts of delightful tales to entertain them, or to make themselves seem more interesting than they really were. Most kids grew up and realized they should take those tales with a grain of salt. Dante obviously hadn't and still believed them. Poor schmuck, she thought.

"He told Tomasso and me all about Atlantis," Dante went on. "About the tall buildings built from a white stone found only there. About the creeping vines that quickly grew to cover the buildings, helping to insulate them from the heat. He said that every summer they would sprout beautiful flowers, much like the flowers we call azaleas today, but larger."

"Dante," she said gently, "Even if Atlantis existed, your grandfather couldn't possibly know what it looked like. No one knows if it even really existed, let alone what it looked like."

"He does know. He lived there," Dante countered quietly.

"Ah, sweetheart," she murmured pityingly. "Surely you know Atlantis is supposed to have collapsed into the sea or whatever ages ago?"

"Yes."

"Well, then your grandfather couldn't possibly—"

"My people are different," he interrupted, repeating his earlier words. "They were advanced technologically, Mary. They were isolated from the rest of the world and had created transportation before the rest of the world even came up with the wheel. And scientifically they were advanced beyond where the rest of the world is even today."

"Dante," she said on a sigh, trying to pull her hands free of his, but he held on.

"Please, just let me tell you," he insisted quietly. "It

will sound incredible and unbelievable and I know this, but let me just tell you anyway."

She hesitated, but then relented and nodded, her posture relaxing. What harm could there be in letting him tell her the stories his grandfather had told him? "All right. Go ahead."

"Thank you," he said, his lips lifting in a charming smile.

It made Mary want to try to snatch her hands away again. He was so damned beautiful, it was almost painful to peer at him. No one should be that good-looking. Or smell this good, she thought grimly as his scent wafted to her, setting her hormones buzzing. Images from her interrupted dreams last night started sliding through her mind: him leaning over her, his naked chest so wide and beautiful, his hair dropping around their faces like a curtain as he kissed her. His hands moving over her body, pushing her T-shirt up to caress her . . .

Damn, Mary thought, bringing her wayward brain to a halt. How had she got here? Holding hands with a handsome young stud half her age or more, and lusting after him like some twenty-year-old hopped up on hormones? She was a dirty old woman!

"As I said, the people of Atlantis were far more advanced scientifically," Dante began again, completely oblivious of her inner turmoil. "They had cures for many of the ailments we still do not have cures for today. But just before the fall of Atlantis, they had begun working with nanos."

When he paused then and hesitated, looking uncertain, Mary guessed he was trying to decide how to explain nanos and said dryly, "I know what nanos are. Or at least enough to follow this tale."

Dante relaxed and smiled again.

Mary followed the movement of his lips, noting that he was growing some serious stubble on his face, and, big surprise, it too looked damned good on him. She probably would have noticed it earlier if she hadn't been studiously avoiding looking directly at him all morning, thanks to her night of torrid dreams. Mary was looking now though, and thought that was probably dangerous. It made her want to run her fingers over his face to see if the stubble now gracing his face would feel as good as it looked. Fortunately, she was saved from herself when he began to speak again, reclaiming her attention to his words rather than how pretty he was.

"They had reached the point where they were experimenting with the use of nanos in health care," Dante continued. "They had bio-engineered nanos that, once introduced to the human body, could use human blood to reproduce and repair themselves as they worked to heal and repair the human body. For instance, if someone had cancer, the nanos recognized those cells as not belonging and would destroy them, and if a person was injured, the nanos would repair the wounds and so on."

Mary raised her eyebrows at this claim. It sounded like an awesome invention if it were possible. She just didn't think it was likely. These nanos would have to be programmed with every single little bit of knowledge about the human body, a lot of info to stick into something smaller than the head of a pin. However, she held her tongue.

"But as a result of a flaw in their design, the nanos had some unexpected side effects," he said solemnly.

"What kind of flaw?" Mary asked, curious, despite knowing none of this could be true.

Dante paused and frowned, and she wondered if he was making up an answer, and then he said, "The human body is attacked by many different illnesses and diseases; cancer, diabetes, Alzheimer's, meningitis and so on. And then there are about a million different injuries a human could sustain, anything from damage caused by a stroke to a punctured lung from a stab wound. Programming nanos specific to each possible need would have meant creating hundreds or even thousands of illness- or injury-specific nanos."

"More than that," Mary said dryly. She couldn't even guess how many different illnesses and injuries humans could suffer from. She'd read something once that had claimed there were at least 100,000 diseases in the world. How many injuries could be added to that? Creating that many programs for the nanos would have been a herculean task.

"Yes. So, rather than program the nanos for each specific need, the scientists developed a program that included the information for both male and female bodies at their peak, and programmed the nanos with the directive to ensure their host was at their peak condition and then self-destruct. At which point they would be flushed from the body naturally like all dead cells are."

Mary nodded. "Sensible."

"They thought so," he agreed with amusement. "However, it did not go quite as they planned. Nanos are ultimately machines, and machines are very literal, so if you gave them to a seventy-year-old man with cancer, not only did they eradicate the cancer, but they set about returning his body to the peak condition they had been programmed with."

Mary raised her eyebrows in question, not seeing a problem there. A fit seventy-year-old would be a good result.

"As it turns out, the human is at their peak condition in their mid to late twenties," he said quietly. "And so the nanos worked to return their hosts to that peak."

Mary sat back slowly as his words flowed over her. What he was talking about was that in a mythical land they had developed a mythical, scientific fountain of youth of sorts.

"Even once they had accomplished that, though, the nanos did not self-destruct and get flushed from the body," he continued. "Because the body is constantly under attack by the environment, the air we breathe, the sun, or just the passage of time, the nanos simply could not get the body to remain at what they considered its peak long enough to self-destruct. They would finish repairs only to find several cells had died from exposure to the sun or just because they'd reached their optimum age. So the nanos remained in the host, continuing to work and repair. Their hosts never sickened, did not age, and were they injured, the nanos quickly repaired them."

Mary let her breath out on a little sigh, thinking that it was a damned shame none of this was true, because that would rock. Or maybe not, she thought in the next moment. She'd lived a long time, gone through a lot and seen a lot, and frankly, Mary was kind of tired. It wasn't that she was suicidal or anything, but death to her was starting to look like a bit of a respite or rest, rather than the scary ending she'd always thought of it as when she was young.

"And that is how I survived being crushed by your RV," Dante announced.

Mary blinked and refocused on him.

"What?" she asked sharply.

"I was badly injured in the accident," he said quietly. "My lower left leg was crushed, my one lung was punctured, I had several broken ribs, and I'm pretty sure several of my organs were crushed or at least seriously banged up in it as well. The tires tore my skin open in several places and the nanos simply couldn't close everything up before I lost a good deal of blood. They do need blood to work with after all and I was losing it quickly."

He shrugged. "Were I mortal, I would have died quickly, I think. But I am not and when you brought the doctors to me, I fed from them and the nanos began to work in earnest. Of course, I couldn't take all the blood I needed from them. It would have killed them, so I had the female fetch—"

"Wait, wait, wait," Mary interrupted with exasperation. "What do you mean you *fed* on them?"

"Their blood," he explained and reminded her, "The nanos need blood to do their work, as well as to power them."

"Their blood," she echoed in a whisper, then tilted her head and asked, "You saying that lady doctor fetched those men from the diner so you could . . ."

"So I could feed on them," he explained with a nod. "I fed on the EMTs too, and between them, the truckers and the doctors I gained enough blood for the nanos to make the necessary repairs. Fortunately, Tomasso and I have always been fast healers. Another immortal might have needed more time to allow the nanos to make the necessary repairs, but—" He paused and peered at her warily when Mary cursed under her breath.

She ran one weary hand through her short hair and shook her head with disgust as she muttered, "You're like a damned roller coaster, Dante. And I'm a bloody idiot."

"You are not an idiot," he said indignantly.

"I am," Mary assured him, pulling her hands from his and urging Bailey off the bench seat so she could get up. She started toward the door, and then paused and swung back, saying, "You pop up in my RV with mad stories of being kidnapped and escaping, and I, like an idiot, believed you," she pointed out. "At least I did until you started spouting off about reading and controlling minds. I smartened up just a little at that point and decided maybe you weren't the innocent victim but a lunatic. But what do I do? Do I call the police like any intelligent woman would? No, I call that idiot friend of yours."

"Er . . ." He cleared his throat. "It might be best not to call Lucian that to his face. He would be offended and no doubt say or do something unfortunate, and I would hate to have to kill him. It would cause trouble in the family."

Mary ignored his interruption and continued, "That *idiot friend* backs you up, claiming you can indeed read and control minds and I think, all right, maybe like Horatio, there are more things in heaven and earth than I'd ever dreamt of, and I go back to at least accepting it's possible and believing that you were kidnapped again." She glared at him. "But then you come up with *this*? I'm supposed to buy that you're some kind of new *vampire*?"

"Immortal," he corrected softly.

"Vampire," Mary snapped. "Let's call a spade a spade here, shall we? You're claiming you drank the blood of those people at the truck stop and got all better, your broken ribs and crushed organs healed. That's a vampire," she spat, and then added, "And I don't believe it, so go sell it to some witless little girl who can't see past her hormones."

Dante frowned and then tilted his head and said something that she was pretty sure was a curse in Italian. Sighing, he tugged out the elastic he'd tied his hair back with, and then ran his hands through his long hair as if his head hurt, before muttering, "You are the most frustrating woman."

"So control me," Mary suggested dryly, snatching up a coffee mug and sticking it in the single coffee server. She placed a single-serve cup into the machine, closed it, turned it on and waited as her coffee was made.

"I have already told you that I am unable to either read or control you," Dante said patiently.

Mary snorted her disbelief. "You've told me a lot of things."

"And everything I've told you has been the truth, Mary. I would not lie to you."

"All men lie," she growled. "If nothing else, I've certainly learned that life lesson."

"Do not judge me by your husband's behavior," Dante growled back, sounding furious. And a lot closer, she noted and turned to find he too had stood up and was directly behind her, his face flush with anger and his hands balled as if he wanted to hit something.

"Every man I've ever known has cheated and lied," she said grimly. "My father, my husband . . . even Dave, according to you."

"Mary—"

"Why do you care about what I think anyway?" she snapped. "I'm surprised you're still even here. I got you away from your kidnappers. Why don't you go find your friends now and go after your brother? I know you want to."

"I do," he admitted grimly. "However, I cannot leave you so long as there is a possibility my kidnappers might stalk you in their hunt for me."

"Oh, yes, we're bait. I forgot," she muttered, turning back to the coffee machine.

Dante immediately caught her arm and swung her back. "*You* are not bait. *I* am bait. You are . . ." He paused, frustration crossing his face, and then he growled that frustration aloud and pulled her forward.

Nine

Mary gasped in surprise and caught at his arms as she stumbled against him, then went still as his mouth suddenly covered hers. Nothing about those dreams she'd had last night had prepared her for this kiss. She'd thought they were hot and exciting in her dreams, but in reality those had been tepid in comparison to the sensations that exploded inside Mary as Dante took advantage of her startled gasp and slid his tongue in to invade her mouth.

Despite all her beliefs about the age difference and the lectures she'd given herself, Mary didn't hesitate more than a moment under the onslaught of passion that tore through her before wrapping her arms around his big shoulders and kissing him back with all the vigor he was dishing out. When Dante responded by immediately catching her under the upper legs and lifting her against his body, to set her on the kitchen counter, she wrapped her legs around him and drew him even closer than he already was. Feeling the hard proof of his response to their kiss grind against her, she moaned into his mouth and tightened her legs around him even more, her hands now moving over his shoulders and then down his chest, to feel and squeeze his hard pectoral muscles.

Dante growled in response, the sound vibrating into her mouth and sending tingles running through her body. It encouraged her to drop her hands to tug at his T-shirt, eager to feel his hot, tight flesh under her fingers.

Dante immediately stopped kissing her to help with her efforts, tugging the shirt up and dragging it off over his head. His hair was caught briefly in the neckline and then dropped around his face like a curtain as he tossed the cloth away. Mary promptly dove her fingers into the silky mess and tugged him back to kiss her again. But she couldn't seem to stop touching him. Her hands were aching with the need to run over his warm skin. He felt so good, his kisses were so hot, and he smelled like every man should. Mary was torn in every direction, wanting his kisses, but wanting to push him away and look at him and feel him up too. It was madness, utter madness, and she could have happily drowned in it.

She was vaguely aware of Dante's hands at the waistband of her shorts, and felt the give as he undid them, and yet she still gasped in surprise when his hand slid between the cloth and her skin to touch her. Mary froze briefly, her hands and mouth stilling, then pulled back and cried out as he reached her core and his fingers slid over the nub of her excitement.

Dante immediately lowered his head to kiss her again, his tongue thrusting into her in concert with his caress and Mary gave up her own caresses to clutch at his shoulders. Her back automatically arched, forcing him to bend over her as she pushed on the front of the cupboards with her feet, urging her hips forward into his touch. The action loosened the cloth of her shorts, somehow, giving him more room, and Dante immediately slid one finger into her while continuing to caress her nub with his thumb.

Mary broke their kiss again and threw her head back on a cry of pleasure, her body beginning to vibrate and shake. She was approaching the orgasm she'd never got to experience in her dreams last night thanks to Bailey constantly waking her, and that's when someone knocked at the door to the RV.

Both she and Dante froze at the sound, their eyes meeting and locking for a heartbeat before the knock sounded again and reality came crashing down on Mary. Who she was, who he was, where she was and what she was doing all suddenly poured over her like a bucket of cold water.

"Mary," Dante hissed desperately, but it was too late, she was already pushing him away from her.

Sliding off the counter before he could stop her, Mary moved several steps away, doing up her shorts as she went. She then ran her fingers quickly through her hair and called out, "Come in."

It was only as she said it that Mary realized how foolish that might have been. It was daytime; the campground gates would be open now and it could be the kidnappers at the door. If there really were kidnappers, she thought to herself as she watched the door open. She relaxed a little when Dave stepped up into view.

"I was starting to think you two weren't here," Dave said cheerfully, glancing from her to Dante.

"I was napping and Dante was in the bathroom when you knocked. I came out of the bedroom just as he came out of the bathroom," Mary lied glibly, wondering if he'd believe her or he'd heard them as he'd approached. Even if he hadn't they probably looked like they'd been doing exactly what they'd been doing. Certainly Dante's lips were swollen from their kisses, his face still flush, and he was still topless and sporting a bulge in his jeans that would not be mistaken for a wallet.

Fortunately, he was standing glaring at her with his back to Dave, so it was only her state that might give them away. Hopefully her claim that she'd been napping would cover any rumpled state. If her lips were swollen and she was flush . . . well, they were all getting older and the light in the RV wasn't that great at the moment. Perhaps Dave wouldn't notice, she thought hopefully.

"Oh, sorry for disturbing you. You did mention you didn't sleep well last night. I would have let you sleep had I known," Dave assured her apologetically, then smiled wryly and added, "We should really get Do Not Disturb signs like the hotels have, but for the RVs. Then we'd know when not to bother guests."

Mary smiled politely at the suggestion, and simply waited for him to explain the reason he'd come. She normally would have been much more friendly, but what Dante had told her about this man was in her mind now and she was looking at him differently.

"I just stopped in to tell Dante there are a group of young people over at the pool," Dave announced into the silence and then winked at Dante when he turned to face him and added, "A lot of pretty girls in the group too. You might like to join them. That way Mary can visit with Carol and I for a bit."

"That sounds like a good idea," Mary said at once, eager to get some time alone to try to straighten herself out. She needed space to recover from what had happened and figure out how to make sure it didn't happen again as well as how she was supposed to act around Dante now.

Mary was looking at Dave, so noticed when his expression suddenly went blank before he turned, and closed the RV door. He then turned back and simply stood there, eyes dull, face expressionless.

"Dave? Are you all right?" she asked uncertainly, moving up beside Dante to see Carol's husband better when he just stood there unmoving. When Dave showed no reaction at all to her question, Mary stared at him with bewilderment, then glanced to Dante and noted the concentration on his expression as he eyed Dave. She glanced slowly back to Dave then, and for one moment believed Dante might really be controlling him. But believing that meant buying his nonsense about being a vampire, and she just couldn't accept that. Mouth tightening, she arched an eyebrow at Dante.

"What is this?" Mary asked now with disgust. "A prank the two of you planned together at breakfast?"

Dante didn't respond, but Dave suddenly dropped to his hands and knees on the floor and barked at them, then lowered his head to begin lapping up water out of Bailey's dish. As he did, Bailey, who had jumped back up on the bench seat at some point, now lifted her head to watch him with interest. But then she just laid her head back down and closed her eyes.

"Dave!" Mary said with dismay and took a step toward him, then stopped and turned to Dante with horror.

"Stop it!" she demanded, moving in front of him and thumping him on the chest with one fisted hand. "Stop it now!"

Dante caught her arms before she could hit him again and peered past her to Dave.

Mary glanced over her shoulder to see Dave getting to his feet. His face was still expressionless and he didn't speak at all, but simply moved in front of the steps leading down to the door, then stood there unmoving. She swiveled her head back to Dante and scowled at him furiously. "If you really are controlling him and this isn't some kind of trick you two cooked up, then you're being exceedingly cruel," she muttered, trying to tug her arms free of his hold.

Dante merely held on and shrugged. "He is unharmed."

"Except for his pride," she snapped, tugging again. "You made him act like a dog."

"His pride is fine. He will not recall this," Dante said gently, and then his voice turning cold, he added, "Although it would serve him right if I left him the memory. He has been sniffing around you like a dog all morning."

"What?" Mary squawked with disbelief. "He has not! He walked with us to the restaurant and joined us for breakfast with his wife," she said pointedly. "Dave and Carol have been friends for years."

"Dave has been lusting after you for years," Dante countered dryly. "And this year planned to take advantage of your missing Joe, get you drunk, and take advantage of you when he so kindly offered to drive you back to the RV last night. The knowledge that I was with you and would return any moment with Bailey is the only reason he didn't try it last night. But he came here this time with the intention of sending me off to "have fun with the young people at the pool" so that he could try it now. Those are the actions of a human dog."

"He was going to take me back to visit with Carol," she reminded him with exasperation. Dante was sounding like a jealous lover, which was just ridiculous. He wasn't her lover and . . . well, hell, Joe had never shown a lick of jealousy in all the years they were married. Why would this young man, when they hardly knew each other?

"Carol is not at the offices," Dante said firmly. "She has driven into town to get the mail. He had no intention of taking you anywhere but to your bed. He is a dog," he growled, and then glared at Dave and added, "Although that seems to me to be an insult to Bailey and her kind. She would never behave in so unsavory a manner."

Mary gaped at him, then turned to peer over her shoulder at Dave again before saying weakly, "I don't believe it."

"Nevertheless, it is true," Dante said quietly. "He thinks you aged better than Carol, and, like me, thinks you have a lovely smile and nice figure. He has been lusting after you for decades and only Joe's presence prevented him from acting on it before this. He was afraid your Joe would beat the hell out of him if he ever found out."

Mary shook her head, finding this impossible to believe.

"Although, he nearly took a chance and tried to bed you that time the four of you were on vacation in a cottage up north and were all in the hot tub. You got out, wrapped a towel around yourself and went in to get more wine for everyone. He followed on the pretext that he needed to use the washroom. But the truth is you were drunk and he hoped to be able to talk you into a 'quickie.' However, Carol followed to see if she could help you and he was unable to make the attempt."

Mary stiffened. The trip he was talking about had been ages ago. At least fifteen years ago, she thought. She hadn't told him about it, and was quite sure no one else had mentioned it today either. How could he have known about that trip without reading minds? Still she shook her head in denial.

"What do I have to do to convince you that what I say is true?" Dante hissed with frustration.

Mary just lowered her head. She had no idea. Perhaps there was nothing he could say to convince her. The truth was, Mary had some serious trust issues and she knew it.

Sighing, Dante released her and moved past her to approach Dave. Mary turned slowly, frowning with concern as she watched Dante stop behind the other man. Trepidation rippled along her back in the silence that followed, and then Dante bent and lowered his head to Dave's neck.

Mary blinked in bewilderment. Did Dante plan to make out with everyone? First her, then Dave. Who was next? Carol? One of the workers here? Did it even matter if it was a man or woman?

Hurt and suddenly angry, Mary hurried forward and caught his arm to jerk him away from Dave. Dante straightened and turned to her and she gasped and took a step back. It was Dante, but not Dante. This Dante looked exactly like the one she knew except that instead of the normal, white teeth she'd seen so many times when he smiled, his canines were now fangs, and they were presently coated with blood.

Dave's blood, Mary realized as she glanced to the other man and saw the marks on his neck. They were carbon copies of the marks she'd noted on the necks of Dr. Jenson and a couple of the truck drivers as they'd come out of the RV, smiling and calm. She'd noted the same marks on one of the EMTs too, she recalled.

Dante shifted and Mary glanced to him sharply.

Noting that he'd turned his attention to Dave again, she glanced to the other man and watched him walk down the three steps to the door. He opened it and walked out of the RV, a calm smile on his face just like the ones the truckers had worn.

Mary took a nervous step back when Dante turned to her, but his fangs were gone and every trace of blood with them.

"Now do you believe?" he asked, moving slowly forward.

Mary swallowed and continued to retreat, one step for every one he took forward.

"I am an Atlantean," Dante said proudly. "Immortal. I need blood to survive. Normally we only feed from bagged blood. In fact, it is against our laws for us to feed directly from mortals, except in emergencies, when we are without bagged blood and in need. Then we may feed on mortals as I just did."

"Dave," she began weakly.

"Is fine and will not remember it so long as I don't spend much time around him," he said grimly.

"Oh," she breathed and then felt her knees give way. Mary was sure she was going to hit the floor and even tried to prepare herself for the impact, but she'd backed all the way to the bedroom and instead of hitting the floor, her fall was brought up short when she dropped to sit on the bed.

Mary blinked in surprise as she bounced on the cushioned surface, and then blinked again when Dante immediately dropped to kneel before her and took her hands in his. He started to look up at her, but then paused and glanced back to her hands with a frown. "You are so cold."

Mary made a sound in her throat that could have meant just about anything. Even she didn't know what it signified other than her confusion at that moment.

Concern on his face, Dante began to chafe her hands. As he did, he said, "My brother and I were born in 1906. I am over a hundred years old. I cannot read or control you. Among my people that means you are a possible life mate for me."

"What's a life mate?" she asked with bewilderment.

"The one person we cannot read or control and whom we may be happy with for all our days. Our mate for our very long lives," he said solemnly.

"And you think because you cannot read or control me I'm this life mate for you?" she asked

"It is one of the signs," he said simply.

"What are the other signs?" Mary asked uncertainly.

Dante stopped chafing her hands and met her gaze. "Shared dreams . . . like the ones we experienced last night."

"What?" Mary stared at him blankly. "You mean you know what I was—?"

"I know what *we* were dreaming. Yes," he interrupted solemnly. "I was there with you every time. I held you in my arms and made love to you while we slept." Pausing, he grimaced and added, "Well, I tried to, but every time we got close, Bailey would wake you and—" He stopped and eyed her warily when her hands jerked in his and she made a choked sound in her throat. Squeezing her hands gently, he said, "Shared dreams too are a sign of a possible life mate. Along with shared passion."

"What's that?" she asked, not sure she wanted to know. This was all madness. She'd gone off her rocker, she was sure.

"When I kissed and touched you earlier . . ." Dante paused and then added dryly, "When we were actually awake before Dave interrupted . . . I was experiencing your pleasure as I gave it to you."

"You were?" Mary asked shakily, and when he nodded, frowned and asked, "How?"

"I am not sure," Dante admitted. "As much as we understand it, it seems that the pleasure between life mates is shared somehow. It bounces back and forth between them, growing with each pass back and forth until it is overwhelming, and when the couple finds their release it is usually so overwhelming they both briefly lose consciousness."

"Oh," Mary breathed, and then simply stared at him for a moment, unsure what to think. After a moment though, she said, "But you keep saying possible life mate. It's not for sure?" she asked, trying to grasp what he was telling her. "It's just possible?"

"Yes, well . . ." Dante hesitated and then sighed and said, "The truth is that for me, you *are* a life mate. But the decision is yours as to whether you agree to be that life mate I can share my long life with."

Mary's eyes widened. He said the word *life mate* as if it was something special, even sacred.

Raising her hands, he pressed a kiss to her knuckles, then met her gaze and said solemnly. "You are my life mate, Mary. And I would like to claim you. Will you accept me as such?"

Dante sounded like he was reciting some kind of marriage vow and Mary stared at him, her heart in her throat. She was tempted to just throw herself at him and say yes, then rip off his clothes, but . . . shaking her head, she whispered unhappily, "But I'm so old."

Her words brought a tender smile to his face and he pointed out. "You are almost half my age."

"Oh, right," she muttered, doing the math in her head. Born in 1906, that made him almost fifty years older than her. It boggled the mind. He didn't look a day over twenty-five and she said, "But you *look* young."

"Oh, Mary," Dante said with exasperation, then smiled slightly and said, "I have lived a long time and seen much. I have learned not to judge a person by the number of wrinkles they have or a few gray hairs." Shifting her hands to one of his, he used his other hand to tilt her face up until she met his eyes and then said, "To me you are beautiful. Your laugh lines and crow's-feet say that you know how to enjoy life, and the scars and marks left by time show that you have *lived* life."

That was so sweet, Mary thought weakly, but . . . "I have stretch marks," she admitted with embarrassment.

Dante shrugged. "They show that you love life and enjoy the pleasure it offers."

"Yeah. Too much," Mary muttered under her breath. She'd long ago given up her battle of the bulge, and had never regretted it so much as in that moment when faced with the possibility of Dante seeing her naked.

"There can never be too much pleasure," he assured her solemnly, drawing her attention back to him.

Mary narrowed her eyes at the smooth line and said a little acerbically, "That sounds like an argument the snake would have used in the garden of Eden to tempt Eve."

Releasing her hands, Dante placed his hands on either side of her legs and slid them up to clasp her by the hips, then asked huskily, "Are you tempted?"

God help her, she was, Mary realized. It was madness. He was telling her vampires existed, that he was old and just looked young. And there he knelt before her, a beautiful olive-skinned Adonis, claiming that he didn't care that she wasn't some sweet young thing with a perfect body and bouncy boobs. He wanted her.

"Please, Mary," he said softly.

She shifted her gaze from his perfectly muscled chest to his face and gave the slightest nod. Truly, Mary wasn't even sure her head lowered more than a quarter inch, but it was enough for him. He lunged upward like a wave, his mouth covering hers as he caught her in his arms, lifted her up and bore her back on the bed before lowering to lie half on her and half on the bed beside her.

Mary moaned at both the combination of his kiss and the feel of his suddenly roving hands. They were everywhere, one holding her head in place as he ravished her mouth, the other sliding from one breast to the other and then sliding down to press the cloth of her shorts against her core. Mary gasped and shuddered and moaned by turn, arching into his caresses even as her own hands reached eagerly for him, first grasping his shoulders in an effort to pull him down on her fully. When that proved impossible, she trailed her hands down his chest and stomach and then finally between his legs to find the spot in his jeans that was again bulging outward as if eager to get to her.

Dante groaned into her mouth and pressed more firmly between her legs as she touched him through his jeans. But just as she reached for the snap of his jeans, he suddenly broke their kiss to shimmy down her body, removing that option from her. Before she could protest, he'd jerked her top out of her shorts and tugged it up.

Gasping in alarm, Mary gave up on trying to get to him and instead turned her attention to trying to push her shirt back down. Kissing was one thing, but she was still not pleased at the thought of his seeing her old body.

However, Dante would not be denied. Catching both of her hands in one of his, he held them out of the way and jerked her shirt up again, then tugged her bra to the side, freeing one breast. He paused briefly then, drinking her in, then raised his eyes to hers and murmured, "Beautiful."

Mary gaped at him, then sucked in a startled breath as he lowered his head and latched onto the revealed breast, drawing eagerly on the nipple with his mouth as his hand squeezed and kneaded the soft flesh around it. Mary bit her lip and twisted her head on the bed at the fire he was breathing over her tender flesh, then cried out, and arched on the bed as his knee suddenly slid between both of hers and began to press against her core.

"Dante, please, let me touch you," Mary begged, struggling to get her hands free. She wanted desperately to hold him just then. Actually, she wanted to rip his pants off, grab him by the hair and drag his head up to kiss him again as he plunged into her, but he was having none of that. He continued to hold her hands over her head with one hand, but the other now left her breast to his mouth's attention and lowered to undo her shorts. She felt the snap giving way and the zipper sliding down, and then he tugged her shorts down around her knees.

Mary cried out as his hand replaced the cloth.

"*Si, cantare per me*. Sing for me," Dante muttered around her erect nipple as he began to caress her. But his words made Mary realize that they were in an RV with flimsy walls and that anyone passing might hear. Instead of "singing" for him, she turned her head to the side and bit into the flesh of her own upper arm to try to silence herself. And then she screamed into the flesh she'd just bit as his finger slid smoothly into her.

"God, Mary," Dante growled. "*Sei cosi stretto*, you are so tight. I want to be inside you."

"Yes," Mary gasped, but instead of rearing up and doing that, he continued to thrust his finger into her and caress at the same time, building the tension until Mary thought she would die if he didn't make love to her.

"Dante, please," she almost sobbed, her hips dancing under his caress. "Please, I need you."

"*Si*, Mary," he muttered, lifting his head. He paused

to kiss her again, then straightened to kneel over her and reached for the snap of his jeans, just as someone knocked at the door.

They both stilled then, eyes locking.

"No," Dante breathed, but the knock came again and Mary bit her lip and glanced along her body toward the door as Bailey leapt off the dinette's bench seat and moved to the door to rear up and paw at it with a bark. A sure sign that it was someone she knew at the door.

"If that is Dave again, I swear I will do more than make him bark and drink out of Bailey's dish," Dante growled, shifting off the bed. "I will make him lick his own balls."

"You will not," Mary gasped, scrambling to get off the bed and pull up her shorts.

"You are right. He probably could not reach them," Dante said grimly, snapping up his jeans.

Shaking her head, Mary did up her shorts, and then ran her fingers quickly through her hair as she rushed ahead of him to get to the door first. If it was Dave, she was going to make sure he didn't step foot in the RV . . . for his own good.

"There you are," Carol said cheerfully as Mary opened the RV door. When Mary smiled and stepped back for her, Carol stepped up into the RV carrying a large box, then stopped abruptly as she got a good look at her. Her eyes immediately went wide and her mouth made a perfect O of surprise. "Oh, you're—did I—you—"

"I was doing my calisthenics," Mary blurted, not sure

what the woman was seeing, but hoping that would explain away whatever it was.

"*Si*, she was working very hard," Dante added, completely straight-faced. Then he stepped between them, placing his back to Carol as he quickly shifted Mary's breast back into her bra and tugged her shirt down. And he was grinning, dammit.

Mary closed her eyes on a sigh and wondered when she had lost control of her life. Or was it her mind she'd lost?

"She will not remember what she saw," Dante murmured softly by her ear, his voice affectionate. Then he stepped aside and she saw that Carol had the same blank look on her face now that Dave had worn earlier. Mary sagged with relief, then straightened when Carol suddenly took on expression and movement again as if someone had pushed a button on her back to activate her.

"I went into town to pick up mail, and two boxes were waiting for you there," Carol announced cheerfully, nodding down at the heavy-looking box she carried before adding, "The other one is still in the golf cart."

Dante immediately moved forward to take the box Carol carried. He set it on the dinette table for her, and then went out to fetch the second box from the golf cart as well.

"Oh, thank you, Carol," Mary murmured as Dante quickly returned with the second box and set it on the table as well. She eyed the boxes curiously, wondering what they held, but she was also thinking that Dante had obviously been telling the truth. Carol hadn't been in the office to visit. Dave had been lying.

"My pleasure," Carol said easily, and then asked, "Have you seen Dave? He was heading out to handle an issue with one of the campers when I left, and still isn't back."

"Oh . . . er . . ." Mary glanced to Dante with alarm, worried that he'd done something to the man. Or made the man do something to himself under his influence.

"I believe he mentioned going down to the river," Dante said mildly in response to her look. When Mary narrowed her eyes suspiciously, he added, "To feed the birds."

Mary relaxed a little and turned to offer Carol a forced smile as the woman said, "Well then I guess I'd better go find him. He'll forget to eat lunch otherwise."

"Is it lunchtime already?" Mary asked with surprise. It seemed like they'd just had breakfast.

"Just about," Carol said lightly as she turned to head out of the RV.

Mary waved her off and closed the door behind her, then turned to peer at Dante suspiciously. "Did you really send him to feed the birds?"

"Yes."

"And that's it?" Mary asked, eyes narrowed.

Dante scowled, but then grimaced and admitted reluctantly, "I may have put the suggestion in his mind that while he was down there he should perhaps fall in . . . a couple or three times," he muttered and when she opened her mouth, added quickly, "He needed to cool off."

"He did, did he?" Mary asked with sudden amusement. He looked so much like a little boy caught being bad in that moment.

"Yes, he did," Dante assured her. "Besides, it is better than he deserved for his thoughts. You are mine."

"Am I?" she asked softly.

"Oh, yes," he assured her and drew her into his arms. His head was just lowering toward hers when Bailey whined and pawed at the door.

They both closed their eyes briefly, and then Mary reluctantly pulled gently out of his arms. "She has to go out."

She turned to collect the leash from the hook, but Dante leaned past and took it from her, kissing her ear as he did and murmuring, "I'll do it."

"Thank you." Mary smiled, and stepped out of the way so that he could put Bailey's leash on. Once he'd finished and straightened to reach for the door, she said, "I'll make lunch while you're out."

"No need," he said lightly, allowing Bailey to trot down the steps ahead of him. "I already know what I want."

"What's that?" she asked with a frown, wondering if he was thinking of going back to the restaurant for lunch or wanted sausages or hamburgers on the barbecue.

"You," Dante growled, and caught her hand to pull her forward for a very thorough kiss that left her shaky legged and breathing heavily. Releasing her hand then, he let his fingers snake up under the bottom of her shorts and glide up to brush across her through her panties.

As he caressed her core through the flimsy cloth, he murmured, "I'm going to strip you naked, spread you on the table and pleasure you with my mouth until we both scream our passion and pass out."

Panting slightly now, Mary grabbed for the counter to steady herself as he withdrew his hand. She stared after him wide-eyed as he turned to continue out the door, and was still staring when the door clanged shut behind him.

Mary remained still for a minute, then sucked in a long breath and sank to sit on the top step. Her whole body was vibrating, and her head spinning with the images he'd put in her mind. Dear God, he was going to kill her with passion.

Shaking her head, Mary got shakily to her legs and turned, only to pause as her gaze landed on the boxes on the table. She'd quite forgotten all about them. Turning to the counter, she opened the top drawer and grabbed a sharp knife, then moved to the table to examine the label on the bigger box. It was addressed to her from Argeneau Enterprises. She pursed her lips briefly, trying to think what Argeneau Enterprises was, what they sold, and why they'd be sending her anything, and then sliced through the packing tape holding the top of the box closed.

Setting the knife down, Mary then opened it and peered down in confusion as men's clothes were revealed. Mary dug through it quickly, noting that there were black jeans, black T-shirts and a leather jacket. All looked to be large enough to fit Dante, she noted.

Mary set it aside and then turned to cut open the

second box. This time a small cooler was revealed with A.B.B. stamped on it. Flipping it open, she stared blankly down at the bagged blood inside for a moment, and then carefully closed it. The boxes may have been addressed to her, but they were obviously for Dante.

She glanced in the big box again and noted an envelope inside. Reaching in, Mary took it out. She really hadn't planned on reading it, but it wasn't addressed to anyone, and the flap of the envelope wasn't sealed, so in the end she slipped her fingers in to grasp the small piece of paper inside and tug it half out. Half was all she needed to be able to read the words on it.

We're here.

Ten

Mary stared at the words for a long time and had no idea why they made her heart race. *We're here.* They were just two little words . . .

But she was recalling that Dante had said they were to wait here until hunters were sent to help trap the kidnappers should they try to grab him again. She was guessing that's who the "We're here" referred to.

Slipping the paper back inside the envelope, Mary set it on top of the clothes and turned to slip out of the RV. She didn't see Dante and Bailey anywhere, but it didn't matter. Mary slipped around the RV and moved to the hookups to begin unhooking her RV from the septic, the water and the electricity.

Mary was rather surprised that she managed the task before Dante and Bailey returned, but simply took it as a sign that she was doing the right thing and checked to be sure that all the storage compartments under the

RV were locked, before going inside and closing the bedroom slide-out. Once the bed had slid all the way forward to press against the drawers under the closets, she left the panel to quickly slide the L-shaped couch back into a straight couch. She then closed the living-room slide-out as well. They hadn't put out the awning, so Mary next got into the driver's seat, turned on the engine and retracted the jacks.

"What are you doing?"

Glancing around at that question, she saw that Dante was leading Bailey into the RV, but merely gestured toward the table and waited for the jacks to finish pulling up as she watched him drop Bailey's leash and move to the table to examine the contents she'd removed from the box.

The jacks finished retracting then, and Mary turned in the driver's seat and patted her leg. Bailey immediately moved to her side.

"Good girl," Mary murmured and leaned down to undo her leash.

Standing then, she hung the leash on the hook and moved up beside Dante. "I'm sorry I opened it. It was addressed to me."

"Yes. Lucian asked for your name," Dante murmured, retrieving a bag of blood from the cooler.

Mary peered at him curiously, noting that his eyes were glowing more silver than black.

"You need blood," she guessed.

He grimaced and nodded. "I was careful not to take too much from the people at the truck stop. It was enough to handle the worst of the healing, but I needed

more and did not take much at all from Dave before
you stopped me."

"I'm sorry," she said softly.

Dante merely shrugged, grabbed two more bags and
turned to carry them toward the bathroom door.

"You don't have to go in there to feed," Mary protested with a frown.

Dante hesitated, but then turned back. "It will not
make you uncomfortable if I feed in front of you?"

"I don't think so," she said honestly. "Actually, I'm
kind of curious to see—" Mary stopped abruptly as
he opened his mouth and his canines suddenly shifted
and slid down like the tips of staples descending out of
a stapler, and then he slapped one of the bags to them.
That was the only way to describe it. He just slapped
it on them like poking a straw into a fast-food drink
glass. Mary watched silently as the bag began to shrink,
crumpling inward as the blood inside dwindled. It was
all rather fast, certainly quicker than she'd expected,
and then he tugged the now empty bag off of his fangs
and slapped another one on.

Not wanting to make him uncomfortable, Mary
turned away then and began to check that all the drawers and cupboards were securely closed so that they
wouldn't swing open with every turn the RV took.
They might still come crashing open if the RV stopped
too abruptly as they had when she'd run over Dante, but
otherwise should remain secure.

"Mary."

She turned to see that he'd finished the third bag. She
opened the door under the sink and he slipped them

into the garbage, then straightened and waited as she closed the door again, before taking her arms.

"I wanted . . ."

"I know," she murmured, ducking her head. Mary certainly hadn't forgotten what he'd said he'd do to her on his return. Clearing her throat, she lifted her head and said, "But if the men poking around the campground gates last night were your kidnappers, they will probably still be around somewhere, and if we let them find and follow us, your friends can catch them and find out where Tomasso is."

"Yes," Dante breathed, obviously relieved at her understanding. Smiling, he pressed a kiss to her forehead, and then hugged her tight. "I am the most fortunate man to have you for a mate."

Mary swallowed, and allowed herself to hug him back briefly, but then pulled away. "Are you driving or shall I?"

"Perhaps I should," he offered. "I know you did not sleep well last night."

"Neither did you," she pointed out with amusement and he nodded in acknowledgment.

"But for my people, an extra bag of blood makes up for that," he said with a shrug. "I'm as good now as if I had a full night's sleep."

"Nice trick," Mary said dryly and took the cooler off the table to secure it in the cupboard over the couch. She placed the box with his clothes in there as well when he handed it to her, then slipped past him to move to the front of the RV and take the passenger seat.

Bailey immediately followed her, squeezing past her

to curl up in the space in front of her legs under the dashboard. It was much more room than you would find in a car, but it was still a bit tight for a dog Bailey's size. Still, she was happy enough there, so Mary left her to it and did up her seat belt as Dante slipped into the driver's seat.

She watched silently as he adjusted his seat and the mirrors, but her mind was all over the place. Part of her was disappointed that they had to leave without doing what he'd said he was going to. But the other part of her brain was straight-up relieved. While she knew he would have shown her great pleasure, and hopefully this time with the actual happy ending, the images that his words had sent floating around inside her head hadn't been pretty ones. Oh, he had been pretty enough in them, but Mary had no delusions about herself. He might *be* older than her, but she *looked* older than him . . . and with an older woman's body. And he could say he liked it all he wanted, but it wouldn't change the fact that she *didn't* like it. At least, she didn't like it next to his young, fit-looking body.

Sighing, she turned her gaze out the window as Dante shifted into gear and steered the RV out of their pull-thru parking spot.

"Should I stop at the office so you can let them know we are leaving?" Dante asked, as they approached the main building.

"No," Mary murmured, glancing to the building. "They have my credit-card number. I'll just call them later to let them know something came up."

Dante nodded, and steered past the building to approach the gate and Mary turned her face away from the offices, knowing she'd probably e-mail rather than call. She also would never come back here, whether Carol and Dave sold the campground or not. She liked Carol and still considered her a friend, but she'd learned too much to want to ever spend time around Dave again. He was, as Dante had said, a dog. Just as her Joe had been, she acknowledged. But Joe had changed, or she'd thought he had, while Dave obviously hadn't. She didn't think she could bear being around the man, always worrying he'd make that pass at her Dante had said he'd planned, and she didn't think that if he did, she could keep herself from telling Carol. She just didn't want to be in the middle of that. She'd dealt with her own husband long ago, and thought they'd sorted everything out, but Carol had never confronted Dave that she knew of.

"What are you thinking?"

Mary glanced to Dante and hesitated briefly, but then admitted, "About the Bigelows, and my husband and my life with him."

"Tell me about your life with your Joe?" he asked softly.

Mary turned her face forward and stared at the passing scenery for a moment. "I was six months pregnant the first time Joe cheated on me," she said slowly, and then grimaced and added, "At least the first time I knew he was cheating on me and I think it really was the first time he did cheat on me."

"I'm sorry," Dante said quietly.

Mary waved the words away. She didn't want sympathy. She wanted him to understand why she would stay with Joe when he did that. Clearing her throat, she said, "He was working late a lot, and came home smelling of perfume sometimes. I started to suspect he was . . . well, doing what he was doing," she admitted wryly. "But of course I didn't want to believe it. Still, I hired a private detective to follow him."

She felt him glance at her, but didn't turn to see what his expression was and continued. "Well, it wasn't long before Joe was working late again one night and the private detective called and gave me an address and a room number. It was a cheap little motel on the outskirts of the city. I went there, and—they hadn't even bothered to close the curtains. He was there with his secretary."

Mary heard the bitterness in her own voice, and paused to take a breath. "I—well, I guess I lost it. I started pounding on the door and shouting." She smiled wryly. "I think every door in that motel opened but the one I was pounding on. I cursed him, and said I was going to divorce him, and yelled that he was cowardly scum that wouldn't even face the music and his secretary was a slut, then I jumped in the car and squealed out of there and crashed into a semi."

The RV swerved slightly and Dante cursed and started to pull over, but Mary stared straight ahead and said, "If you stop, I'll stop talking. Please just drive."

He hesitated, the RV still slowing, and then put his foot back on the gas.

Mary let her breath out, but waited another moment. Even after all these years the memories hurt and she was afraid her voice would crack if she didn't get herself under control before she continued. But it was harder than she expected and Mary cursed and undid her seat belt.

"Do you want a coffee?" she asked, getting out of her seat.

Dante nodded and glanced at her, and the sadness in his eyes was nearly her undoing. Turning abruptly, she moved back to the coffee machine and switched the inverter on. As she waited for the machine to heat up, Mary took the time to compose herself. By the time she'd made two coffees she felt more like her old self and even managed a smile when he thanked her for the coffee she set in his cup holder.

Settling back in her own seat, she continued abruptly, "I woke up in the hospital to learn that not only had I lost my baby, but due to complications, I'd never be able to carry another."

"Mary," Dante said, sounding pained.

"Drive," she instructed, and continued, "Joe was crushed that I'd killed our child with—as he put it—my foolish hysterics."

"Bastard," Dante breathed.

"Yes well, I didn't see that at the time. I was so awash in guilt for killing my baby, I agreed with him. I never should have gone there. I should not have driven so recklessly."

"The private investigator should not have given you the address. He should have taken pictures and presented those to you. Was he even licensed?" Dante demanded furiously.

Mary grimaced and shrugged. "Who knows? I found him in the phone book."

"So your husband cheated on you, then made you feel responsible for what followed . . . presumably so that you would not leave him?"

"That seems likely," she agreed, and then added, "And I let him."

"What?" he asked with disbelief. "You are going to take responsibility for his—"

"No," she interrupted quietly. "I am not responsible for what he did. But I am responsible for my decisions, and I—" She paused then sighed. "It was a bad time for me. My mother was dying of cancer; I'd just lost my baby and learned I would never have another. I felt anger, guilt, loss . . . I was a mess," she acknowledged. "And I was scared."

"Of what?" he asked with a frown, glancing toward her again.

Mary bit her lip, and then sighed and said, "Joe and I met in high school. I was in grade nine and he was in grade twelve when we started to date. He graduated and went on to further his education, but we continued to date. He proposed to me on my prom night." She smiled wryly and said, "It was all terribly romantic. He'd already graduated from the University of Winnipeg with his degree a few months before and had got a good job with a big local company. He was making money and spared no expense that night. He rented a limo, brought me roses, took me to dinner at the finest restaurant and got down on one knee right there in front of everyone to propose." She smiled faintly at the memory. "I didn't even care about the prom after that, but he insisted I'd regret it if I didn't go, so we went to prom and I showed off my ring to everyone."

Sighing, she shrugged those memories away. "Anyway, I'd kind of planned on going on to get some kind of degree too, but hadn't really settled on anything yet and he said he didn't think I should. That I didn't need to waste our money on that. I'd be his wife, the mother of his children, a housewife."

"Dependent on him," Dante said quietly.

"I didn't see it that way," Mary said sadly. "Or maybe I did and didn't care. I thought we'd be together forever and live happily ever after. So if he wanted me to be a housewife, I'd be the best housewife there was."

Dante grunted. She didn't know what the sound meant, so continued.

"We got married, and quickly got pregnant and . . ."

"You caught him cheating," Dante said grimly.

Mary nodded, and picked up her coffee. "I could have left him then, but I was scared. I'd gone straight from my parents taking care of me to Joe taking care of me . . . at least, financially. And I did feel guilty about crashing the car and killing my child. On top of that, I couldn't have babies anymore. Who would want me for a wife when I was so useless?"

"Me," Dante growled. "And you are not useless."

"No I'm not," she agreed quietly. "But I didn't see that then."

Mary took another sip of coffee before continuing.

"Of course, after his first outburst, Joe was very sweet. He was constantly at my bedside until I was released from the hospital, then took care of me at home."

"Guilt," Dante said shortly. "And he *should* have felt guilty."

Mary just smiled wryly and went on, "He apologized for his affair with his secretary. Promised to have her transferred to work for someone else and swore it would never happen again. He said he could live with not having biological children so long as he had me. We'd adopt, or use a surrogate, whatever it took to make me happy. So, I said I forgave him and stayed."

"But I didn't really," Mary admitted in the next breath, and explained, "Forgive him, I mean. I was angry for a lot of years." She grimaced. "We pretended all was well, and set about adopting children. A little boy first, and then a little girl. But things were not all right. I couldn't bear him touching me. I could hardly look at him. I know he had other affairs then, he warned me he would if I didn't stop treating him like a leper, but I didn't care. I was angry, at myself and at him, so I punished us both for it."

She smiled wryly. "I'm surprised he didn't give up and divorce me. He didn't though. Joe told me years later that he felt he deserved the punishment. Anyway, while I was a horrible wife, I was a good mother, and we acted as if all was well for the sake of the children."

Mary took another sip of coffee and then said, "We probably would have stayed like that till his death if things had just continued as they were going. As it was it went on for fifteen years."

"What happened to change things?" Dante asked with curiosity.

"I found out about one of his children. A son," she said quietly. "An angry fourteen-year-old who showed up at our door one day. His mother had finally told him who his father was and he wanted to confront him. He was faced with me first."

Mary peered down at her coffee mug. "I was furious. There I was unable to have children of my own and Joe had gone and had them with another woman. Not only that, but he'd just abandoned him. I didn't know what made me angrier. I hired a private detective to find out if there were any others and . . ." She paused and swallowed the bile rising up in her throat at the memory of how she'd felt when the detective had given his report. "Joe had at least four children by four different women that he knew of. The one boy I'd met, and three girls. There may have been more though; he couldn't be sure. But he was sure that Joe wasn't a part of their lives. He'd just been dropping his seed and leaving it to grow as he danced on to the next victim."

Mary glanced to Dante and smiled wryly. "Joe admitted that most of the women he had affairs with had no idea he was married. He said a friend had helped with that. I'm guessing now that it was Dave, but Joe wouldn't tell me who it was at the time. I suppose that was to prevent me outing Dave to Carol. Joe would only say he was just a chum from work. But he told me that they went out together to meet women, often double dating. A woman who met two male friends hanging out didn't imagine that he would be married and carry on an affair with his friend's knowledge. And his "chum" backed up any story he gave to explain why he couldn't see her at certain times, or why she hadn't met his family or any other friends."

Mary shook her head with remembered disgust. "Of course, once the girlfriend started pushing for those kinds of things, it was time to end it and move on anyway in his mind. Or if she got pregnant," she added grimly. "As far as Joe was concerned, birth control was the woman's problem and he always asked if they were on the pill when they started up. If she said no, he moved along. He wanted no chance of having to explain why he had condoms in his wallet when we weren't having sex. So, they were all supposed to be safe, and if a woman got pregnant, he was sure she was just trying to force him into marrying her. Joe claimed he offered to help with an abortion and if she refused, it was "sayonara sweetheart.""

"He really was a bastard," Dante muttered.

"Yes," Mary agreed solemnly, "And I was a total psycho bitch."

"Mary!" He gaped at her with dismay, and she smiled slightly.

"I was," she assured him. "I was making his home life as miserable as possible. For instance, he traveled a lot then and one time when he was gone for two months, I bought the kids a cat. Joe was deathly allergic to cats. But the kids had had it for two months by the time he returned. He could hardly take it away from them then. He had to get an inhaler and start taking allergy shots twice a week just to be able to breathe at home. Joe hated shots."

"Diabolical," Dante said on a laugh.

"Hmm. I did other things as well."

"Like what?" he asked with amusement.

Mary considered the various things and said, "Oh, if I knew he hated something, I made it a lot for meals, saying I was sure he'd said he'd liked it last time. If he liked something, I never made it again. I deliberately used his razors on my legs so the blade was always dull when he went to shave his face. I constantly washed his whites with reds to turn them pink. I bought him the loudest and ugliest patterned shirts and ties every birthday and Christmas and then acted wounded if he didn't wear them. And I used to cook him something with mushrooms in it as his meal before each flight. It didn't matter what, so long as it had mushrooms."

When Dante glanced away from the road to give her a confused look, she explained with amusement, "Mushrooms gave Joe gas, you see. Which made the flight miserable for him. Gas expands as the plane climbs in altitude and causes terrible stomach pains."

Dante's mouth dropped a little at this news, and then snapped shut. Turning back to the road he muttered, "Remind me not to anger you."

Mary grinned faintly, but shrugged. "He was the only one I did those kinds of things to. I'm pretty sure I was a good mother. I worked very hard at it. And

I was perfectly lovely otherwise." She pursed her lips and admitted, "I think getting all my aggression out on him made me much more patient with the children and everyone else."

"Thank God," Dante breathed.

"Yes, I could really have screwed up those children had I allowed my anger to stretch to them. Fortunately, torturing him was enough." Mary paused and frowned and then admitted, "Although, I did influence their opinion of him a great deal. It was inevitable, of course. He was often away and I was always there. I shuttled them to school, practice, friends etc. And I never praised him to them. I didn't put him down either really. I mean I never said he was a lying, cheating louse or anything, but I did often use the term, "Oh, your *father*," in that derogatory manner you really shouldn't use in regard to the other parent in front of children." She made a face and admitted, "I'm pretty sure I undermined his position with them without even really trying."

"But that may not have had much affect had he been there to spend time with them," Dante pointed out reasonably. "Had he been there, they would have got to know him as his own person rather than the man who occasionally showed up at the house and the one you 'oh, your fathered' about."

"True, but then I didn't make his being home an attractive proposition," she pointed out.

Dante frowned, but Mary continued before he could argue further. "As I say, that went on for years. Fifteen to be exact."

"And then his son showed up at your door," Dante said quietly.

Mary nodded and fell silent as the pain of that discovery washed over her anew. She loved her children and had considered them her own from the minute they'd been placed in her arms, but in that moment, looking at the young carbon copy of her husband . . . Mary thought she might have killed Joe if he'd been home at the time. But she knew without a doubt that after she'd heard what else the boy had to say, she definitely would have killed her husband had he been there.

Eleven

Dante glanced toward Mary with a frown. She'd quite suddenly gone silent, and considering the topic, he was concerned about her. After another moment passed in silence, he said gently, "You must have been very hurt."

"Hurt?" she asked dryly, and then snorted. "I was freaking furious."

Dante's eyes widened and he glanced quickly her way, taking note of her anger now just at the memory. She was nearly vibrating in her seat with it. Shifting his gaze back to the road, he cleared his throat and asked, "Because the boy was proof Joe was continuing to have affairs?"

"No," she assured him. "Not about the affairs. I didn't give a rat's ass about the affairs by that point. I had been completely asexual since the miscarriage, shutting down that part of myself. What I cared about was his children. I was furious that he'd had them, and paradoxically, furious that he hadn't been a part of their lives or taken any responsibility, even monetarily, for their existence."

"Ah," Dante murmured, and wasn't sure what to say to that.

Another moment of silence passed and then she announced, "I left him that afternoon. I packed up the kids and checked into a motel and made an appointment with a divorce lawyer, all by dinner." She swallowed and then admitted, "But I never went to see the lawyer."

"Why?" Dante asked at once, and when she didn't answer right away, glanced over to see that she was peering out the window at the passing scenery. Her expression was closed and he shifted his gaze back to the road, simply waiting.

After a moment, she sighed and said, "Carol came to see me at the motel. We were good friends even then. Dave and Joe often traveled together, and we were each other's support when they were gone. So, of course, I called her with the crushing news of Joe's betrayal. She came rushing to the motel and we talked and cried for hours. She thought I should leave him, of course," Mary added wryly. "And then she gave me the number of a therapist her sister had been trying to get her to go see. She had no interest in counseling, but if I wanted the number . . ."

"Surprisingly, I did. I knew I was angry and had contributed at least somewhat to things, and I didn't want to carry that anger and self-destructive streak on out of the marriage and into any future relationships. So, I called this therapist. Her name was Linda and she just happened to have a cancellation the next morning, so I went to see her. It was the best call I ever made."

"Really?" he asked, and couldn't hide the doubt he was feeling on the subject. She had stayed with Joe, after all, something he thought was just wrong after everything the man had done. He would have thought a good therapist would have insisted she leave, not convince her to stay.

"Yes, really," Mary assured him solemnly, and then explained, "Linda listened patiently to my tale of woe about my marriage. How he'd convinced me not to go on to further my education. How he'd cheated on me. How he'd refused to face me, forcing me to drive madly off and crash, and how he, how he, how he . . ." She let her voice trail off and then he heard her sigh and she said, "And then Linda asked if I'd even been in the marriage."

"What?" he asked with confusion, casting another glance her way.

She smiled at his expression and admitted, "That was my reaction, but then she said that the way I told the story, I hadn't made a single decision or choice. Linda said I was taking the victim's role. That, yes, Joe had suggested I didn't need an education, but was it possible it was because he'd realized that I was unsettled about what to take and perhaps a little afraid and so had tried to make my decision easier by giving me the option to be a housewife? If I'd really wanted that education to fall back on, wouldn't I have spoken up about it and insisted? Even if only to take part-time courses to see what I liked? After all, as I'd told her, he was making good money, and I wasn't pregnant for the first three years of our marriage. I could have taken courses until we were blessed with that baby if I'd really wanted to. Wouldn't he have allowed that?"

Mary paused and out of the corner of his eye, he saw her raise her coffee cup for a sip. After swallowing, she continued. "I had to admit that yes, he probably would have been fine with that. And she said, so, I hadn't really been interested or wanted a degree. He hadn't forced me not to go on to further my education."

"Hmm," Dante murmured. "I suppose she is right."

"Yes, well that was the first of the revelations," Mary said wryly. "By the time I left her office, I was thinking less like a victim, and acknowledging my part in things. I had told even myself that I wanted my marriage to work, but my actions said something else entirely. In truth, I hadn't wanted Joe back as a partner; I'd wanted to punish him pure and simple. And I had. I'd got exactly what I'd wanted," she said wryly. "And then Linda made me begin to question Joe's motives in all of this. Why had he put up with my punishing him? Why had he stayed married to me when I offered him nothing but food he disliked, a cat he couldn't breathe around, and children who grew increasingly distant from him? What had been in it for him?"

"She suggested I put off the divorce, and that we work together first, her and I, and once we got to a space where I felt comfortable, bring in Joe for couples counseling."

"I was sure Joe would never agree to couples counseling," she admitted quietly. "But I was wrong. We set the divorce aside. I moved back to the house with the kids and he got a temporary apartment close to work while I started therapy. But it wasn't long before my whole attitude was changed and I was able to see things more clearly. And then the couples counseling started. I found out the first session that after I'd spoken to him about the couples counseling, Joe had called Linda and asked if he could see her one-on-one like I was doing. So he'd been working too. We both knew what our motivations were, and understood what we'd each been doing, and it was just a matter of admitting it to each other, and finding out a way to deal with each other without falling into old patterns."

"And what was he doing?" Dante asked dryly. "Aside from having affairs at every turn?"

"Joe hadn't intended on having the first affair," Mary said quietly. "That had developed over long hours together working a project. He said he knew he should have arranged for her to be transferred the moment he realized what was happening, but he'd been afraid of looking stupid or weak at work. It had been a mistake."

"I'll say," Dante muttered.

"No one's perfect," she repeated solemnly. "And there were extenuating circumstances. We'd been married three years when I finally got pregnant. I expected it would happen right away, but it didn't. It took three years, so for three years I was just a housewife, cleaning house and cooking meals and getting comments from friends and family like didn't I want to do anything?

Didn't I feel I should stop being a burden to Joe and get a job?" She paused and then admitted, "It wasn't very good for my self-esteem. I felt like a failure because I wasn't getting pregnant and started having problems with depression. I doubt I was great fun to live with after the first year or so."

"That does not—" Dante began, but she continued over him.

"Then when I finally did get pregnant? Well . . . I was over the moon, of course, and sick as a dog. I spent more time hanging over the toilet than anything else. Joe used to come home from work to a mess, no food and would spend hours just rubbing my back and holding my hair out of the way as I threw up. My doctor said he'd never seen such a bad case of morning sickness. Which is a misnomer by the way, it was morning, noon and night sickness."

"Then Joe had a big project come up. If it was a success, he'd get a promotion. If not . . ." She shrugged. "He started working late hours on it, probably partially because he needed to, but maybe also a little to avoid coming home to my misery."

"And he started the affair with his secretary," Dante said quietly and glanced over to see her nod in response. His mouth tightened as he shifted his eyes back to the road, and he growled, "You were carrying his child, Mary, and apparently very sick in doing so. It is not okay that he had an affair."

"Oh, of course it isn't," she agreed. "Don't misunderstand me. I'm not saying it was okay that he had the affair. He should have talked to me. I was so miserable myself; I didn't realize how miserable he was. He should have suggested I see a specialist and see if anything could be done about the nausea. Or, he could have suggested I get a friend or family member in to help me. Or found any other way to handle it. But he didn't. He had the affair. That was his choice, and what he had to live with afterward."

"My choice was in what I did when I began to suspect he might be having an affair. I didn't talk to him either. I too turned to someone else and hired a private detective. And then when the detective gave me that address, I chose to go to the motel and catch him rather than simply confront him with the information when he came home. And when he didn't satisfy my need for confrontation and my "Ah ha!" moment at the motel, I was the one who drove out of there like a maniac, straight into a semi."

"Most of my anger was at myself for doing that, but I buried it under my anger at him and blamed him for everything. He, in turn, felt guilty about his part in it and so let me punish him for the next fifteen years rather than leave me to find a healthier relationship and happiness. He even refused to see his own biological children because he felt that would be the ultimate betrayal."

"The affairs were not?" Dante asked with disbelief.

"The first one was, but after that, as I said, I wanted nothing to do with him in that area. He figured I didn't care anymore if he slept around, but acknowledging and being a part of the life of a child he'd had a part in creating when I couldn't have children anymore . . . ?

To him, that seemed like the ultimate betrayal. Especially when he felt guilty for his part in the accident that caused the miscarriage and my inability to have those children. He felt like he'd ruined everything, especially me. And I felt the same way. So I punished him, and he took it. But it was a punishment for me too. I wasn't any happier than he was."

"And yet you stayed together," he said grimly.

"We almost didn't," she admitted. "I mean, when I realized how much time I had wasted on punishing us both . . . And I think he felt the same way. Like we'd done enough damage. But Linda suggested we at least see if anything could be salvaged. We'd been in love once. Could we get past the hurt of the past and find that love again?"

"She sounds like a quack to me," he said abruptly, anger sliding through him for everything she'd been through. Mary was a beautiful, smart, and caring woman. She should have been loved and cherished, not cheated on and betrayed and that quack counselor should have said as much and encouraged her to get the hell away from Joe Winslow.

"Joe said the same thing," Mary said with a chuckle. "He'd liked her until then, but that suggestion convinced him she was a quack and he said it to her face. She just smiled and asked, "What's wrong? Are you afraid? Besides, what have you got to lose? If it doesn't work, you divorce, just a couple months or so later. But if it works . . .""

"So, we both agreed to give it a try with her counseling. He continued to live in the apartment and we started to have dates that we then dissected in her office during our appointments." Mary sighed. "At first, it was hard. There were still a lot of emotions to work through, but she helped us get through them. And eventually, we started to find each other again, but this time it was better."

Dante couldn't keep the skepticism from his voice as he asked, "How?"

"I'd always looked up to Joe and kind of put him on a pedestal," she said, trying to explain. "First he was the "senior boy" to my freshman in high school, and then he went and got his degree while I didn't, and then he got the big impressive job while I was a housewife. In my mind, we weren't so much a couple as he was the star and I was just the supporting cast," she admitted quietly. "But after everything that happened, he was no longer on that pedestal. He was just Joe. On top of that, I realized that I needed to boost my self-esteem and think more of myself, so I started taking classes at the university."

Dante glanced to her with surprise. "In what?"

Mary hesitated, rolled her eyes and then admitted, "psychology."

His head swiveled toward her, his eyebrows flying up in surprise and she shrugged helplessly.

"I wanted to better understand myself so I didn't mess up again," she admitted wryly, then added, "And I wanted to help others who might be going through the same things I had. Joe and I had wasted so many years on useless emotions we didn't even understand." Mary was silent for a minute, then sighed, and said,

"So I got a bachelor's, then a master's, then went on for my doctorate."

"You're a *doctor*?" he gasped, unable to hold back his shock. That surprised the hell out of him. He'd got used to the idea of her being the housewife she kept talking about. This news was a bit surprising.

"Dr. Winslow, psychologist, at your service," Mary said lightly with a nod, and then admitted, "It took me a while to get it. I was thirty-four when I started taking courses, and that first term I only took a couple classes. But then I started going full time, and even taking summer courses and I got my doctorate just before turning forty-four."

Dante didn't care how long it had taken; it was damned impressive.

"A psychologist," he said with a smile. "Nice."

They were both silent for a minute, then he glanced to her and teased, "So how does a psychologist end up with body issues?"

Mary's eyes narrowed and then he saw her nose rise before he turned his gaze back to the road, and wasn't really surprised when she snapped, "Actually, I don't have body issues."

He was starting to smile at the show of spirit when she added, "At least not with *my* body."

Dante's head snapped around with shock. "Surely you are not suggesting you have problems with *my* body?"

"Eyes front," Mary said sweetly, using his own line on him. Once he turned his attention back to the road, she said, "Yes, I'm afraid I do have issues with your body. If you looked more like Dave I'd be dancing around the RV naked and jumping you at every turn."

Caught briefly by the image of her dancing around the RV naked, it was a moment before the rest of what she'd said sank through his muddled brain. Once it did, Dante squawked, "*Dave?*"

"Well, not like Dave," she said quickly, and then soothed his ego by adding, "I'm not attracted to him like I am to you. I just meant if you looked like you but more his age."

Dante relaxed a little, a slow smile coming to his lips before he reminded her, "I am older than him."

"Yes, but you *look* twenty-five," she pointed out with exasperation.

"So?" he asked mildly.

"So my children are older than that," she said with disgust.

"And that bothers you," he said gently, and then pointed out, "Many women would take pleasure and pride in being able to show off a handsome younger man as their lover."

Mary snorted. "Then they're idiots. Because everyone is snickering behind their hands and assuming he's there for money or something."

"I have a great deal of money, Mary. I am not with you for anything but yourself," he assured her solemnly.

She fell silent for a minute, and then said quietly, "It's okay when you're kissing me. Then I forget about how young you look and how old I am. But when you aren't kissing me, all I can think about is that you look twenty-five to my sixty-two, and I feel like a dirty old woman contemplating raping a child."

Dante chuckled at the claim, and then assured her, "I am *not* a child. And trust me, it would not be rape." He glanced in the side mirror as a car whipped past them on the highway, then cast a smile her way and offered, "I could tie you down the next time so you can be sure you are not raping me."

Mary's eyes widened and he could hear her heart rate speed up at the very thought, then she swallowed thickly and said, "Anyway, Joe and I—"

"Coward," Dante interrupted, affectionately. "I know you would like me to tie you up. Your heart sped up at the suggestion."

Mary flushed, but forged on as if he hadn't interrupted. "Joe and I got back together, but this time it was totally different than the first part of our marriage. We were equals, and friends. We had learned how to communicate with each other, and made sure we did. The last twenty-eight years of our marriage were wonderful. We enjoyed ourselves and each other and did everything together." She paused then added, "But maybe it wasn't as great as I thought. Because I trusted he was faithful to me after that, but apparently Dave—"

"Dave was much younger in his memories of his catting-around days with your husband," Dante interrupted solemnly. "It is most likely they occurred during those fifteen years when you and Joe were having your war of a thousand tortures."

Mary breathed out a little sigh of relief at this news,

obviously glad Joe hadn't betrayed her again after all the work they'd done to save their marriage. Dante supposed it would have put a pall on what she presently considered the happiest years of her life. But he intended to show her what true happiness was. He would spend the rest of his days doing so. He would never betray her, would always want her, and once he turned her, she would be able to have those children she had always longed for. And Dante would be happy to give them to her. In fact, he knew without a doubt that he would enjoy planting them in her belly and fully intended on practicing doing so the first chance he got. And he would continue that practice until he could convince her to accept being his life mate and agree to the turn, then he would keep her in bed for a year whether she got pregnant quickly or not.

Dante glanced to her again and almost sighed aloud. The woman might think she was too old for him, but he could not look at her without thinking about getting her naked. The things he wanted to do to her . . . and would already be doing to her if not for the constant interruptions and then the arrival of the box and the need to save his brother. But once they had captured his and Tomasso's kidnappers . . .

By the time he was done, Dante was determined the woman would know how beautiful and sexy she really was.

"War of a thousand tortures?"

Dante glanced to her at that squawk. She'd obviously just realized what he'd called the fifteen years of misery during the first part of her marriage. Shrugging, he said, "That is what those years sound like to me." Smiling to soften his words, he added, "And I will be most careful not to anger you ever."

Mary chuckled at the claim, and then fell silent for a moment before glancing at him curiously. "Can you really hear my heartbeat?"

"*Si*."

"How?" she asked curiously. "I mean the engine is humming, the windows are cracked open and a breeze is coming in, and everything is jingling and rattling in the back. How can you possibly hear my heart over all of that?"

"The nanos—"

"And where the hell did the fangs come from?" she burst out suddenly, bringing up something that had been nagging at the back of her mind since he'd bitten Dave. "You said the nanos kept your people at peak condition. Peak condition for humans does not include fangs for sucking blood."

"They—"

"Come to that," she interrupted again, growing a bit agitated. "Reading and controlling minds isn't a usual condition for humans either, at their peak condition or not."

"Mary?" he said softly.

"Yes?"

"*Sta'zitto*," he suggested gently, and then added, "*Per favore*."

Mary blinked. "What does that mean?"

"Please, shut up," he translated, his tone affectionate. "I will explain if you just let me."

Mary narrowed her eyes, but nodded, and waited for these explanations.

"In Atlantis, the nanos kept their hosts at their peak condition. "But, as I mentioned, Atlantis fell and the survivors, the ones with the nanos, found themselves in a world much less advanced. There were no more transfusions. No more blood. But the nanos had work to do, and kept using the blood that was in their host." Dante paused briefly to narrow his eyes at the rear camera screen, and then continued, "Grandfather says it was a bad time. When the blood is low in the veins, the nanos seek it out in the organs. It is very painful. Many of the survivors died. Often killing themselves."

"So you can die?" she asked. "You aren't really immortal?"

"We can die, but it is hard to kill us. You must cut off the head and make sure it is kept away from the body for a certain amount of time. Or we can burn to death."

"So these immortals that killed themselves . . . ?"

"Set themselves on fire, usually. Or convinced someone to cut off their head for them."

"Oh," Mary breathed, thinking the agony must have been extreme to drive those poor people to such a terrible end.

"Those who survived did so because they did not give up. The nanos eventually forced a sort of evolution on their hosts to get the blood they needed to continue their job."

"The fangs," she guessed solemnly.

Dante nodded. "Our people developed fangs to

gather the blood we needed. But they also developed increased speed and strength to help them in the hunt, as well as better hearing, better vision and even night vision."

"Is that why your eyes glow silver?" Mary asked curiously. "The night vision, I mean? Cats' eyes kind of glow in light at night and they're supposed to have good night vision."

"I am not sure," he admitted. "I know the silver has something to do with the nanos. All immortals have silver or gold flecks in their eyes that glow in certain circumstances."

"What kind of circumstances?"

"When we need blood," he answered. "Or when we feel . . . . passionate."

"Ah," Mary muttered and lifted her mug to her lips. Finding it empty, she set it in the holder, and clasped her hands in her lap, simply waiting.

"We also suddenly had the ability to read minds and control people, which made hunting without being discovered much easier."

"I imagine so," she said dryly, and then frowned and asked, "But how did the nanos do that? I mean, they weren't programmed to do that."

"No, but their main directive was to keep their host at their peak condition," Dante pointed out.

"Yes."

"And they needed blood to do that."

"But they use more blood than the human body can produce," Mary remembered his earlier words.

"*Si.*" He nodded. "So, I presume the nanos just added getting blood as part of their task to complete the original task."

"You presume?" she asked. "Don't the scientists who developed this have some idea—?"

"The scientists who developed the nanos did not survive the fall of Atlantis," he interrupted.

Mary raised her eyebrows. "None of them had the nanos?"

"Apparently not," he said with a shrug.

"So, only the human guinea pigs survived Atlantis," she said slowly. "And they have no idea about how the stuff in their bodies works?"

"We have some knowledge now," Dante assured her. "We have scientists among our ranks who have discovered much and are always working to discover more. However, as I say, technology in the new world our people found themselves in was far behind Atlantis. And none of them were scientists. They had to wait for science to catch up a bit. Most of the discoveries about our nanos have been made in only the last century."

"So your people wandered around for centuries with no clue about what they had in their own bodies," Mary muttered. "Weird."

"How much do you think most people with a pacemaker know about the mechanism inside their chest?" Dante asked with amusement. "Or the people who have been given artificial hearts until a transplant is found, how much to you think they know of the mechanics of it?"

"Probably not much," she admitted wryly.

"Hmm." He nodded.

They fell silent for a moment and Mary was comfortable enough with him to allow it until she noted the worry on his face. She suspected it was because of the black van that had started tailing them some miles back. It was probably the kidnappers, and she had no doubt they would probably try something. The problem was they didn't know where or when or what it might be.

"Tell me about your childhood," Mary said abruptly to distract them both. "What was it like growing up a vampire in 1905?"

Dante winced, and his voice was pained when he said, "We prefer the term *immortal*."

"But you can die, so you aren't immortal," she pointed out. "You do, however, have fangs and drink blood like a vampire."

"*Si*, but we were around before the English invented the vampire. Before even the Dacians and their *strigoi*. We are Atlanteans, and immortals," he ended with finality.

Since he was so touchy on the subject, Mary decided to let it lie for now, and said, "So? 1905? Italy? I imagine it was beautiful? No pollution, no cars, no—"

"No," he said dryly.

"No?" she asked with surprise.

"Mary, I was a baby in 1905. I don't remember much," he pointed out gently. "But I do know pollution was no better than it is now. In fact, it may have been worse."

"Really?" she asked with surprise. "I always thought it was a more modern problem."

Dante shook his head. "From what my grandmother says, pollution has been a problem for quite some time. Especially in more populated areas. She said it was a problem even in Roman times."

"Well," Mary murmured, "That's depressing."

Dante smiled faintly.

"So, tell me about growing up then, instead," Mary suggested.

He glanced from the rear camera view to the road and shrugged. "What do you want to know?"

Mary considered the question. She almost asked what it was like being a twin, but didn't want to make him think of his missing brother, so instead asked, "Did you like school growing up?"

"Tomasso and I were homeschooled," Dante said sadly.

So much for not making him think of his brother, Mary thought wryly.

"Most born immortals are," he added. "It is safer."

"Safer how?" she asked curiously.

"Well, children are not known for their self-control or consideration of consequences," he pointed out.

"And they might fang out and attack another student in a school?" she suggested, trying to follow his reasoning.

"They might," Dante acknowledged. "Or they might get injured on the playground, which could be equally dangerous. A serious injury could land them at a hospital before adult immortals could get there to prevent it, which might lead to blood tests or something else that might reveal the nanos in their blood," he pointed out, and then added, "But even small injuries could cause problems because they would heal so quickly, which would draw attention."

"Yeah, I guess it would," Mary agreed thoughtfully.

"And then there is the risk of a young immortal sharing the knowledge of what they are with a mortal friend, thinking they may never betray them," Dante went on. "Unfortunately, friendships do not always last a lifetime, and even if they do, friends have falling-outs and the mortal might reveal that secret in a moment of spite."

"So, basically immortal children are . . . what?" she asked. "They keep you only among other immortal children?"

Dante shook his head. "Usually immortal children lead very solitary lives. At least, in regard to other children. They have their families of course, but in the past, immortals were very spread out and they rarely had friends their own age. Unless they were lucky and had a twin like I did," he added quietly.

"Like you do," Mary said firmly, afraid he was giving up on his brother. To get his mind off Tomasso, she asked, "Why were immortals spread out?"

"Having too many hunters in the same area was risky."

"How?" she asked at once.

Dante hesitated, and then said, "Life for us was different before blood banks were started. We had to hunt."

"Humans you mean," Mary tried not to sound too angry as she said it, but knew some of her disgust at the thought of her fellow humans being hunted like animals showed in her voice.

"We need blood to survive," he reminded her gently. "But we did not hunt willy-nilly. It was not necessary to take so much blood we killed the human, and immortals have been careful from the beginning not to do so."

"Don't kill the cow that supplies the milk?" she suggested dryly.

"Just so," Dante agreed calmly. "However, just taking blood from too many people in the same area can cause problems. It raises the possibility of discovery of our kind. We lived very carefully throughout history, everything we did meant to keep knowledge of our kind hidden."

"So you basically wanted a big herd to feed from, like a whole city to one family?" Mary said, and then sighed to herself as she realized how bitchy that had come out when she hadn't really meant it to. She did understand their need to feed, and knew it wasn't even their fault that they had to. It was a matter of survival. Still, that didn't make it any easier to accept that she and every other human on the planet were basically cattle to them.

Dante didn't react to her attitude. He merely said, "We did what we could to minimize our need for blood. In an effort to reduce the amount of blood we needed, immortals took to keeping mostly night hours and sleeping during the day to avoid sunlight and the extra damage. Most were careful about their diets and eschewed drinking as well. And despite the fact that we could easily win any battle, engaging in one was always a last resort, to avoid injuries that would need extra blood for repair."

"So your people were a bunch of vegetarian pacifist night owls?" Mary asked dubiously.

"Not exactly," Dante said on a laugh. "I said they were careful with their diets, not that they gave up every pleasure. And war was a last resort, not forsworn entirely."

"Hmm," Mary murmured, frowning as she glanced to the side mirror and noted that the van that had been keeping back a bit was now moving up closer behind them. She glanced at the road around them, noting with some concern that other than a dark SUV almost on their front bumper, the traffic appeared to have cleared out almost entirely. It was a lonely stretch of highway with little in the way of witnesses.

"Of course, war should always be a last resort," Dante added, regaining her attention. "But it was more so for our people."

"Dante," Mary began worriedly as the van moved to the left, out of sight of her side mirror.

"I know," he said quietly. "They are about to pass us. No doubt they plan to get in front of us and force us to stop or—" He broke off abruptly and cursed as something, no doubt the van, rammed into the left back end of the RV.

Mary instinctively braced herself, pressing her right hand against the window next to her and grabbing at her armrest with her left as the RV jolted and swerved. Her gaze slid to the window. Spying the embankment along the side of the road, she knew without a doubt that they would be in serious trouble if Dante couldn't regain control of the RV, and nearly released a relieved sob when he did. However, he'd barely straightened them out when they were hit again. Harder.

As the back end of the RV began to swing toward the side of the road, she glanced down to Bailey who was trying to straighten under the dashboard. Mary instinctively lifted her legs, blocking the dog in and then closed her eyes as the RV's back tires slid off the road and over the embankment. She felt them tipping, and then everything seemed to explode around her as the vehicle rolled. Mary thought she heard Dante shout her name, but never got the chance to respond before something slammed into her head and the lights suddenly went out.

What sounded like a gunshot made Dante open his eyes and while he heard the squeal of tires and the scream of one engine, and then another, his attention was taken up with trying to make sense of the confused world around him. Everything was such a jumble that for one moment, he couldn't place where he was, and then his gaze landed on Mary, below, rather than beside him.

He was hanging from his seatbelt in the driver's seat of the RV, he realized and recalled what had happened. The back tires had gone off the road and over the embankment, dragging the front end along for the ride before it had toppled. The vehicle had done at least one complete roll, before coming to a stop on its side, the passenger's side.

Mary's side, Dante thought as he peered at her. She lay crumpled on her side with the lower half of her body still strapped into the passenger's seat, but her upper body having slid off to rest against the wall of the RV, which for all intents and purposes was now the floor of the RV if he stood up.

Mary looked like a broken doll amid the debris surrounding her. She was pale and still, covered in blood, and Bailey lay in front of her, her back legs still tucked between the dash and the floorboard, but her upper body out. She was whimpering and licking her mistress's face, trying to wake her.

The scent of gas reached Dante's nose then. It was followed by a waft of smoke and he glanced toward the back of the RV. It had pretty much crumbled under the impact of the roll, the walls collapsing. Dante couldn't see much of anything but a jumble of household items mixed in with the crumbled walls. He didn't see fire, but he could smell the smoke it was producing somewhere in that mess.

Cursing, Dante started feeling for the buckle of his seat belt. He nearly undid it the moment he found it, but then realized that would let him drop on top of Mary and Bailey. Pausing, he glanced around, then braced his feet on the motor cover between the two seats, and tangled his arm in the upper strap of the seatbelt before releasing it. Much to his relief, while he dropped a bit and swung, Dante was able to keep himself from simply dropping onto the pair on the floor. Grabbing the belt with his free hand now, he quickly untangled his arm, and then carefully let one foot drop to the floor, positioning it behind the passenger seat at Mary's back. Then he lowered the other as well before releasing the belt to stand behind her.

"It's okay, girl," Dante murmured to Bailey, as he bent to examine Mary. The amount of blood covering the pair of them was terrifying, but he could hear Mary's heartbeat, and while it was slow and weak, it was there. Spotting the nearby empty cooler that had held the blood; he glanced around and noted that the empty bags were all around them. It gave him hope that they were the source of most, if not all, of the blood he was seeing.

Bailey whimpered again, this time licking his hand, and Dante turned back and gave the dog a quick, reassuring pet, then undid Mary's seat belt.

"It's all right Bailey," he said as he scooped Mary into his arm. "Come on, let's get her out of here."

Dante straightened slowly with Mary in his arms, and then paused. The RV was lying on the side where the only door was situated. The only way out was through one of the windows. The front windshield was the obvious choice. It was huge. He'd guess about eight feet wide and five feet high. At least it was when the RV was upright. Right now, with the vehicle on its side, the opening was eight feet high and five wide. But there were shards of glass still in the frame, most of them small pieces, but a couple of larger ones that he had to be careful of.

"Come on, Bailey," Dante murmured and carefully

maneuvered his way through the opening, moving slowly to ensure he didn't scrape Mary up against any of the glass shards. Once outside, he paused to glance back, frowning with concern when he saw that while Bailey was following, she was moving very slowly, and limping and whimpering in pain as she did. She'd obviously not escaped unscathed, but she was still mobile, so he left her to follow at her own speed and carried Mary several feet away from the vehicle to lay her in the grass.

Kneeling beside Mary, Dante began to run his hands over her, searching for injuries. His heart began to sink as he realized there were many of them. The blood was not all from the bags. She had cuts, bruises, broken bones, and a fearsome head wound, he saw as he turned her face to see both sides. What scared him most, however, was the jagged piece of glass he found protruding from her side. The blood was oozing out around the glass. Too much blood. Her weak heartbeat was growing slower with each beat.

"Mary," he whispered helplessly, and then did the only thing he could; Dante slid one hand under her neck so that her head fell back and her mouth dropped open, then he raised his other wrist in front of his mouth, let his canines descend and bit viciously into his own flesh. Dante pressed the gushing wound to her open mouth, and kept it there, hunching over her protectively as the RV exploded behind him.

Twelve

Mary smiled sleepily and reached up to pet Bailey when the dog ran a wet tongue up her cheek. She frowned in confusion, however, when her hand encountered a curtain of long soft hair instead of short, dog fur. Blinking her eyes open, she peered blankly at Dante. He was leaning over her, but his head was presently turned away as he did something out of her line of vision. When he swung his head back, his eyes widened as he saw that she was awake, and then chagrin filled his expression.

"I am sorry. I was hoping to clean you up before you woke, but I did not intend to wake you. I expected you to be unconscious for a couple more hours at least."

"Clean me?" Mary asked weakly, sure she'd misunderstood.

"Yes." Dante raised a washcloth she hadn't noticed in his hand and gave her face another swipe. "Francis,

Russell and I were so busy trying to hold you down and keep you from harming yourself I did not get the chance before now. You only calmed this morning and by then we were so exhausted . . ." He shrugged. "But when I woke from my rest and saw your face I thought I'd best clean it. I did not want you to wake up, see your face all covered with blood and . . . What?" he asked uncertainly when she suddenly closed her eyes with relief.

"I thought you were licking my face," she admitted.

"What?" he asked with disbelief.

"Well, really I thought Bailey was licking my face, but then when I opened my eyes and it was you here I—" She shook her head and waved the matter away. "Never mind. I have more urgent matters to attend to. Where is the bathroom?"

"Oh, it is there," Dante said, turning to gesture to a door in the wall behind him.

The moment he turned his face away, Mary tossed the blankets and sheets aside. All she had on was an overlarge T-shirt. She'd rather been hoping for more than that, perhaps joggers and a T-shirt or something else that would cover her from throat to toes. Unfortunately, that wasn't the case. Equally unfortunately, she had to relieve herself so badly that she couldn't wait for him to leave so that she could get up. So, Mary leapt from the bed and sped around it to dash to the bathroom door. She was inside and slamming it closed so quickly she even impressed herself. Adrenaline was apparently a truly amazing thing, Mary thought as she hiked up the T-shirt and dropped to sit on the toilet.

As she tore some toilet paper off the roll, Mary remembered a time when she was young and being chased by a boy at school. He was known to like to grab the boobs of all the girls while they were out on the playground at recess. Mary had seen him coming up behind her one day, hands out and at the ready, and she'd taken off at a dead run. Her feet had moved so fast they'd barely touched the ground. It had felt to her as if she'd almost just flown across the playground.

Mary hadn't thought she still had it in her. But it seemed even an old broad could practically fly when faced with humiliation. And having handsome, young-looking Dante get a gander at her dimpled thighs was definitely a humiliating prospect to her. He was so damned perfect, and she so wasn't.

Grimacing, she finished her business, flushed the toilet, and stood to wash her hands. It was as she soaped her hands that Mary actually looked at any part of herself for the first time, and then she paused and frowned with confusion. Her hands were pale and as smooth as a baby's bottom, the nails long.

Actually overly long, she thought with a frown and turned her hands over then back. She hadn't seen these hands in years—many, many years. Time had scarred and wrinkled them, marring them with age spots and—but no more. Now they looked like they belonged to a young woman. Someone maybe twenty or twenty-five and—

Thoughts dying, Mary stilled and stared blindly at

her hands, her mind suddenly racing, and then she slowly lifted her head and peered into the mirror over the sink. An old friend stared back.

"Dante!" Mary called, her voice coming out strangled.

"Yes?" He answered right away. It sounded like he was right outside the door. "Are you all right?"

Mary merely stared at the woman in the mirror. Her hair had grown a bit and now hung almost to her shoulders. It was also a golden blond for the first couple of inches, before becoming the platinum white age had turned it to. It actually looked kind of cool, she noted with surprise. Like some kind of young, hip hairdo.

Her face also looked young under the smudges of dirt and blood still on it. Mary picked up the folded washcloth on the counter and dampened it, then ran it over her face, cleaning away the smears of blood that Dante had missed. Then she let the cloth drop into the sink and simply stared at herself. Her cheekbones were high, her lips full, and her eyelids no longer looked like they were drooping with exhaustion. But her eyes themselves? They were a beautiful cornflower blue mixed with a silver that had never been there before.

"Oh my," she breathed.

"Mary?" Dante asked through the door with concern. "If you do not answer me I am coming in."

"What did you do?" she asked in almost a whisper. "Look what you did to me."

The door opened behind her and Mary shifted her gaze briefly from herself to Dante. He looked worried.

"I am sorry I had to turn you without asking permission," he said quietly. "But you were dying. I could not let you die."

"Ah," Mary breathed and shifted her gaze back to her own face again. He'd turned her. This was her peak condition. She must have been badly injured in the accident after they'd been forced off the road.

"The RV?" she asked, her gaze still sliding over her face.

"The council will replace it," Dante assured her.

"Ah," Mary said again. The RV had been totaled then. She wasn't surprised. She had a vague recollection of them rolling. RVs were not good at rolling. Meeting his gaze in the mirror, she asked, "And the kidnappers?"

He shook his head unhappily.

"I'm sorry," Mary said sincerely.

Dante's mouth tightened, but he merely said, "They will try again. Russell is sure they followed us here from the accident sight."

"Russell and Francis," Mary murmured slowly. He'd mentioned both names earlier as she recalled and she tilted her head and then asked, "Are they the men Lucian sent?"

"Yes." Dante nodded and then asked, "You are all right?"

Mary blinked in surprise at the question, and then recalled that he'd entered because she'd called out in shock when she'd first seen herself. Shifting her gaze back to her reflection in the mirror, she marveled over it again. It was incredible, and made her wonder how long she had been out. How long did a turn and this kind of transformation take? Before she could ask, a knock sounded at the door of the bedroom. Mary turned to peer at him in question.

"Wait here. It is probably room service," he said, turning away. "I was getting hungry and ordered food."

Mary watched him go, and then turned her gaze back to herself. It was probably horrible of her to admit it, but she was quite enthralled by the wonder before her. Dante had turned her. She was at her peak condition. *All of her*, she thought suddenly, and losing interest in her face, reached for the hem of the overlarge T-shirt she wore and jerked it up.

Mary pulled it all the way up to her neck, leaving only her throat and shoulders covered. She then stared at what she could see of her body in the mirror. High, full, firm breasts, a much smaller stomach than she was used to seeing, but still with a soft roundness, and the tops of curvaceous hips. Wishing she had a full-length mirror, Mary continued to hold up the shirt and turned to look over her shoulder to see what her peak-condition butt looked like. She had to get up on her tiptoes to be able to see it, but once she did . . .

Damnnnn, Mary thought with wonder, she had one fine ass. It was bigger than she'd expected. Apparently, a female body in peak condition was not a body that looked like a skinny boy's body minus the penis as all of today's models seemed to have. Who knew?

Shaking her head, Mary turned back around to look at her front again. This time she didn't just look though. Releasing one edge of the T-shirt, she slid that hand over her body, running it lightly over smooth, taut skin, amazed it didn't all disappear and turn into the body she'd become used to.

"Oh, *mio dolce Dio*."

Mary jerked her gaze upward at that comment and positively beamed at Dante's reflection when she saw that he'd returned, and that he was staring at her with a combination of shock and pure unadulterated lust. Apparently, he hadn't expected to return to find her feeling herself up, she thought with amusement and slowly let her T-shirt drop back down as she turned to face him. "*Dolce* means 'sweet' in Italian, yes?"

"*Si*," he breathed, staring at her chest as if he could see through the cloth.

"So you said, 'My sweet God'?"

"*Si*," Dante repeated and started forward. Mary immediately grabbed the door and swung it shut in his face. Just before the door closed, she saw shock claim his expression as he realized what she was doing.

"You said you were hungry. Go eat," Mary ordered as she locked the door. "I'm all greasy and want a shower."

"But Mary," he groaned. "*Sei cosi bella mia uccellino. Permettetemi per lavare la schiena.*"

Mary raised her eyebrows at the sudden spate of Italian. She didn't understand a word of it. She'd only understood the *dolce Dio* thing because she'd seen *La Dolce Vita* several times on the Classic Movie Channel and had been curious enough to look up what it meant. As for the *Dio* part, well, everyone knew *Dios mio* meant "oh my God," didn't they? Although she suspected that might be Spanish, but she'd always heard that the two languages were quite similar.

She started to turn away, but curiosity got the better of her and she asked, "What did that mean?"

" 'You are so beautiful, my little bird. Let me wash your back,' " he translated. "Please, Mary."

She hesitated briefly, but when she'd run her hand down her body, it had come away feeling slightly greasy. The only thing Mary could think was that during the turn the nanos had probably forced a lot of gunk out through her pores or something. That was a guess, however. She'd have to ask Dante about that later. In the meantime, she wanted to be clean, and knew without a doubt that if she let him into the room, cleaning would be the last thing to happen.

"Next time," she said softly, quite sure he'd hear, then turned and walked over to open the shower door and turn it on. She adjusted the knobs until the water temperature was to her liking and then closed the door again and whipped off the T-shirt she wore. Letting it drop to the floor, Mary grabbed one of the rolled up towels on the counter and slung it over the shower door. She then glanced over the selection of tiny bottles on the counter and selected the body wash, shampoo and conditioner, then carried them into the shower with her.

Mary was usually quick about her showers. "Get in, get it done, get out" had always been her motto for showering. Today was the exception. After years of not bothering to look at her body, today she inspected every inch of it, starting at the top. Much to her surprise, this peak condition came up short in a couple of areas. For instance, she hadn't suddenly sprouted lovely longer legs. Mary supposed she could live with that however, considering her derriere was now so awesome. Sadly, another thing was that, while she hadn't had to shave her legs much at all since going through menopause, she'd now sprouted five-o'clock shadow all over them. She looked like a damned porcupine, and wasn't that sexy?

The only bright side Mary could think of for that situation was that it was all just stubble and not two or three inches of extra hair growth like on her head. That would have been a horror to find for sure.

Once she'd finished cleaning and inspecting herself, Mary used the shampoo and conditioner, and then opened the shower door. Stepping out, she called out, "Dante can I use your razor?" as she grabbed the man's travel kit that had been set on the end of the counter. Something fell to the floor as Mary snatched up the kit and she glanced down to see that it was exactly what she needed, a razor.

"Everything I own is yours, *mio amore*," Dante assured her through the door as she set the travel kit back on the counter and bent to retrieve the razor. She was walking back to the shower when he added, "But I do not think Russell and Francis brought me a razor."

"They did," she sang out on a laugh as she stepped under the shower and pulled the stall door closed again.

"What was that?" Dante called.

"Never mind. You'll see," Mary responded as she picked up the body wash and began to lather some in her hands.

Mary had quite forgotten how time consuming and just plain annoying shaving your legs could be. But she simply wasn't going back out there to the bedroom in just the T-shirt, her legs bare and imitating Bigfoot, so she took her time, performing the chore in a leisurely manner to ensure she didn't cut herself all over the place. Going out there with bleeding legs or bits of toilet paper stuck to the cuts would not be attractive either, she was sure.

When she finally finished with her legs and under her arms, Mary stood under the water for a minute to rinse away the last of the body wash, then turned off the taps and grabbed the towel she'd slung over the door. She dried her hair and then her body, tossed the towel aside to reach for the T-shirt, then paused and grimaced. She didn't really want to put her nice, newly clean body back in the shirt she'd worn while so slimy. There must be some residue on it and just the idea of pulling it on made her grimace.

Sighing, Mary picked up her towel again and wrapped it around herself sarong style, then used Dante's brush to brush out her hair. He didn't have makeup, of course, but she didn't really need it. Her skin was flawless, her lips a healthy rose pink. She actually looked good without it, and Mary didn't think she'd ever thought that about herself. Even when she had been young the first time.

Shrugging, she smiled at her reflection, then turned and opened the bathroom door.

Dante was seated at a small table beside the bed, a half-eaten feast on the table before him. He got quickly to his feet when she entered, though.

"I didn't want to put the dirty T-shirt back on after showering, but I have no clothes," Mary announced as she entered the bedroom.

"They are hanging in the closet," Dante said. "Russell had the hotel launder them. You can put them on later. Sit now. Eat."

Mary glanced toward the closet, but then made a beeline for the table. Now that food was on offer, she was suddenly aware that she was *very* hungry. Pausing beside the table, she admitted, "I'm starving."

"I am not surprised," Dante said, his voice a little husky. "You have not eaten in four days."

"Really? All it took was four days for me to turn?" she asked with surprise. She would have expected longer for a transformation like this.

"You are still turning," he assured her solemnly. "You are just through the worst of it. The rest will complete over the next weeks or months."

"Oh," she murmured, turning her gaze back to the food.

"As for how long a turn takes, it varies. For some it is faster, for some longer. Your injuries probably contributed to the length as well."

"Right," she murmured, wondering what her injuries had been. From what he'd said, they'd been life threatening, but had it been head trauma, or had she been pinned? Crushed? Skewered by a piece of metal?

Maybe she didn't want to know, Mary decided, and admitted, "I don't remember much. I know they drove us off the highway, and then it was like the RV exploded."

"The RV did explode," he said, but quickly added, "after I got you out."

"Oh." She sighed her relief and grimaced. "I don't remember that. I just remember everything flying at me and—" She whirled and glanced around the room with alarm. "Where is Bailey?"

"She is fine," Dante said quickly, taking her arm and urging her into the chair across from the one he'd been seated in. "She broke a leg in the accident, but—"

"What?" Mary cried, jumping to her feet again.

"She is going to be okay," he assured her, placing a hand on her shoulder to push her back down onto her chair. "She is at the veterinary hospital."

"And they've kept her four days?" Mary asked with alarm, popping to her feet once more. Vets did not keep dogs that long unless it was terribly serious. Hell, she'd had dogs that were operated on and sent home the same day.

"Russell . . . convinced them to keep her for a few days because we thought it best she not be here while you were going through the turn," Dante explained soothingly.

Mary didn't need to ask to know he was talking about mind control when he said *convinced.*

Dante added, "It was for the best. We had enough on our plates looking after you and trying to keep anyone from calling the police to report a murder. We couldn't watch Bailey too."

"What murder? Why would anyone call the police?" she asked with a combination of alarm and confusion.

"Mary," he said solemnly. "The turn is very painful.

You have been screaming your head off for four days. We had to take turns, two of us holding you down to ensure your bindings did not snap and loose you to hurt yourself, and one of us out in the hallway controlling anyone within hearing distance."

"You tied me down?" she asked with amazement.

"We had to. You would have hurt yourself otherwise," Dante said apologetically.

"I would not," Mary assured him indignantly. "I'm not into cutting or any of the other self-abuse things."

"It is not a matter of being a self-abuser," he assured her. "It is a matter of the pain being so great that . . ." Dante paused as if searching for an example, and then sighed and said, "I heard once of a turn who stabbed himself in the eye trying to end the agony."

"Ewww," she said, sitting down abruptly.

"Si. Exactly." Dante nodded. "I wished to avoid your doing something like that."

"Thank you," Mary muttered, trying to imagine how bad pain had to be to make a person do something like that. She couldn't even imagine it though. It just seemed so alien. Shaking her head, she admitted, "I don't remember suffering any pain."

"That is a blessing then," Dante said and began to move the plates with food still on them closer to her.

Mary stared down at the food before her, and then glanced up and asked almost apologetically, "You said Russell is sure the kidnappers followed us back here?"

He nodded.

"So they drove us off the road and then just let this Russell and Francis collect us and bring us here?"

"Not exactly," he said dryly. "When the kidnappers forced us off the road, Russell and Francis were in the SUV directly in front of us. I do not think the men in the van even realized they were there. The RV probably blocked their view of them."

Mary nodded. She had noticed the SUV he was talking about. It had practically been riding the RV's front bumper. She had no doubt the kidnappers hadn't known they were there and had probably thought the road empty when they forced the RV off the road.

"Russell and Francis pulled over at once when we were forced off the road," Dante continued. "Apparently shots were exchanged and then the kidnappers must have decided not to risk themselves. The van pulled away and Russell and Francis gave chase, but we were only miles from town. Russell and Francis had to slow down once they reached the more populated area to avoid harming innocent mortals. The van, however, did not and they lost them. Russell and Francis then came back for us."

"I see," Mary murmured, accepting the fork he handed her. She managed to wait until he'd reclaimed his seat, then dug in. Literally. She was suddenly starving, her stomach churning with it, so she started with some sort of pasta dish that was quite nice, then halfway through it, picked up a chicken leg and began to alternately gnaw on that and scoop pasta into her mouth until she realized that Dante was watching her with amusement. Realizing what a disgusting picture she must make, she set down the fork as well as the chicken leg and reached for the glass of water he pushed toward her.

Mary took a sip of the cool water, then set it down and asked, "Is it the nanos that are making me this hungry? Am I always going to be wolfing down food? And if I am, how the hell are the nanos going to keep me at my peak condition?"

Dante chuckled and shook his head. "You will not always be this hungry. No doubt this is a result of a combination of the turn and not eating for four days. As for the nanos keeping you at your peak, they will. It is as simple as that. You can eat all day and night and they will keep you at your peak. They will also use a great deal of blood to do it, however, which means you would have to consume more of it."

"Oh." Mary had picked up her fork again, but now lowered it to the table and glanced down at her new hands worriedly. She hadn't considered that part of the deal. It was awesome and lovely to look and feel young and strong again, but he had turned her to do it. She would have to feed . . . on blood. Mary wasn't sure she could do that. She didn't even like rare steak. The blood turned her off.

"Eat Mary, you can worry about everything else later," Dante said gently.

She hesitated, but then gave in and picked up her fork again. Her stomach was still churning with hunger, and she hadn't eaten for four days. She reminded herself of that and then decided that starving herself would probably mean taking in extra blood too.

Once Mary started to eat again, Dante picked up his own fork to continue eating. They were both silent for a bit, and then Mary said, "Everything smells so . . .

much," she ended finally, because she couldn't think of another way to put it. The good smells still smelled good, but were stronger, and it was the same for bad smells. Mary had never cared for blue cheese, the smell had always bothered her, and there was a very small, thin slice of it on a steak on a plate in the center of the table, probably more as a garnish than anything, but it smelled to her like there was a pound of blue cheese under her nose.

It was just one of the scents assaulting her, though. Mary could smell everything as if it were concentrated and set directly under her nose . . . including Dante. He had a deep, almost smoky scent combined with a higher note that was slightly coppery. It was quite wonderful, and to her, smelled more delicious than any of the food on the table.

"I did tell you that the nanos improved skills and senses," Dante reminded her softly.

"You said they improved speed, strength, eyesight and hearing," she countered. "You did not mention smell."

"Ah." He shrugged. "I was born immortal, so have never experienced the difference myself. I can only tell you what I was told by others," he pointed out. "I suspect the truth is the nanos improve pretty much everything."

"Hmm," Mary murmured and turned back to her food. After a moment, however, she jerked her eyes to him again and said, "This means I won't need my glasses anymore, doesn't it?"

Dante's eyebrows rose. "You wore glasses?"

"Oh." She flushed, and dropped her gaze. "I only needed them for reading. I never needed them when I was younger. I had better than twenty-twenty vision then. It was only as I got older that I started having trouble with reading and such."

"I see. Well, you will not need glasses anymore," he said softly, and then grinned and added, "Although that might be a shame. I suspect you were sexy in glasses."

Mary laughed at his teasing, but merely shook her head and returned to eating. Between the two of them they finished off everything on the table, and still she was hungry.

Giving a little dissatisfied sigh, Mary set her fork back on her plate and leaned back in her seat, her gaze shifting to Dante. Now that all the food was gone, the smells in the room had been reduced a great deal. The primary smell filling her nose now was Dante, and he did smell delicious.

"Your eyes are glowing," Dante announced quietly after a moment.

"Are they?" Mary asked with disinterest. Then she smiled seductively and stood to walk around to where he sat. Pausing in front of him, she whispered, "I must be feeling passionate then."

Dante stood at once, but rather than take her in his arms as she'd hoped, he moved around her and walked toward the small fridge in the entertainment center, asking, "Are you thirsty? Would you like something to drink?"

Mary scowled at his back. No she didn't want a bloody drink. She wanted him to take her in his arms so that she could lay her head on his shoulder, bury her face in his neck and lick, nuzzle and nip her way along the vein pulsing there and—

"Dear God!" Mary gasped and turned away in horror.

Hearing Dante approaching from behind her, she turned, mouth opening to warn him to stay away. She never got the words out; the moment she turned to warn him, he slapped a bag of blood at her mouth. Mary blinked in surprise, automatically reaching for the bag, but he dumped the other two bags he'd brought with him onto the table and caught her hand with his now free one as he held the bag in place with the other.

"Relax," he instructed. "Your fangs will do all the work."

Mary tried to relax, but it was the oddest sensation. She could feel the cold liquid moving up her fangs. She couldn't feel it after that, but she could feel it in her fangs and she wasn't sure she liked it. In fact, she was quite sure she didn't. It was blood after all. She was consuming *blood*. She was a *vampire*. One of those horrid creatures that fed on mortals like a leech, filling its belly on blood from people like her friends, her children and grandchildren.

Mary's eyes widened with horror as it occurred to her to wonder how this would affect her life in more ways than just her looks. How was she to explain this to her children and grandchildren? How was she—?

"Mary," Dante moved closer.

She glanced to him and saw the concern on his face. It seemed pretty obvious that he could see her mounting distress. Sliding one arm around her, he pulled her close, and then tugged the blood bag from her teeth. She waited to be splashed with the red liquid, but wasn't. The bag was already empty, she saw with surprise as he tossed it to the table. Dante then caught her chin in his hand, turned her face back to his, and kissed her.

Mary hesitated, but quickly gave in and kissed him back. She didn't want to think about what she was now and everything it meant. She didn't want to consider the complications, and his kisses seemed a good escape from her thoughts.

The moment she opened her mouth to him, Dante caught her by the bottom and lifted her to sit on the table, pushing the dishes back with her behind as he did. Mary didn't protest, she merely wrapped her arms around him and then her legs and kissed him hungrily. She didn't realize her fangs were still out until she tasted blood in her mouth and realized she'd nicked him.

Moaning, Mary immediately found herself sucking on his tongue, drawing the warm, coppery liquid from the small wound and swallowing it eagerly. Some part of her mind immediately stepped back from her when she did that, horrified that she could enjoy the crimson liquid, and she feared Dante was doing the same when he suddenly broke their kiss, but then she found another bag popped to her fangs. She blinked at him over the bag, worried and grateful all at once, and Dante kissed her on the forehead. It was a sweet gentle kiss and made her feel better at once.

When she relaxed against him, Dante took her hand and placed it to the bottom of the bag. Mary automatically grasped it, and the moment she did, Dante grabbed the third bag and placed it in her free hand, then scooped her up off the table and carried her to the bed. Once there, he dropped to his knees, lowering her to sit on the end of the bed as he did. He then sat back on his heels in front of her.

Eyes wide, Mary tipped her head down and watched wide-eyed over the bag of blood as he took one of her feet in hand and lifted her leg so that it was extended. He paused, seeming to examine it, then ran his fingers lightly up the leg he held and murmured, "You have the loveliest most shapely legs. I noticed that when you came out of the bedroom in shorts the morning we breakfasted at the Round Up."

Mary's eyes widened even further. He'd liked her legs even then? When she'd looked her age? The thought startled her, but not as much as Dante did when he suddenly bowed his head and began to nibble his way up the inside of her calf.

Grunting in surprise, Mary dropped the third bag of blood she'd been holding and reached out to try to catch him by the hair and stop him, but he merely caught her hand in his and then continued to kiss his way up to her knee. He then set her foot back on the floor and it wasn't until he moved forward to kneel between her legs that she realized he'd set her foot down so that her legs were spread.

Before she had even fully processed that, Dante was tugging at her towel.

Mary immediately released the bag at her mouth and tried to grab at his hands. Fortunately, there was so little left in the bag at her mouth that it didn't fall away and splash everywhere. Unfortunately, Dante was quicker than her and by the time her hand reached his he'd pulled the sides of the towel apart, exposing her. Mary clutched his wrist anyway and squeezed her eyes closed as she felt a blush rise up over her face. She hadn't been bothered at all at his seeing her when he'd walked up behind her as she'd been examining herself in the bathroom mirror. But then, she hadn't been so exposed then, her legs spread to him. Then too, the body in the mirror hadn't really felt like hers yet in that moment. In truth, it still didn't, but she wasn't looking at a mirror, she was sitting with her legs wide open as Dante—

Her stomach gave a sharp jolt and Mary blinked her eyes open as he pressed a kiss to her stomach. It was such a sweet, tender action . . . and then his hands closed over her breasts and his mouth moved to claim one already erect nipple.

Mary nearly bit right through the dwindling blood bag then. Managing to restrain herself, she eased her grip on it and then moaned around the plastic as he suckled first one nipple, then the other. He was so enthusiastic in his attention that she was surprised when the moment the last drop of blood had been drawn from the bag at her mouth, he was aware of it and reached up to pluck it away and toss it to the floor. Dante immediately wrapped his hand around her neck and drew her forward for a kiss. Mary kissed him eagerly back, one hand covering his where he was still caressing her breast, and the other sliding around his shoulder to pull him closer against her.

Dante let her have her way and, releasing her breast, slid both arms around her, pressing her close and then shifting his chest across hers. Mary moaned and found her legs wrapping themselves around his hips as the soft cloth of his T-shirt brushed across her erect nipples. Hearing, sight, taste, and smell were only four of the senses. Touch was the fifth one, and Mary was quite sure the nanos had improved that too and made her more sensitive. Certainly she had never been set afire by such a light caress. A butterfly's wings probably would have been stronger than that brush of hair, but her body responded eagerly to the caress and her kiss became a little more desperate.

Dante responded by thrusting his tongue into her mouth and urging her back onto the bed until she lay flat with only her legs hanging off from the knees down. He kissed her thoroughly, once, then broke the kiss and slapped the last bag of blood to her fangs before rising up and backing off of her.

This time Mary groaned in disappointment at losing his kiss as well as his touch, but he was not done. She could feel his hips still between her knees, then he began to press kisses to her stomach, blazing a trail down to her hip and nibbling there briefly before moving between her legs.

Mary cried out against the new blood bag, her hips bucking as his mouth found her sweet spot. It was really quite amazing that she didn't split the bag with her hands right then, but she somehow managed to keep from crushing it, all while twisting her head on the bed, her body jumping and trying to move simultaneously away from his caress and into it at the same time. It didn't move anywhere, however. Dante was holding her down with his hands and arms as he worked and Mary was left to tremble helplessly under his ministrations until the bag at her mouth was finally empty and she could tear it away.

Throwing it to the side, Mary promptly sat up then and reached for Dante. The moment her hands touched his shoulders, he lifted his head, then rose up on his knees again. Now able to reach him, Mary immediately began tugging at his shirt, eager to get him as naked as her. Much to her relief, he helped, pulling the T-shirt off over his head the moment she got it free of his jeans. His hands then lowered to the snap of the black jeans he wore, but Mary already had that undone. He however, lowered the zipper and stood to push the heavy cloth down his legs. When he stepped out of them, kicked the jeans aside and turned back to face her, Mary simply stared. She'd seen him naked when they first met, of course, but not really, not fully, just glimpses and peeks before forcing herself to look away, and then she had been full of guilt for doing so. Now Mary took a good long look without that attendant guilt . . . and he was absolutely beautiful.

A small sigh slipping from her lips, she raised her gaze to his face, then shifted and stood up on the end of the bed to wrap her arms around him and kiss him. Dante's arms immediately closed around her in response and he quickly took over the kiss, his hand tangling in her hair and tilting her head to the angle he wanted as his tongue thrust between her lips.

Moaning, Mary accepted his offering, her tongue dueling briefly with his before he broke the kiss in favor of latching on to one of her nipples. While she was five four and shorter than him by a foot and four inches, standing on the bed had placed her breasts at his face level. He took advantage of that now, his hands closing around them and kneading as his mouth closed over first one nipple to tease it with his tongue before suckling, then shifting to the other to do the same.

Groaning, Mary leaned her lower body against him and closed her arms around his head. It was all she could do really; everything on him was out of range except for his head. She bore the attention as long as she could, but it wasn't long before she moaned his name and tugged at his hair.

Releasing her breasts, Dante lifted his head to her kiss again, and then caught her under her legs, urging her to wrap them around him. Once Mary did, Dante let her drop down a bit until her face was lower than his. Now he was the one having to bend his head to continue the kiss, rather than her. It also positioned her so that the core of her rubbed against the top of his penis, pressing it flat against his stomach between them as he shifted to kneel on the end of the bed. When he then moved forward across the bed on his knees, the movement drew a groan from Mary's throat as the friction sent shockwaves of pleasure through her. She was almost sorry when he stopped moving and dropped to sit on his heels with her straddling him.

Almost. Until Dante caught her by the waist and

raised and lowered her against him, pleasuring them both with the friction.

"Dante," Mary moaned, tearing her mouth from his. "I need—Ah!" she gasped as this time rather than just rub them against each other, he lifted her high enough for his erection to slide forward, then lowered her onto it.

Mary stared at Dante through wide, incredulous eyes as he filled her. She had been so wrapped up in the pleasure the caresses had given her, that until that moment Mary hadn't realized she was experiencing his pleasure too, but when he filled her . . . it was like nothing she'd ever experienced and she dug her nails into his shoulders, holding on for dear life as wave after wave of keen need drove through her.

"Dante," she gasped uncertainly, not sure she could handle this, and then he covered her mouth with his and rose up slightly, pressing forward. Mary felt the headboard of the bed at her back, and reached out to hold on to it with her hands in an effort to keep from scratching his back and shoulders to ribbons. Dante immediately raised one hand to the wall behind her to brace himself. His other hand, though, slid down between them to caress her as he began to pound into her.

Mary kissed him furiously as the pleasure grew inside her to unbearable levels. She felt like she would die from it, like her body would just shatter and explode, and then the pleasure inside her seemed to do just that and she broke their kiss to throw her head back on a scream that quickly died as she lost consciousness.

Thirteen

They were in a little heap when Mary woke up some time later. She was still straddling his legs, but was slumped back against the headboard, her arms draped over it and her head back and to the side in a most uncomfortable position. Lifting it with a grimace, she glanced to Dante and then smiled crookedly. He too had apparently lost consciousness as she recalled him saying they would. However, he'd fallen back on the bed, one arm splayed out, the other falling across his chest. His hair lay around his head on the bed like a dark nimbus, and his face . . . it was perfect in repose. He looked even younger than his normal appearance of about twenty-five without the usual worry that had shadowed his face since she'd encountered him.

Mary stared at him silently, slowly becoming aware that she was hungry again. This time she knew better than to assume that it was for food. Dante smelled just too delicious. She found her gaze focusing on the vein pulsing in his neck, sure she could hear the blood rushing through it, and felt saliva fill her mouth one second before she became aware of a sliding sensation in her mouth and felt something poke her bottom lip.

Her fangs had descended, Mary realized. She needed blood.

Unhooking her arms from where they hung over the headboard, Mary sat up cautiously, grimacing when Dante immediately stirred. He didn't open his eyes, but reached blindly for her. He caught her arm and tried to drag her down to lie on top of him, but Mary resisted, sure that if she got any closer to his throat she'd rip it out.

"Dante," she muttered, tugging at her arm to try to free herself.

"Mmmm?" he murmured sleepily, still pulling at her.

"You need to let me go. I think I need more blood," she said apologetically, almost ashamed of her apparently endless thirst for the red liquid.

Dante reacted as if she'd stuck a tack in his butt at that announcement and was suddenly moving. In a heartbeat he'd lifted her off of him and set her on the bed and then he was gone, crossing the room so quickly he was almost a blur. She watched him open the fridge in the entertainment cupboard, and then he was returning with several bags in hand. Dante handed her one, and set the others on the bedside table, then lay down beside her on his back.

Mary glanced from the bag of blood he'd given her

to his supine body and licked her lips as her gaze slid down along his length. His hands were under his head, his legs crossed at the ankles, and he was sprouting an erection as she looked at him, Mary noted with interest.

"Feed," Dante growled.

Mary hesitated, then tried to emulate his earlier actions and brought the bag quickly to her mouth, relieved when it popped smoothly onto her fangs.

"Good," he murmured and let his eyes close.

Mary watched him silently as she waited for the bag to empty, noting that now that his eyes were closed, his penis had stopped growing and was only semi-erect. She thought he'd actually dropped off to sleep again, but when the bag was empty and she pulled it from her mouth, he blinked his eyes open, took the empty bag and reached to the table to retrieve a fresh one for her.

"How many times a day am I going to have to do this?" she muttered with irritation as she took the bag from him.

"It is different for different people, but this constant need shouldn't last long,"

Dante said reassuringly. "I think it is because we did not have an IV to give you blood while you were turning and had to try to feed the bags to you orally while you were thrashing about. I suspect more landed on the bed than in your mouth," he admitted with a grimace and then added, "That might have contributed to the length of the turn too."

"We were in the room next door," Dante said when Mary glanced down at the mattress they were on. "This is Francis and Russell's room. We moved you here shortly before you woke up so that they could clean up our room and replace the mattress and such."

"Oh," she murmured.

"Now feed," he ordered gently.

The moment Mary slapped the bag to her mouth, he nodded and closed his eyes again. Mary stared at him briefly, noting that his erection was smaller still and then reached out to clasp him gently. She didn't really plan it or anything. In fact, her hand seemed almost to have a mind of its own as it closed around him.

Dante's eyes immediately popped open, air hissing through his teeth as his hips bucked in response to her touch, and Mary stilled, shocked to feel a shaft of pleasure shoot through her as well. Knowing this was the shared passion he'd spoken of, and fascinated by it, she tightened her grip and then slid her hand down his shaft and slowly back up. Her own eyes immediately closed, a moan slipping around the bag at her mouth and her hips shifting where she sat as her body responded. She might have been touching herself, she thought faintly as she continued to caress him. Only touching herself had never felt this good. This was—

Mary gasped and blinked her eyes open with surprise when Dante suddenly rose up, caught her by the waist and lifted her, setting her down on top of his erection as he dropped back to lie flat again. She stared at him over the bag of blood, her eyes uncertain. He'd set her down so that her body held his erection flat between them. She could no longer touch him as she'd been doing, but he could touch her and smiled slowly as his hands reached for her breasts and cupped, then caressed them as she fed.

Mary closed her eyes on a sigh as he played with her. Her caress had brought on sharp, hard pleasure, but this was a slower, milder pleasure. At least it was until Mary shifted her hips against him, her core rubbing across his erection. The hands at her breasts immediately tightened briefly and Dante muttered something in Italian that sounded beautiful, but could have been anything from an insult to a grocery list. He did tend to switch to Italian when excited, she thought as she shifted herself across him again.

"*Si*, Mary, ride me," he groaned, his hand dropping to grasp her hips to urge her forward and back along his length again, pressing her tighter to him as he did.

Mary moaned around the bag at her mouth, and did exactly that, helping to move herself over him. But the moment the bag at her mouth was empty, she tore it away and leaned forward to kiss him.

Dante cupped her head and kissed her back almost violently, then turned, rolling her beneath him on the bed. Mary slid her arms around him, and then reached down, trying to grab his butt, but he was already pulling back slightly. He was positioning himself, she realized as she felt him press against her opening, and then he was sliding home and she arched and groaned into his mouth as he filled her.

When Dante suddenly broke their kiss, she cried out in protest, then gasped in surprise when he caught her ankles and drew them up to rest against his shoulders on either side of his head. With nothing else within reach, Mary grabbed at his forearms and almost screamed as he slammed home again, this time seeming to thrust deeper and fill her more fully. She opened eyes she hadn't realized she'd closed and simply watched his face, her mind full of amazement as wave after wave of pleasure began rolling through her, seeming to expand with each surge, and then her eyes squeezed closed and she cried out as those waves all suddenly crashed against her brain at once, carrying her under as they did.

Mary woke to find herself wrapped in Dante's arms . . . and it felt perfect. In all the years she'd been married to Joe she'd never woken feeling so content or as if she belonged right where she was. Joe had been her husband for the better part of her life. For a while he'd also been her enemy, and then he'd been her partner and best friend, but Dante felt like . . . a part of her. And she was quite sure that she could have lain there forever. At least she could have if she didn't have to pee so badly.

Grimacing, Mary glanced toward the bathroom door and then at the hand dangling off her shoulder. After a hesitation, she slowly eased downward, trying to get out from beneath his arm without waking him. At first Dante's arm went with her, but then it dropped away and she quickly sat up, then slid from the bed and rushed to the bathroom door.

Mary spotted the toothbrush by the sink while she

was washing her hands afterward. The sight made her slip her tongue around the outside of her teeth and her eyebrows rose slightly when she didn't find them furry. She didn't even know when last she'd brushed her teeth. Her last morning as a mortal, she supposed. Which meant it had been . . . what? Dante said she'd been asleep for four days, but how long had they slept this time? She didn't know, but even four days was a long time to go without brushing. There should be some serious buildup on her teeth, but there didn't appear to be any. Did nanos take care of that too? Is that why she hadn't woken up with bad breath and a desire to brush and gargle? Man, if they did, that was pretty super cool. Mary had always hated the dentist.

Adding that to her growing list of things to ask Dante, she picked up the toothbrush, squirted some toothpaste on it and quickly brushed her teeth. She followed that by brushing her hair, then considered herself in the mirror.

She looked good. At least Mary thought she looked good. Her hair fell softly around her face with a natural wave that didn't need much fussing. She'd already recognized that she didn't need makeup. She wouldn't feel at all subconscious going out like this. Well, with clothes on, of course.

Making a face at her reflection, she turned and opened the door and stepped out into the bedroom.

Dante was still sleeping, his beautiful body splayed out on the bed, completely uncovered from the waist up, and one leg also free of the sheet that just draped across his hip and trailing down to cover one leg after tenting slightly over his groin, which didn't appear to be sleeping like he was. He was a feast for her eyes. And other parts of her body as well, she recognized, as a tingling started between her legs just from looking at him. Mary almost tossed aside her desire for food to crawl on top of the man and settle herself on that morning erection pushing at the sheet, but she was hungry again. Crazy hungry.

Turning from the sight of Dante's beautiful body, she walked to the closet and eased the door open. Mary immediately spotted the shorts and T-shirt she'd worn the day of the accident among the male clothes inside. Her gaze slid over what appeared to be a dozen pairs of jeans, and twice as many black T-shirts, followed by several more colorful T-shirts, and finally a black leather jacket. Her eyebrows rose. The man was apparently a clotheshorse, she thought, wishing she had more of a selection herself. However, she didn't.

Retrieving the two hangers holding her T-shirt and shorts, Mary turned away, and then paused and glanced around the room, wondering what Dante would have done with her bra and panties. Mary hung the clothes on the bathroom door, and then made a quick, quiet search of the drawers in the room, but there was nothing resembling panties and a bra anywhere. And then something made her look in the garbage bin. They were there, right on top.

Mary lifted out the two scraps of material, her breathing slowing as she noted their state. Both were ruined, and it wasn't just because they were so caked with dry blood as well as a more oily substance. It looked like they'd both been cut off of her. She let them drop back into the garbage bin, and rushed into the bathroom to wash her hands, not liking the oily feel to them.

Drying her hands quickly, Mary grabbed the hangers from the doorknob and then closed the door and quickly pulled on the clothes. The first thing she noticed was that they were both now quite large on her. The shorts were at least four or five sizes too big. Although she automatically unsnapped and unzipped them to put them on, she didn't have to. Mary figured that out when she did them up and then reached for the hanger holding the T-shirt and her shorts dropped to pool around her feet on the floor.

Muttering under her breath, she left the shorts where they were for the moment and pulled on the T-shirt. While it had been almost clingy before her turn, it was now quite blousy on her. Shrugging, Mary pulled the shorts back up and tucked the shirt in, hoping the extra bulk would help keep them up. It wasn't enough, however.

Holding them up herself, Mary went back out to the bedroom and considered her options. She already knew there was nothing in the closet to use as a belt. That left the room at large. The only thing in there that she might have used was the drawstring from the curtains. She even actually considered that, but it was vandalism, or theft or something, so she let that idea go.

Mary glanced toward the closet, considering using one of Dante's T-shirts, but then her gaze dropped to her own T-shirt instead. It was longer than she needed, if she cut the bottom couple of inches off . . .

Raising her head, she glanced around until her gaze settled on Dante's jeans lying in a puddle on the floor by the bed. A lot of men carried pocketknives. Did he? A quick search of his pockets proved that no he didn't, or at least he didn't have one in them now.

Grimacing, Mary straightened and scowled as she looked around the room, and then recalled the razor in the bathroom.

It would do, she decided and slipped back into bathroom again. Mary ended up having to break the razor blade casing to get the actual blades out, but decided she would explain to Dante and replace it first thing. Even before she found food. There must be a drugstore somewhere nearby. Or maybe they'd have razor blades in the hotel store. They often carried necessities like that in those places, she thought as she took off the T-shirt and began to slice the bottom couple of inches off of it.

Mary's next thought was that she hadn't seen her purse anywhere in the room when she'd been searching for things. Which probably meant it had gone up in flames with the RV. Good God, she had no money! She was completely dependent on Dante!

Just like he'd been dependent on her at first, she realized. Only she at least had clothes, even if they were too big and had several slits and tears from the accident.

Sighing, Mary finished slicing off the material she needed, then pulled the T-shirt back on and tucked the bottom of it into her waist again. She then strung the strip of T-shirt she'd cut off through the belt loops of her baby blue shorts and tied it up in front. It wasn't pretty, she decided as she checked out her handiwork in the mirror, but it would have to do for now.

Shrugging, Mary turned and slid back into the bedroom, then simply stood there, unsure what to do next. If her purse had been there she would have simply slipped out, found a store or restaurant and bought herself something to eat. However, her purse wasn't there.

It was an odd feeling being without it. Mary had been carrying a purse since she was a teenager. She'd never thought about it much, but now realized that the leather bag was freedom of a sort. So long as she'd had her purse, she'd had pretty much anything she might need in an emergency; money, credit cards, keys, usually a couple of bandages, a lipstick, a tiny deodorant stick, perfume, often allergy pills and aspirin, a little packet of Kleenex, sunglasses, reading glasses, her phone, Handi Wipes, safety pins, a tiny emergency sewing kit, and a brush and compact.

Mary could have used several of those items right then, like the deodorant and perfume. Certainly the sewing kit and safety pins might have saved Dante's razor. If she hadn't been able to just pin the shorts so that the waistline was smaller and stayed up without a belt, the sewing kit had tiny scissors in it she could have used to cut her T-shirt.

Man, she'd never really considered how much she depended on her purse. Until now, when she didn't have it, Mary thought grimly and then simply went over and sat on one of the chairs at the table. Her gaze slid to Dante, but he was sleeping soundly and she didn't want to wake him. She glanced to his jeans, but while she might have used a pocketknife while he was sleeping and then returned it to his pocket, she was not taking his money. Even though she would have returned it the first chance she got, taking it without permission just seemed wrong to her.

Sighing, Mary raised her hands and peered at them silently, then spread them to the side so she could see her legs. It was a new and pretty body, and exactly what she'd often fantasized about having, but really, it didn't feel comfortable to her yet. She was used to having more bulk and taking up more space; now she felt kind of scrawny.

The thought made her smile faintly. Mary had always bemoaned her figure for being too voluptuous and wished she was smaller. Now that she was, however, she felt like a foreigner in her own body . . . and wasn't at all sure she liked it. Perhaps that's why her diets had always failed and she'd never seemed to be able to get down to that more desirable weight the world seemed to insist on. Maybe she'd actually felt more comfortable being larger.

The hotel room door opened suddenly and Mary stiffened and glanced to it with alarm. Her alarm did not ease when she saw two men entering, one fair haired, and one with dark hair, but both tall and strong-looking. Standing, she started to move toward the bed to wake Dante, but was caught by the arm just as she bent to shake his shoulder.

"Let him sleep. He has been without it for days while watching over you."

Mary turned slowly and stared at the fair-haired man

who had somehow crossed the room so quickly. Her gaze then zeroed in on his eyes, noting the golden color and sheen to them and she asked uncertainly, "Are you—?"

"Friend not foe," he assured her with a smile that made the skin at the corner of his eyes crinkle. Releasing her arm, he offered her his hand, and introduced himself. "Russell Renart Argeneau Jones."

"Argeneau," she murmured, accepting his hand and shaking it. "Like that Lucian fellow."

"He is my great uncle," Russell confirmed. "My grandfather, Ennius Argeneau, was one of his younger brothers."

"Oh," she said simply. Mary could hardly tell the man that she didn't like his great uncle.

"Do not worry. Most people do not like Lucian," Russell said with amusement as if she'd spoken aloud.

Mary's eyes widened and then she glanced to the man with dark hair as he appeared beside them. His eyes were a deep brown with shiny flecks of metallic bronze in them. Both men were obviously immortals then, she reassured herself as he said dryly, "Lucian is an antiquated ass who has no idea how to be civil." He wrinkled his nose, and then added almost reluctantly, "Sadly, he is also one of the best people you could ever have on your side."

"Why?" Mary asked dubiously.

"Because he is frightfully strong," the man said solemnly. "In character as well as physical strength. He always judges fairly, always does what needs doing, and, if he approves of you or your cause, he will fight to the death for you."

"Oh," she breathed and had to admit that sounded pretty admirable, which was a shame; it made it harder to dislike him, and Mary really hadn't liked him by the time she'd finished the one and only conversation she'd had with him. She did not enjoy being threatened, by anyone.

"This is Francis," Russell introduced quietly.

"Francis Renart Argeneau Jones," Francis said, extending his hand now as well.

Mary raised her eyebrows over the shared last names, and as she shook the offered hand, asked, "Are you brothers or something then?"

Russell exchanged a glance with Francis and they both smiled faintly, before the fair-haired man took her arm to urge her away from the bed.

"Or something," Russell murmured, as he led her to the chairs by the table. There were only two chairs. He urged Mary into one, held the other for Francis to sit down, and then bent to press a kiss to his neck before moving to lean against the window ledge next to the table.

Mary glanced from one man to the other as they shared an affectionate smile and breathed, "Ohhhhh," with sudden understanding.

Francis chuckled at her wide-eyed look. "You are not scandalized."

It wasn't a question.

"And you are not disgusted," Russell said with equal certainty.

Mary blinked at the comment. "Of course not. Why would I be disgusted?"

Russell shrugged mildly. "Some people are."

Mary clucked with irritation. "Some people need to keep their minds out of your pants then."

Both men blinked briefly, then burst into laughter that they both quickly quelled when Dante murmured sleepily and turned on his side in bed.

They were silent for a moment, each of them practically holding their breath as they peered at Dante, but when he didn't stir again, they relaxed and glanced at each other.

"I like that," Francis said quietly, and then echoed her words slowly as if savoring them. "Some people need to keep their minds out of your pants then."

"Well, they do," she said quietly. "Love is love and shouldn't upset anyone. So what else are they thinking about when they get upset at your partner preferences?" she asked reasonably, and then answered the question herself. "Their minds are in your pants and on what you do. And while they're welcome to bury their brain in their own pants, they have no business in yours."

Francis glanced to Russell and grinned. "I like her."

"Me too," Russell said with a smile.

Mary blushed and turned to glance at Dante for a minute, but then turned back and asked, "You said Dante hasn't slept for a while?"

"This is the first time he has slept since the accident," Russell said solemnly. "He watched over you throughout your turn. We helped of course, but we did take breaks, and we offered to spot him so that he could rest as well, but he refused to leave your side even for a twenty-minute nap."

Mary turned to peer at Dante again at this news, her eyes traveling slowly over his sweet face in repose. The man must have been exhausted when he'd finally collapsed that first time they had sex, and yet he'd not made a single complaint when she'd woken him up for another go round . . . or for the third one, or the fourth. Mary felt bad about her greediness now. She almost felt like she should apologize to him : . . except she'd have to wake him up to do so.

"There is no need to apologize," Russell assured her solemnly. "He will be fine."

Mary turned slowly back to stare at the fair-haired man as another realization struck her. "You're reading my mind."

"I am afraid so," he acknowledged. "I apologize, but it is hard not to."

"Why? Because you're so used to reading everyone?" she asked, curious.

"Not quite, although that is a factor too," Russell allowed.

It was Francis who explained, "Mary, honey, as a new turn and a new life mate, it is difficult *not* to hear your thoughts. It would be like trying not to hear what someone was shouting in your ear."

She tilted her head and eyed him uncertainly. "You're suggesting I'm somehow shouting my thoughts at you?"

"Basically," Francis said with a shrug, and then leaned forward to pat her hand. "Do not worry. It is common among new turns as well as new life mates, and you are presently both."

"Right," she breathed, sitting back in her seat as

questions immediately began whirling through her head.

"You wish to know more about this life mate business," Francis said with a smile.

Mary shrugged. "Wouldn't you?"

"I did," he admitted with a grin. "I wanted to know absolutely everything when I found out I was Russell's life mate. And I imagine you do too."

"Yes, definitely," Mary admitted sitting forward again and resting her arms on the table as she peered curiously from Francis to Russell. "So you weren't both born immortal?"

"No. Russell was and turned me," Francis said, sharing another smile with the man. Turning back, he added, "I was not even gay when we met."

Mary blinked in surprise at this and he burst out laughing at her expression.

"Sorry, I am just teasing," he said, patting her hand again. "I was 'in the closet,' as they say now, but definitely preferred men to women. It was Russell who had no idea of his sexual preference."

Her gaze shifted to Russell then to see that he was watching Francis with amused affection. She glanced back to Francis and narrowed her eyes. "You're teasing me again, right?"

"Not this time," he said with wry amusement, and then assured her. "He really had no clue. Russell was just wandering through the centuries with a bad haircut and worse fashion sense, waiting for his dream girl to pop up." He smiled and added, "But what *popped up* was no girl."

"Behave, Francis," Russell said with wry amusement, and then glanced to Mary and said, "I was old enough by the time we met that I had not bothered with relationships, sex or food for a millennia. And then this annoying fellow," he said the words affectionately and smiled at Francis to take away any sting before continuing, "appeared in my life and just would not go away. Worse yet, I could not take control of him and make him leave me alone. And then of course, I found I was suddenly eating again and . . . well, other interests were reawakened and . . ." He shrugged.

"I don't understand," Mary said slowly. "You weren't eating or . . ."

"Apparently," Francis said, taking over again. "When immortals are old and alone for centuries, they become sad old men who lose interest in everything." Taking on a horrified expression, he added, "Including food and sex. Can you imagine?"

Mary's eyes widened and she glanced to Russell for verification.

He nodded solemnly. "It is quite common."

"But Dante was eating and—"

"Oh, he is not old," Francis said dismissively. "He and Tomasso are just baby immortals. Heck, I am two hundred and I am a baby by immortal standards."

"Oh," Mary said slowly. "So Dante was still interested in—"

"Yes, he and Tomasso were both still scarfing down everything and anything, and banging every female from—" He paused abruptly when Russell stuck a foot out to nudge him. Grimacing, he said instead, "He was still active on the dating scene."

"Ah," Mary said with amusement. She wasn't surprised that Dante had been "active on the dating scene." Between his looks and his size, she was sure women would have been throwing themselves at him left, right, and center.

"But don't worry, Mary," Francis said now, patting her hand. "Now that he's found you, he will want only you."

She tilted her head curiously. "Why?"

"Why?" Francis asked blankly. "Because you are his life mate, honey." Frowning, he asked, "Did he not explain about life mates to you?"

"He said something about a life mate being the one person an immortal couldn't read or control and that they could live happily with or something," she said slowly, trying to recall his exact words.

"Oh, dear," Francis muttered and rolled his eyes. "He is a good-looking brute, but not big on talking, that one."

Mary raised her eyebrows in surprise at that claim. It seemed to her that Dante had talked a lot since she'd met him. Or had she done all the talking? She worried suddenly.

"All right, I shall have to fill you in," Francis said determinedly, then scooted his seat closer, took her hand, looked her in the eyes and announced, "Mary, sweetheart, you are like the holy grail to Dante."

She raised her eyebrows, but didn't speak her doubts aloud and he continued.

"Now that he has you, Dante will never ever be the least interested in another woman, mortal or immortal."

"Why?" she asked at once.

Francis's eyes narrowed on her forehead, and then he clucked impatiently. "You *know* why. You have experienced the shared pleasure with him. That alone is enough to ensure he remains always faithful. Sex with anyone else simply could not compare. It would be like choosing Alpo for dinner over a gourmet meal."

"Aside from that though," he added, "If the nanos put you together, you were meant for each other." When Mary looked dubious, he said, "I know, I know . . . you have not known each other long, but trust me, you will suit each other beautifully. The nanos are never wrong. Dante is your happy ever after."

Mary merely nodded, unsure how she felt about what Francis said. On the one hand, she'd like to believe in happy ever after, but had learned through her own marriage and the people she'd counseled over the years since getting her doctorate, that happy ever after really didn't exist . . . at least, not without work. Mary had been happy the last two thirds of her marriage, but it had been after years of misery and it had taken a choice and a lot of hard work. Even then it hadn't been perfect. No one was perfect.

Francis patted her hand and said, "You shall see."

Mary was saved from having to answer by the sudden ringing of a phone. Turning toward the sound, she watched Russell take a cell phone out of his pocket. He looked at the caller ID on the face, and then tapped it and pressed it to his ear.

"Lucian," he said cordially, straightening from the window ledge and moving to the door.

Mary grimaced at the name.

"He'll want to know if you are awake yet and that the turn went well," Francis said quietly as Russell slipped out of the room.

Mary nodded and then movement caught her attention, and she glanced to the bed to see that Dante was sitting up. The phone must have woken him, she realized, and smiled as she watched him wipe sleep from his eyes.

"Sleeping Beauty is awake," Francis sang out. Getting up and smiling at Mary, he said, "I shall go wait outside with Russell while the Hulk here dresses and then we will take you for breakfast. I know you are starved." His gaze slid over her as she stood up and he added, "Then we will take you shopping."

"Shopping?" she asked, reluctantly tearing her gaze from Dante's naked chest to peer at him uncertainly.

"We need to buy you clothes," he decided and then pointed out apologetically, "Darling, you are dressed like an old woman."

"I *am* an old woman," she said with amusement.

"Yes, but you look like Barbie. We should dress you accordingly." He grinned suddenly. "It will be such fun."

Mary smiled faintly, thinking it might very well have been fun. Unfortunately, she didn't have her purse, and therefore didn't have money until she found a bank. Actually, she realized with sudden concern, even then she'd have a problem, since she had no way to prove who she was so that she could gain access to her accounts. She had no ID. Not that that would help since she no longer looked like the sixty-two-year-old woman she was.

"Stop fretting," Francis said lightly, heading for the door. "The council will take care of everything."

"The council?" Mary murmured with confusion, but Francis had already slipped out the door and was closing it behind him.

"The council is basically our governmental body," Dante explained, his deep rumble sounding directly behind her.

Mary turned sharply and he immediately drew her into his arms.

"Good morning," he growled just before his lips covered hers.

Mary sighed into his mouth and slid her arms around him as they kissed. But when he began to back toward the bed, pulling her with him, she broke the kiss and dug her heels in to stop him. "Francis and Russell are outside."

"Good. They can stay there," Dante muttered, his mouth moving to nuzzle her neck.

"They're taking us to breakfast," she breathed, tilting her head to give him better access despite her hunger.

Dante paused, then sighed and slowly straightened. "Food."

Mary chuckled at his expression. It looked to her like he was weighing his different hungers in his mind. Food or her? She helped him out by saying, "I'm hungry."

"So am I," he admitted, and then muddied the water

by grinding against her so that she could feel the morning erection he was sporting.

Mary moaned, and then pushed herself away from him. "Food first."

"You are a hard woman, Mary Winslow," he complained, turning to move back to the bed to grab up his jeans.

"I'm not the one who's hard," she said on a laugh and headed for the door.

"Sassy wench," he said with affection as she slipped from the room.

Fourteen

"**D**id you have any trouble replacing the mattress?"

Mary glanced up from the bacon and eggs on her plate at that question from Dante and followed his gaze to Russell as the man shook his head. They were in a mom and pop restaurant up the road from the hotel. The décor wasn't much to look at, but Francis had assured her the food was extremely good when she'd joined him and Russell in the hall back at the hotel. He'd then led her to the room next door to the one she'd woken in, and made her feed on three bags of blood in a row while they waited for Dante to dress.

Mary hadn't thought she'd been feeling that kind of hunger at the time, but Francis had insisted it was better to be safe than sorry, especially since they were going out among mortals, and the moment he'd handed her one of the bags, her canines had dropped down into fangs. So Mary had gone through the three bags he'd handed her and even asked for a fourth when those were gone. As he'd said, better safe than sorry. The last thing Mary wanted was to find herself attacking some poor waitress or store clerk on her first outing as an immortal.

"The store manager was very accommodating," Russell said now, drawing her attention back to the conversation. "She arranged to have the new mattress delivered right away and even had her deliverymen take away the old one."

"Yes, and we did not even have to use mind control to get her to do that," Francis said, then added with amusement, "After Russell gave her one of his sexy smiles, she was smitten. I think she would have dragged the mattress out herself to please him if she had not been able to get ahold of her moving men."

Russell just shook his head and said, "We did have to use a little mind control with the movers. They were a bit alarmed when they saw the blood on the hotel mattress."

Dante grunted and nodded as he took a bite of his toast, apparently not surprised. Once he'd chewed and swallowed, he said, "Thank you for handling it."

"It was no problem," Russell assured him, and then cast Francis a teasing look and said, "Francis likes to shop."

"Shopping for mattresses is not my idea of the fun kind of shopping," Francis said with a sniff, then smiled at Mary and added, "Now clothes shopping for *you*, though? That *will* be fun."

"Clothes shopping?" Dante asked slowly.

Mary smiled with amusement at his expression. He looked as pleased at the prospect as she would at the idea of visiting the dentist.

"Yes, clothes shopping," Francis said with exasperation. "Just look at her, Dante. Mary *needs* clothes."

Dante didn't look convinced. Mary wasn't surprised. Joe had always hated going clothes shopping too. Taking pity on him, Mary said, "Dante doesn't have to come with us. He could head back to the hotel and get some more sleep while we shop."

"No," Dante said at once. "I will come with you."

"Are you sure?" she asked, thinking it would probably actually be nicer for her if he wasn't there, looking miserable and bored.

But Dante nodded firmly. "I will accompany you."

"Mary, honey," Francis said with amusement. "Now that he has found you, Dante probably will not let you out of his sight for . . . oh . . . a good century or so. We will just have to deal with it. Although," he added, turning to Dante. "Your coming with us means I will finally get the chance to tweak your wardrobe a bit."

"Tweak my wardrobe?" Dante asked, stiffening, and then he shook his head. "My wardrobe is fine."

"Everything you own is black," Francis said at once with a shudder that showed his opinion of that. "We need to change you up from faux funeral to fashion fabulous."

Dante scowled at the suggestion. "No. If I let you dress me, I would end up looking like one of the Village People."

Mary blinked at the comment, surprised at the reference to a band that had been around in the seventies. It reminded her that while he looked too young to know the band, he wasn't.

"You wound me," Francis said with irritation. "I have better taste than that."

"You are wearing pink," Dante pointed out and Mary had to bite her lip to keep from laughing at the comment. It wasn't that long ago Dante had been wearing her pink joggers and flowered T-shirt.

"That comment just shows how much of a Neanderthal you are," Francis assured Dante. "This is salmon and—" Pausing abruptly, he turned to stare at Mary wide-eyed. "Really? Pink joggers and a flowered—Oh, my, those did not fit him well at all, did they?"

Mary's eyes widened incredulously, and she found herself covering her forehead with her hands as she realized he was plucking the memory and image right out of her mind.

"That will not help," Francis informed her, and then added apologetically, "But I shall endeavor not to see and hear the things you are projecting."

Mary lowered her hands slowly, her eyes narrowing. "The *things* I am projecting?" she asked. "Plural?"

He nodded, his expression almost pitying, and Mary's eyes widened.

"What kinds of things?" she asked with alarm.

"Oh, you know," he muttered, suddenly seeming fascinated with the food on his plate. Picking up the end of a piece of bacon, he turned it back and forth on the plate from one side to the other. "Things you have seen . . . and done . . . and stuff."

When Mary then glanced to Dante, he grimaced and gave a slight, almost apologetic nod.

"You are not the only one. Dante is projecting too," Francis said reassuringly as if that should make her feel better. "Like we said, it is a new-life-mate and new-turn thing. It will pass eventually."

Mary stared at him with dismay. If she was running around projecting images of her memories, things she'd seen, and the *stuff* she'd done . . . Good Lord! She couldn't even look at Dante without thinking of him naked or all the things he'd done to her and they'd done together. That meant that, basically, her mind must be projecting what amounted to homemade porn.

"Pretty much," Francis agreed as if she'd spoken her thoughts aloud. "But as I said, it will pass eventually."

"How long is eventually?" Mary asked at once.

Francis shrugged helplessly. "It varies with each couple. And how it ends does too. For some it stops abruptly, and for others it just slowly fades over time, like a radio being slowly turned down."

"How long though?" Mary insisted.

Francis glanced to Russell. "How long would you say it was for us?"

Russell shrugged. "A year and a half, maybe closer to two."

"Years?" Mary breathed with dismay.

"I have heard of couples that were only projecting for one year though," Francis reassured her. Biting his lip, he then added, "Of course, I have also heard of couples that projected for as much as four years or more too."

"Years?" she repeated with horror.

Francis nodded, his expression sympathetic. "I suspect that is part of the reason new life mates tend to spend the first year or so mostly at home."

"That and the fact they cannot drag themselves out of bed long enough to actually do much else," Russell said with amusement.

"That too," Francis agreed.

Mary stared at them blankly for a minute, and then stood up abruptly, muttering, "I need to visit the ladies' room."

She didn't wait for anyone to comment, but moved quickly through the tables to get to the hall with the sign reading WASHROOMS. It was a long hall and while she expected the bathrooms to be at the front, they weren't. She passed a door with a sign that read EMPLOYEES ONLY, and then another that had a small window in it that looked into the restaurant's large kitchen. Then there was a long stretch of wall before she reached a door with a male symbol on it. The women's bathroom was the next door, the last one before the hallway ended at an emergency exit.

Sighing, she pushed her way inside the ladies' room.

The tiled room had three stalls, all presently empty, she noted with relief. It also had a counter with two sinks in it and a mirror over the sinks. Mary immediately moved to the sink and turned the cold tap on, then automatically glanced up and blinked in surprise at the young woman peering out of the mirror at her. She stared at her reflection for a moment, and then shook her head. Her reflection did the same and Mary lowered her head, wondering how long it would take for her to get used to this new her.

Probably about as long as she would be projecting her thoughts to everyone, Mary thought grimly, and cupped her hands to catch some of the cold water splashing out of the tap. She then splashed it on her face.

It was a bit alarming to think that every little thought she had was being broadcast to any and every immortal around her. But it was positively humiliating to think that every time she glanced at Dante and thought about . . . well, anything, someone would be picking up on it.

Sighing, Mary turned off the tap and straightened to look at herself again, ignoring the water that slid from her face to run down her neck in rivulets before it was absorbed into the collar of her T-shirt.

"You can do this," she told herself solemnly. "You may look like Barbie, as Francis put it, but you are a beautiful, intelligent and mature woman. We are all grown-ups. They've been through this themselves and obviously been around others who went through this. Stop acting like a shrinking virgin and deal . . . and maybe try not to think so much about Dante naked," Mary tacked on with a grimace, and then added, "And sex with Dante."

Yeah, that would work, she thought dryly, and turned the tap back on. Just saying the words had brought a tsunami of memories and images to her mind. Every one of them X rated. Mary splashed her face twice this time, then stayed bent over the sink and reached out to grab paper towels from the paper towel dispenser. Her top was already a mess with a hole in the side and a couple stains that laundering hadn't removed. She didn't need to add to its disheveled state, so she quickly dried her face before straightening this time.

"Think of something else," Mary instructed herself firmly. "That article, the 'Profile of Cognitive Aging,' that you read last week, was interesting. Think of that."

Mary paused for a minute and focused on the article she'd read in one of the medical journals she still got. Once she was satisfied that her thoughts were purely boring and safe and miles away from anything to do with sex or Dante, she nodded to her reflection and turned to leave the bathroom.

There was a man in the hall when she stepped into it. He was leaning against the wall outside the men's room. She automatically offered a polite smile as moved toward him, but then paused as he raised his hand and she heard a sharp hiss-thump sound and felt something punch her in the chest. Glancing down with confusion, she stared at the red tipped dart protruding from her shirt just above her breast. Instinct made her reach for it, but before her hand could connect, she noticed that the floor was leaping up to meet her.

Mary had barely left the table when Francis pulled a notepad out of his pocket and began writing down items.

Dante immediately leaned toward him and began to

read the list aloud, "Toothbrush, men's and women's razors, panties?" Pausing, he straightened and asked, "What are you doing?"

"What does it look like I am doing?" Francis asked dryly. "I am making a shopping list."

"Oh," Dante murmured, and asked, "For Mary and me?"

"For Mary and *I*," he corrected. "You said you did not want help shopping."

"Why do you have a man's razor on there then?" Dante asked. "I saw your shaving kit in the bathroom."

"Mary thought it was yours and used the razor," he explained. "And then she broke it to slice up her T-shirt. She also used my toothbrush thinking it was yours."

"Oh. Sorry," he muttered.

Francis shrugged. "It is fine. I am not afraid of getting cooties or anything. I just thought it would be nice to get her a toothbrush of her own, as well as her own razors and such." He paused briefly and then began to write again, muttering, "A hairbrush too."

"Dante," Russell said, drawing his attention away from the dark-haired man busily scrawling on his notepad. Once he had Dante's attention, he suggested, "Now that the worry of Mary's turn is out of the way, perhaps we should discuss ways we can set up another trap for the kidnappers."

Dante nodded slowly, and then frowned and added, "If they are still around and have not given up."

"They are still around," Russell assured him.

Dante stiffened at this news and glanced worriedly toward the hall Mary had disappeared down.

"Relax. I kept an eye out for them when we left the hotel for here, and there was no sign of them. However, there was a dark van following Francis and me when we went to the furniture store and back. They left when the delivery truck pulled up, but I suspect they will pop up again, and we have to decide how to deal with them."

"Yes," Dante agreed, but glanced toward the hall to the bathrooms again and muttered, "Mary is taking a long time."

Francis glanced up from his list at that comment and said, "Relax. I am sure she is fine. She was just embarrassed and wanted some time alone to compose herself."

"Hmm." Dante scowled at him. "That is your fault. You are the one who told her about that projecting business."

"What? I should have left her ignorant?" Francis asked dryly. "Knowledge is power, my friend. She needed to know."

"Yes, but—" Dante paused and sat back in his seat as their waitress rushed to the table.

"Um . . . hi," she greeted them, her expression flustered, almost panicked. "Er . . . I was out having a cigarette and I think—I mean I saw— That lady who came in with you guys? I think she's in trouble. Some guy just carried her out the back door of the restaurant and put her in a van. She was unconscious."

Dante was out of his seat and rushing for the door before she'd finished speaking.

Mary woke to the hum of an engine and rumble of voices and for a minute, didn't have a clue where she was. She also couldn't open her eyes at first, or even move, she realized, and felt panic well up within her as she tried to sort out what was happening.

"Dr. Dressler is going to be mighty pleased with this shipment," a man said, his voice filled with what sounded like glee. "Five vampires, two of them twins, and one a new turn. He'll give us a huge bonus for this."

"Don't count your chickens before they hatch, Ernie," another voice cautioned. "Right now we only have the woman and the one twin. We haven't captured the rest of them yet."

"We will," Ernie said with certainty. "That waitress told the fangers like you paid her to, and they're following us. Once we stop at the warehouse, they'll rush the van to save the girl and Danny and Jackson'll take 'em out with the darts. Easy peasy."

Mary frowned at this news, and actually felt her mouth move. Whatever they'd shot her with must be wearing off, she thought, and opened her eyes, happy when she was able to. She opened them all the way, and then closed them to slits in an effort not to give away that she was stirring. Mary then glanced around to see that she was lying on the floor in the back of a van. She had been placed along the wall behind the driver's seat with her head toward the front of the van and her feet toward the back.

Mary tried to tilt her head back to look at the men who were speaking, but her head didn't move. She didn't think it would be long before it would; her fingers already had movement again, as did her hands, although she couldn't move them far. She seemed to be tied up or something. She could move her feet too though, and they were bound. Still, the rest of her felt like she'd been given some kind of numbing agent. Whatever the darts held was definitely wearing off quickly.

"How much do you think our bonus will be for this one?" Ernie asked, his voice excited.

"I don't know," the driver muttered. "All I'm thinking about is making sure those fangers don't catch up with us before we get to the warehouse."

"They're still two car lengths back," Ernie said, his voice growing a little louder and Mary stilled, her eyes closing. She was quite sure the man had turned to glance back toward her as he spoke so stayed as still as she could, practically holding her breath.

"We still have six blocks to the warehouse," the driver said grimly.

"Yeah, but they won't try anything on a busy street," Ernie said, his voice returning to the quieter level, suggesting he'd turned away again.

Relaxing a little, Mary carefully opened her eyes and glanced toward the front of the van. This time she was able to tilt her head. Her gaze slid over the driver and passenger, Ernie. All she could see was the backs of their heads over the seats. Both had dark hair.

Lowering her head again, Mary started feeling around with her fingers, trying to sort out what she'd been tied up with. A quick inspection of whatever was around her wrists told her she hadn't been tied. Instead, something that felt very like shackles to her were around each wrist. The shackles both had chains flowing away from them. Following the chains with her fingers, she found that it was actually one chain connecting both shackles. But that it was threaded through some sort of metal circle attached to the sidewall of the van, she noted, wincing as the chain made a clanking sound behind her.

Mary stilled, her eyes instinctively closing in case the sound made one of the men glance back, but their conversation continued, unhindered.

"The bonus has to be huge," Ernie muttered. "Hell, even if we don't catch the others, he's gonna be pleased with the woman. Especially once he finds out that the hottie in the back was an old broad just yesterday. He said he thought the fangers could turn mortals and she's proof they can."

"Maybe, but we still don't know how they did it, and he'll want to know that more than anything else," the driver pointed out. Mary dubbed him Bert rather than keeping thinking of him as "the driver."

"So? She'll know," Ernie said with certainty. "He'll make her tell him."

"Actually, I almost feel sorry for the woman," Bert said, "From what Jackson says, some of the experiments the doc performs on the fangers are pretty nasty."

"This is no time to be going soft," Ernie said firmly. "Just think of the bonus we're going to get."

Mary's mouth tightened. Dante had said people had been going missing in San Antonio. What he'd meant was immortals, she realized, and she and the others were going to join their ranks if she didn't do something about it. It seemed to her that she was the only one who could. Dante, Russell and Francis had no idea they were being led into a trap. She did. If she could somehow warn them, or get out of her chains . . .

She wasted a moment trying to force her hands out of the shackles, but quickly gave it up as a lost cause. They were too tight. She considered the situation briefly as the men continued to talk and then she grasped the chains higher up their length, closer to the metal circle they were threaded through and gave a tug.

Mary wasn't terribly surprised when nothing happened. While Dante had said the nanos made them stronger and faster and all that, she suspected they didn't work so quickly that she would suddenly be as strong as the Hulk.

Despite that, she blindly felt her way up to the metal circle and, just for shits and giggles, tried to turn it like it was a wing nut. Much to Mary's amazement the circle apparently wasn't well affixed to its base, that or her tug had loosened it. The metal turned under her pressure, just a little, but it turned. Grasping it more firmly, she tried again, and it snapped off.

Mary was so surprised by her success that she just lay there for a minute, her heart pounding and eyes wide, but then she started trying to figure out what she should do next. She was free and needed to stop the van before it reached this warehouse they'd mentioned. How much time did she have? Mary wondered. And how the hell was she supposed to stop the van?

Her gaze slid to the side door of the van. It was just feet in front of her, and Mary supposed she could probably leap the short distance, slide the door open and leap out before Bert or Ernie could stop her. The only problem was she didn't know what kind of road they were on. Was it one lane or two lanes? If it was two lanes, she might get run over by a vehicle coming along in the next lane when she tumbled out of the van. Or even a vehicle behind them if it was one lane.

Mary knew she'd probably survive getting run over, but there was the possibility that she might get injured badly enough that she couldn't warn Dante, Russell and Francis. They would no doubt stop and jump out to rush to her, and then Bert and Ernie would just shoot them with their darts . . . maybe. It depended on how willing they were to abduct them all in public.

Maybe she could stop them without leaping out, Mary thought hopefully, and slowly eased one foot back and up behind her butt, trying to find and poke it through the chain now lying between her hands. All she needed to do was get the chain in front of her rather than behind her and she could use it as a weapon.

Fortunately it was a longish chain. It wasn't huge or anything, but it was long enough that Mary was able to ease first one foot into it and then the other and then draw the chain slowly forward until it was around her knees, and then in front of her.

Mary kept her gaze on the men in the front as she did it, watching to make sure that the small clinks and clanks of the chains didn't attract attention. But Ernie, she saw, had his window open and the traffic noises appeared to mask any noise she was making. At least he didn't glance around, and neither did Bert.

"They're right behind us now," Ernie announced grimly.

"Good, we're almost there. One more block," Bert said, sounding just as grim, and she heard the vehicle accelerate.

Time's up, Mary thought.

Sending up a quick prayer, she rolled abruptly onto her hands and knees and then pushed upward with both hands and feet to lunge toward the front of the van. Dante had said that the nanos improved speed, but to her it seemed almost like time slowed. She saw Ernie's head slowly turning, as if the noise she'd made had drawn his attention, but she was behind the driver's seat, swinging the chain that dangled between her hands over Bert's head and down to his throat before Ernie had turned his head halfway around.

"Stop the van," Mary snapped, tugging the chain tight behind Bert's neck. When he didn't obey at once, she snapped, "Now!" then glanced quickly toward Ernie as he began to move, reaching for a dart gun that lay on the dashboard.

"I'll break his neck!" Mary barked in warning.

Ernie froze, his hand halfway to the gun. Turning back to peer at her, he eyed her briefly with calculation, and then pointed out, "We'd crash."

Eyes narrowing, Mary said calmly, "I'd survive. Would you?"

Ernie started to frown, but before the expression was fully formed he paused and smiled instead. "You're a nice old grandma. You won't kill him."

"Sonny," Mary growled. "I'm a crotchety old lady in

a strong young vampire body and right now you look an awful lot like a walking blood bank to me. Do you really want to test my patience?"

Apparently, he did. Ernie tried for the dart gun, and Mary instinctively shifted to jump at him, intending to stop him. Unfortunately, she forgot about poor old Bert and the chain around his neck. She heard the crunch of what could only be bone breaking as she unintentionally snapped his neck, and then the van swerved wildly.

"Crap," Mary breathed as she looked out the front windshield and saw the telephone pole they were about to crash into. *That's gonna hurt*, she thought just before impact.

Fifteen

Mary turned over sleepily and snuggled into the pillow under her head with a little sigh, then sniffed with interest as the scent of lavender teased her nose. Wondering where it was coming from, she opened her eyes and stared at the alarm clock radio sitting on the bedside table in front of her. It wasn't her clock radio; that was her first thought, and then she rolled over and glanced around the room she was in, which also wasn't hers.

Sitting up abruptly, Mary peered around at the pale blue walls, the sitting chairs by the window, the mirrored sliding closet doors, and the two normal doors in the room. This definitely was not her home or the RV. Not a hotel either, though, she thought and then glanced curiously at the contraption next to the bed. An IV stand, she noted, and followed the tubing coming out of it down to the back of her hand. She raised her hand and eyed it curiously, wondering why she'd needed it, then glanced down at herself, eyebrows rising when she saw that she was wearing a pretty white cotton nightgown with spaghetti-string shoulder straps . . . also not hers.

A hospital? She considered the possibility, but hospitals didn't look this nice; at least none of them that she'd been in had. Besides, they usually smelled of disinfectant, not lavender.

Sighing, Mary pushed the blankets aside and slid her feet off the bed, then paused and glanced around the room again, before deciding to try the door to the right of the bed first. She had to go to the bathroom, and knew that one of the two doors in the room would either lead to a bathroom or a hallway that would lead to a bathroom. Either one would get her closer than just sitting there, so Mary pushed herself to her feet and then paused and grabbed the IV stand to balance herself when the room started a slow spin. It only lasted a minute before the room settled and her equilibrium was restored, but it was kind of startling. Keeping her hold on the IV stand, Mary pulled it along with her just in case the room decided to do another dance move. Much to her relief, however, she made it to the door without anything else happening.

Opening the door, Mary was relieved to see that it was indeed a bathroom. She'd figured a bedroom wouldn't have two exits, but one never knew. Especially since she had no idea where she was. She wheeled the stand into the room with her and positioned it between the toilet and the counter holding the sink and then hiked up her nightgown and sat on the toilet.

It was while she was sitting there that the first shaft of agony struck. Mary gasped in pained surprise, and immediately grabbed her head, trying to keep it from blowing apart. However, the pain eased and waned just as quickly as it had struck, leaving her breathing cautiously in and out as she waited warily to see if it would strike again. After a little time had passed without a recurrence, she let out her breath slowly and reached for the toilet paper.

It wasn't until she stood and moved to wash her hands that Mary even glanced to the mirror, and then she froze, the room spinning around her as she stared at her forehead. There was a large, ugly scar cutting across the top of her head, from her forehead back and the top of her head around it was slightly misshapen, like it had been caved in but was pushing its way back out.

Mary grabbed for the counter to steady herself, then screamed and grabbed for her head as another shaft of pain crashed through her skull, sending her to her knees. She thought she heard someone shout her name, but she was already losing consciousness.

The next time Mary woke up, the IV was gone and there was a warm body in front of her as well as one at her back. Opening her eyes, she peered at the furry body she had her arm around.

Bailey.

She was back from the vet, Mary thought, and smiled, her arm tightening slightly around the dog.

Bailey immediately turned her head and tipped it back slightly to look at her and Mary gave her another squeeze, whispering, "Hello, sweetie. It's okay. Go back to sleep."

The German shepherd laid her head back down with the little huff of sound that she usually made when she was content, and Mary lifted her head slightly to glance to the rather large arm that was wrapped around her from behind.

Dante, she thought. At least she hoped it was. Otherwise, she and Bailey were in the wrong place.

"Mary?"

She stilled at that whisper, then turned her own head and tilted it back to look at the handsome man presently wrapped around her.

Dante smiled and bent to press a kiss to her nose, then asked solemnly, "How is your head?"

Mary stiffened, her smile freezing, and then she sat abruptly upright, knocking his arm away and nearly sending Bailey tumbling to the floor as she grabbed her head and began to feel it. It felt fine. Normal, she thought with relief, but—

Climbing out of the blankets and over Bailey, she stumbled to the door next to the bed and into the bathroom to see if it truly was all right. Mary's breath left her on a sigh of relief when she saw that her head was back to normal. Even the scar was gone, she noted, parting her hair to get a look at her scalp. There wasn't even a thin line to show where the injury had been.

"It is all healed," Dante said gently. "At least on the outside."

Mary turned to glance at him and started to nod, but paused when she saw that he was naked. Again.

"Honestly, do you have an allergy to clothes or something?" she asked with exasperation. "Every time I turn around you're naked."

Dante's eyes widened and he opened his mouth to respond, then gasped in surprise when she suddenly leapt at him . . . literally. She jumped him like a monkey, wrapping her arms around his shoulders and her legs around his hips as she covered his mouth with hers.

Dante chuckled into her mouth and caught her under the bottom to keep her from slipping before he turned and set her on the bathroom counter. Breaking their kiss then, he nuzzled her ear and murmured, "I think you like me naked."

"I do," Mary admitted huskily, pressing kisses to his shoulder as he nibbled at her ear. "You should always be naked."

"Always?" he asked, tugging her nightgown off one shoulder.

"Always," she assured him, pulling back to run her hands over his chest as he tried to bare hers. "Thank you for getting Bailey back."

"She is a good dog, and you love her. I would not leave her behind," he assured her solemnly, and then giving up on getting her nightgown down, he simply bent and closed his mouth over one nipple through the cloth.

Mary moaned as the cloth grew wet and his tongue moved it across her immediately erect nipple.

"How long was I out this time?" she asked on a gasp, arching her back.

Dante reached down to begin pushing her nightgown up her legs before answering. "Two days."

"Two?" Mary muttered, lifting one butt cheek off the counter and then the other so that he could get the nightgown out from under her.

"You took a very serious head wound," he said solemnly, and dropped her nightgown to cup her face between his hands. "You must never allow yourself to be so harmed again. I thought my heart would stop when I found you after the van crashed."

Dante leaned down to kiss her gently and Mary sighed against his lips. "I'm sorry. It was my fault. I accidentally broke Bert's neck when Ernie went for the dart gun."

"Bert?" he asked with confusion. "One of the men was Ernie, but the other was Bob, not Bert."

Mary smiled crookedly. "I didn't know his name so I gave him a nickname."

"Ah." He nodded. "Bert and Ernie are dead."

"Both of them?" she asked with surprise, and then grimaced. She'd seen her own head wound. Surely it would have killed a mortal? Why would she think Ernie would have made out any better?

"Yes, both are dead," he said quietly, then raised his eyebrows and said, "You broke Ernie's neck?"

"No, Bert's," Mary corrected. "Couldn't you tell when you saw the bodies?"

"There was not much to see," he said solemnly. "The van exploded on impact. If you had not flown out the windshield and into the post, you too would now be dead. Immortals are highly flammable."

Her eyebrows lifted at this news, and then she bit her lip and asked, "And Tomasso?"

His shoulders drooped and he shook his head silently. "Lucian has people looking in Venezuela, but nothing yet."

Mary sighed and leaned her forehead against his shoulder. "I'm so sorry."

"No, I am the one who is sorry. I promised to keep you safe and failed you. Twice. You have nothing to be sorry for," he assured her quietly.

"Yes, I do," Mary said unhappily. "I killed Bert, which led to Ernie dying too. And you needed one of them alive to find out where Tomasso is." Raising her head, she added quickly, "I was only trying to make them stop. It was all a trap. They were leading you to a warehouse about a block away from the crash, or maybe a half a block by that time. There were two men waiting there." Mary paused and then muttered with frustration, "They said their names, but I can't remember. I think one was Jack or something."

"You took a lot of trauma to the head," Dante said soothingly. "The nanos are probably still making repairs. Your memory may be shaky for a while until the repairs are finished."

"Right." She took a deep breath and then continued, "Anyway, they set it up for you to follow. Once at the warehouse, there were men waiting to shoot you and Russell and Francis with darts, and then we were all going to be shipped to wherever with Tomasso."

"Tomasso was there at this warehouse?" he asked sharply.

"I'm not sure, but I think so," she said unhappily. "I was going to tell you what I'd heard once I forced them to stop the van. I thought maybe we could drive in, in the van. They wouldn't have been expecting that. But then dumb Ernie ignored my warning and went for the dart gun. I tried to grab him and broke Bert's neck and we crashed."

Sighing, she dropped her head to his shoulder again. "I'm sorry, Dante. I messed up. It's all my fault."

"No," he said firmly, wrapping his arms around her. "It is not. If you had not done what you did, we might all now be in the same position Tomasso is in. Instead, we are alive and safe and able to help look for him."

Mary thought it was sweet of him to try to soothe her conscience, but she still felt guilty. Relaxing against him, she closed her eyes, then glanced up with surprise when Dante pulled back. But he merely scooped her up in his arms and carried her back out to the bedroom.

Bailey was still lying on the bed and Mary frowned with concern as she noticed the cast on her leg.

"She is fine," Dante said softly. "She has had her pain killers and the cast barely slows her down. She is not even limping anymore."

"Oh," Mary murmured as he carried her around the bed and set her down next to Bailey.

Dante quickly covered her with the sheets and blankets she'd tossed aside just moments ago, and then straightened and turned to open the cabinet door of the table on his side of the bed. Curious, Mary watched as he bent to retrieve something, her eyes widening when he turned to set two bags of blood on the bed.

Catching her surprise, he smiled and said, "It is a hidden fridge. Mortimer," he paused to explained, "He's the head of the rogue hunters. He had them custommade. Now everyone wants them for their homes," he added with amusement as he retrieved two more bags to set next to the others. He closed the door as he straightened, then scooped up the four bags and set them down right next to her before leaning forward to kiss her on the forehead. "I have to go tell Lucian what you told me. He will want to send someone to search the warehouses in the area and see if there is any information that might be of use." He straightened, and then asked, "Is there anything you want me to bring you when I return? Something to eat or drink?"

Mary hesitated, but then aware that he wanted to leave, just shook her head. "Maybe later."

Nodding, he bent to kiss her again, then leaned past her to give Bailey an affectionate pet before straightening and crossing the room.

"Feed," Dante said firmly as he opened the second door in the room to reveal a hall beyond. Glancing back he added, "I want all four bags empty when I come back." Then he slipped from the room and pulled the door closed behind him.

Mary picked up one of the bags, but then just stared at it. She had no idea how to make her fangs come out. Before this, they'd just popped out whenever she was hungry. She hadn't had to—

The thought died as she felt a shifting in her mouth. Mary waited, and then ran her tongue cautiously along her teeth until it rubbed up against a fang. Well, that was handy. But then she *was* hungry, although she hadn't realized it until she'd actually picked up the bag. Or, perhaps, it was better to say she hadn't been able to identify what she was hungry for until then. Although, Mary thought, she wouldn't mind food either, just then. However, she didn't have any, so she simply opened her mouth and popped the bag toward it, relieved when it landed correctly and remained in place.

Keeping her hand in place on the bag to support it, Mary glanced to Bailey then. The dog appeared to be asleep. She suspected it might have something to do with the pain pills Dante had mentioned. On the other hand, Bailey slept a lot. Most dogs seemed to. They'd run around like crazy chasing balls, animals and anything else that caught their attention, and then would drop and sleep for a while before getting up to do it again.

It was a tough life, Mary thought with amusement and glanced to the bag to judge how much more blood there was in it. It was going down pretty quick, and didn't bother her as much as it had at first. She didn't exactly like the feel of cold fluid moving up her teeth, and she wasn't pleased to have to actually consume blood, but at least she didn't have to actually drink it cold from a cup or something. That would have been disgusting. This way she didn't have to taste it or anything.

The moment the first bag emptied, Mary tore it off and slapped on another, eager to get the chore over with. It seemed to take forever, although she knew that was probably because she was waiting through it with nothing to distract her. Still, she was surprised when she finished the next two bags and Dante hadn't yet returned.

Tearing the last bag from her mouth, she scooped up all four of the empty bags, crawled off the bed and took them into the bathroom to throw them in the small garbage can there. Mary then went right back to the bed.

Her getting up had apparently disturbed Bailey and the dog had raised her head to watch for her return. Mary smiled at the shepherd as she climbed back into bed, and then settled back onto her side and ran a hand down her side.

"We're a pair, huh?" she asked softly, petting her. When Bailey just closed her eyes on a little huff of sound, Mary stopped petting her and instead curled her arm around her, careful not to get anywhere near her broken back leg. She then closed her eyes, surprisingly sleepy again. She never heard the door open when Dante returned.

"I hear Mary woke up."

Dante turned from watching Bailey sniffing her way around the yard and smiled when he saw Russell approaching.

"*Si*," he said, before turning back to continue watching Bailey. Mary had been asleep by the time he'd finished talking to Lucian and returned to the bedroom. He'd lain down with her for a while, but hadn't been able to sleep. Instead, he'd simply lain there, his mind racing.

He'd worried about Tomasso, wondered where he was, and hoped that the men Lucian sent to look for the warehouse Mary had mentioned found it and got some information that might help them find Tomasso. When those worries had proven useless and raised his stress level and concern for his brother, Dante had then turned his thoughts to Mary and the future he planned to have with her. He wasn't sure how long he'd been doing that when Bailey had got off the bed and pawed the door, letting him know she needed to go outside.

Leaving Mary sleeping, he'd immediately got up to bring the dog out. She was a fine animal: good-natured and well behaved. Mary had done a fine job with her.

"How is her head?" Russell asked, pausing beside him and turning to watch Bailey as well.

"It is back to its proper shape," Dante said with a frown. Nothing in his life had terrified him as much as seeing Mary with the top of her head caved in. It was not a moment he would ever want to relive.

"Any pain?" Russell asked.

Dante's mouth tightened. "The first time she woke up, yes, but not the second. However, she was not long awake."

"I am sorry to say it, but she might yet have headaches then," Russell murmured.

"*Si*." Dante sighed the word unhappily. "And you are no sorrier to say it than I to think it. After the explosion and turning and now this accident, she has suffered enough." He shook his head. "I should have accompanied her to the ladies' room."

Russell shrugged. "Hindsight is twenty-twenty, my friend. None of this is your fault."

Dante didn't agree, but merely changed the subject. "Where is Francis?"

"At the gate," Russell glanced back the way he'd come. "He asked me to come check on Mary for him." He turned back and smiled at Dante. "He likes her. So do I."

"I always knew you were both intelligent men," Dante said solemnly and Russell laughed. Smiling faintly, himself, he asked, "So you are back on the gate. Does this mean Francis is done with wanting to become a hunter?"

"Oh, hell no," Russell said dryly. "He was all ready to rush right down to Venezuela to hunt down the bastard behind those men who fried in the van. It took a lot of talking to convince him to wait until he has had some more training."

"Has he not already had training?" Dante asked with surprise.

Russell grimaced and nodded reluctantly. "Yes, but—"

"But you have convinced him he needs more because you do not wish him anywhere near danger. You do not wish to lose him," Dante suggested sympathetically.

Russell ran a weary hand through his short fair hair and nodded. "I waited a millennia for him, and while I did not recognize that he was my life mate immediately on encountering him, once I did . . ." He shrugged. "I could not bear to lose him now, Dante. I could not go back to the lonely existence I was living before him, especially now that I know what I would be missing." He paused and shook his head. "I do not know how Lucian bore it all those millennia after losing his first life mate in the fall. I could not do it were I to lose Francis."

Dante nodded, understanding completely. He already felt the same way about Mary.

They were both silent for a minute, and then Russell cleared his throat and said, "The reason Francis wanted me to check on Mary was because, as he reminded me, we never did get to that shopping trip, and he would still very much like to help her shop."

Dante glanced at him with surprise. "He wanted you to ask that for him?"

"Francis has issues with rejection," Russell said quietly. "His family turned their back on him when they realized he preferred men to women." He smiled wryly and added, "In a way, he was more alone than I when we met. I, at least, had my family."

Dante nodded. "I am sure Mary would enjoy his company when we shop. But . . ." He hesitated, not wanting to offend either man.

In the end, he didn't have to figure out a way to word his request. Russell grinned and suggested, "But you want to ensure he dresses her like Barbie and not Stripper Barbie?"

Dante nodded with relief, and then grinned and said, "Not that I would mind one or two Stripper Barbie outfits for at home."

"But the majority of the clothes should probably be more Next-Door-Neighbor Barbie," Russell said with amusement. "I understand completely and shall pass that along."

"Thank you," Dante said with a smile.

"Give us a shout when she wakes up and wants to go. I shall talk to Mortimer about arranging someone to take over the gate."

"There will probably be no need," Dante said, glancing toward the house and the window of the bedroom Mary inhabited. "I suspect she will sleep through the night. We probably will not shop until tomorrow afternoon."

"Just call then and we'll come," Russell said and slapped his shoulder before turning to head back around to the front of the house.

Dante watched him go, and then turned to see Bailey walking back toward him, her duty done. He squinted his eyes and watched her legs carefully as she walked. She was not yet used to the somewhat clunky cast, and it slowed her down a little, but as he had said to Mary, she wasn't limping at all.

Thoughts of Mary made him pat his leg.

"Come on. Let us go check on our Mary," he suggested and turned toward the house.

Bailey immediately turned toward the house and began to move more quickly. In the end, she reached the door before he did and waited patiently for him to open it so that she could rush inside and up the stairs, eager to see her mistress.

Mary was woken up by more than eighty pounds of dog leaping on top of her. It was accompanied by angry whispers in Italian that could only be Dante, she thought with amusement, as she reached out to pet her dog and try to calm her.

"Oh, *Dio mio*, do not pet her, Mary. Go back to sleep. She is being bad waking you, and you are rewarding her," Dante said with exasperation.

Chuckling, Mary rolled onto her back to see him approaching the bed.

"I know. I guess I'm just a bad mother," she said with amusement, absently stroking Bailey's head as the dog laid it on her stomach.

"Your fangs are out," Dante said rather than respond to her comment.

Pausing at the side of the bed, he opened the hidden refrigerator and grabbed a bag of blood and then climbed onto the bed on the other side of Bailey. He passed the bag of blood over to her and then curved around Bailey so he could lay his head on the pillow next to Mary's.

Gripping the bag of blood, Mary sat up and ran her tongue cautiously around her teeth. Yep, there they were, long and sharp and apparently hungry again, she thought with resignation and slapped the bag to her hungry fangs. They did seem to constantly be popping out on her. Every time she woke up she seemed to have to consume the red liquid, and usually several bags of it.

"How is your head?" Dante asked as they waited for the bag to empty.

Mary raised her eyebrows at the question, wondering how he expected her to answer. But then he asked, "Does it hurt?" and she was able to shake her head in answer.

"Good," he murmured, toying with the top of the blanket covering her. "And you are a wonderful mother, Mary. Bailey is lucky," he added, finally responding to her comment of a moment ago. "And our children will be too. I have no doubt you will spoil them at times. But you will discipline them too, and they will always know they are loved."

Mary stared at him silently. She had been smiling around the nearly empty bag at her mouth, but now that smile faded and tears glazed her eyes. Mary immediately turned her head away from him so he couldn't see the tears. She was relieved when she could tear the bag away from her mouth a moment later.

When Dante immediately took it, she began to fiddle with the edge of the blanket covering her and muttered, "What's this talk of *our* children? I think you're getting a little ahead of yourself, mister. Heck, I've only known you for a couple of days."

Dante caught her chin and turned her head toward him. He peered at her silently for a moment, taking in her glassy eyes, then said solemnly, "It was a week yesterday that you ran me over. True," he added quickly, his fingers tightening to keep her in place when she started to turn her head away again, "You have slept through most of the week."

For some reason, that brought a wry laugh from her, and he smiled, but continued.

"However, it does not matter. We are life mates, Mary, and I do not intend to lose you. We will love each other, and we will be together for however long we both shall live, and we will have many, many babies. It was meant to be," he assured her.

Mary swallowed, trying to shift the lump suddenly lodged in her throat. She suspected that, despite the little time they'd been together, she was already half in love with the big idiot. How could she not be? He was sweet, and strong and caring. The fact that he was beautiful didn't hurt either, but it was just gravy.

After years of counseling people, Mary had become adept at judging character, and Dante was a man of substance. She had loved her husband, Joe. Once they'd worked through their issues, theirs had been a caring and contented relationship of friendship and love. It had been hard won and appreciated all the more for it. But with Dante, Mary suspected she could have that special, once-in-a-lifetime love many of her patients had talked about yearning for, and she'd always thought was just fantasy. Mary didn't think it was fantasy anymore, and she was quite sure she could have it with Dante, and that it would actually last as long as they lived, whether that was another twenty years, or two thousand. But, she could not have children. She did not mind for herself. Mary had long ago got over the fact that she couldn't give birth. The moment she had held her adopted son in her arms, he had been hers as surely as if she had carried him for nine months, and when her adopted daughter had followed, it had been the same. She had her children. But she could not give Dante children.

"Dante," she said softly. "I told you. The accident caused a miscarriage. I was six months pregnant. I lost the baby and . . . there were complications. I can't have your children."

Her voice cracked on the last word, and Mary was holding on to her composure by a very fine, very short thread, so was a bit taken aback when he smiled.

"And as *I* told *you*, Mary," he said gently. "The nanos return their host to their peak condition. You *will* be able to have children, and I cannot wait to watch your belly grow with my child."

He covered her mouth with his then, but Mary was too stunned to respond at first, and quickly pushed him back slightly.

"Wait," she said uncertainly. "When I lost the baby, they had to—"

"The nanos will repair whatever has been damaged, and replace whatever has been lost," he interrupted solemnly, "covering pretty much everything up to and including a hysterectomy."

He started to kiss her again and this time, Mary began to respond, but the moment he urged her lips apart, she broke the kiss and pulled back again. This time she was frowning as a myriad of thoughts assaulted her.

"Are you saying I could get pregnant *right now*?" she asked, actually alarmed at the prospect. It was wonderful to know she could give him children, but she wasn't at all sure she wanted to do it right now, or nine months from now, she supposed. It didn't seem like a good way to start a new relationship.

"Probably not," Dante said, looking slightly quizzical that she seemed so alarmed at the prospect. "Do you not wish to have my child?"

"Well, sure. At least I think I do," she added, trying to be levelheaded about this. They had just met, after all, and common sense and all her training told her she shouldn't be jumping so wholeheartedly into this relationship. Sighing, she added, "But not right now. I mean, it would be nice to feel a little more settled in the relationship before we add a baby, don't you think?"

"Oh. Yes," he agreed, relaxing, and then grinned and urged Bailey away. Once the dog had shifted herself to the foot of the bed, he scooted closer, and drew her into his arms. "You are right. It is better to wait on having a baby. Especially since once we get Tomasso back I intend to keep you in bed for a good year or so. A baby would interfere with that. So we will wait a year or so."

Mary relaxed and nodded with relief. That was definitely the smarter route, she thought, as he began to kiss her again. She kissed him back this time, her body coming alive at once, but when he broke their kiss to lean back and begin tugging at the blanket and sheets covering her, she asked, "So you have protection?"

Dante glanced to her with confusion, and his voice was distracted when he asked, "Protection?"

"A condom?" Mary explained as he turned his attention back to removing the coverings between them. She pointed out, "It's not like I'm on birth control or anything."

"Oh." Dante murmured with a nod as he finally got the blankets and sheets out of the way.

Mary relaxed at his nod that he had protection, and

smiled faintly as his gaze moved hungrily over her in the white cotton nightgown.

"We—" Dante began as he reached toward her breast, but whatever would have followed was pushed aside by a groan as his hand closed over the soft globe and he squeezed, sending shivers of pleasure through them both.

"We what?" Mary gasped, arching into the caress.

"Yes," he muttered and covered her mouth with his again, his kiss almost violent with need.

Mary responded in kind, her body quickly melting beneath his touch and kiss. The man was fire to her tinder, sending her up in flames with just a touch. She had never experienced anything like it before. She'd thought her marital bed a satisfying one before she and Joe had had their problems, and after they'd sorted them. But he had never lifted her to these heights, even after loads of foreplay. Mary knew it had to be a chemical reaction, and most definitely a result of something to do with the nanos. It was the only explanation for this madness, she thought faintly, as Dante shifted to his knees, and lifted her to her own without breaking their kiss.

His hands were immediately everywhere. Sliding down her back to urge her forward until she knelt between his spread knees and they were chest to chest. His hands then slid down to cup her behind and squeeze eagerly, before gliding up and around to find her breasts.

Mary moaned, and arched and shifted into each touch and caress, then broke their kiss and cried out when his hands suddenly dropped again, this time to slip under her nightgown. One hand slid up to cup her between the legs, while the other slid around to cover both of her bare cheeks in his big hand so that he could urge her to move into his caress.

"God, Mary," Dante muttered against her cheek, his fingers beginning to explore the damp heat that waited for him.

"I want your clothes off," Mary moaned against his shoulder, and then gasped and began pulling at the cloth herself as he found her sweet spot. "Please."

Cursing, Dante retrieved his hands and quickly tugged his T-shirt up and off over his head.

"Your pants," Mary said breathlessly, when he started to reach for her again.

Dante was immediately off the bed, undoing and pushing his pants down.

"Where are the condoms?" she asked as he raised one foot and started to push the black denim off of it.

Turning, she opened the bed table drawer to see if there might be any there. There weren't and she turned back to ask if they might be in his wallet, or one of the other drawers, but paused when she saw that he had frozen, standing exactly as she'd last seen him, on one foot, bent over to push the cloth off. Except for the confusion on his face, he looked like a stork.

"You do have a condom?" Mary asked with a frown.

Dante shook his head, his expression blank.

"But you said you did." Mary said with accusation, and then her eyebrows drew together and she added, "At least, you nodded."

"Did I?" he frowned now too, obviously trying to

recall, then relaxed and smiled faintly. "I nodded that I understood. But I was going to explain that we do not need them, and then got distracted."

Mary recalled him starting to say, "We," and then pausing on a groan. She'd then asked, "We what?" But she couldn't remember whether he'd said anything then or not. She'd been a bit distracted by what he was doing. Apparently they both had been.

Taking a deep breath to try to ease some of the excitement still rushing through her body, she said, "What do you mean we do not need one? Of course we do, Dante. You said I can get pregnant now and we agreed we were not ready for that."

"Yes, but no," he said at once and she blinked in confusion. Fortunately, he continued, "I mean, yes you no doubt can get pregnant now, but no, you probably will not."

"*Probably?*" Mary asked grimly, arching one eyebrow.

Dante frowned slightly, and straightened, setting his foot back on the ground. His black jeans were still pooled around his ankles as he explain earnestly, "Mary, your body is still going through the turn, which has no doubt suffered something of a setback thanks to the accident. It is not likely it could support a child just now."

"It's not *likely*?" she asked archly.

Grimacing, he sat down on the side of the bed, and took her hand. "For an immortal woman to become pregnant, she has to take in a lot of blood. More than she usually would need to take in. Otherwise the nanos will see the fetus as a threat to their getting the blood they need and will abort it."

"I've been taking in an awful lot of blood," she pointed out.

"Yes, yes," Dante agreed waving the issue away with one hand in the same moment. "But that will all be taken up to finish the turn and repair the damage from the accident," he explained. "It is highly unlikely that you could get pregnant right now."

"Highly unlikely," she said slowly, and then raised one eyebrow and asked, "But not impossible?"

"Well . . ." Dante hesitated, and then his shoulders drooped. "You are going to insist on a condom."

"Yes," she said dryly.

"Right," Dante muttered and stood to pull his pants up, then headed for the door, muttering, "I shall be back directly."

Mary lay back on the bed with a sigh. If someone had told her that birth control would be an issue for her at sixty-two, she would have laughed in their face. "Who knew?" she muttered with disgust.

Sixteen

Dante hurried up the hall and then jogged downstairs, wracking his brain for a way to get condoms. Buying them was the obvious answer, but while it was only 7:30 in the evening and most stores would be open right now, the Enforcer House was in the country, a good fifteen minutes from the nearest store. He really didn't want to wait that long to get back to Mary.

Perhaps one of the men would have condoms, he thought and grimaced even as the possibility struck him. That just wasn't likely. Certainly Russell and Francis wouldn't have them. And Mortimer and his life mate Samantha were apparently hoping to get pregnant, so they wouldn't have them. Hell, most immortals wouldn't. They knew all they had to do to guard against pregnancy was not overindulge in blood. But Mary wasn't willing to take that chance because she had to take in so much blood just now. He understood, but it was frustrating as hell.

Maybe Mortimer kept condoms on hand for guests who stayed at the Enforcer House, Dante thought suddenly. The man had recently taken to ensuring they had most things an unexpected guest might need: everything from clothes in various sizes to shoes, extra vehicles—even brand-new toothbrushes and toothpaste still in their packaging. Condoms might also be on that list, Dante thought hopefully, as he stepped off the stairs and turned into the kitchen.

He was hoping to find Mortimer in there, since that was where the head of the enforcers had been when Dante had gone upstairs. However, he wasn't, and the first person he ran into on his quest for condoms was Mortimer's wife, Samantha. The sight of her made him pause abruptly several feet into the room.

"Oh, hello, Dante," the slender woman said with a smile when she glanced up from the pot she was stirring and spotted him. "How is Mary? Is she hungry? I made some soup."

"Er . . . no," Dante murmured, backing toward the doorway. When her eyebrows went up at his strange behavior, he added, "I was looking for Mortimer."

"He, Bricker, and Lucian went into his study," she said, and then added, "I'm sure they won't mind you interrupting. Although if there's something you need that I can help with—"

"No!" Dante barked with dismay, and then forced a smile and said more calmly, "Thank you, but it is better I talk to Mortimer."

"Okay," Samantha said easily, glancing down into the pot she was stirring. But as he left the room he could have sworn he heard her murmur, "No glove, no love, huh?"

Assuring himself that he must have misheard her, Dante hurried along the hall toward Mortimer's study. He could hear them talking before he reached the door, but was distracted enough he didn't bother really listening. He also didn't wait for a response after knocking at the door, but simply opened it and walked in.

Mortimer, Lucian, and Bricker were all there, as Samantha had said. They were standing around Mortimer's desk, looking at a map of some kind. All three glanced up with mild curiosity at his entrance.

"Sorry to interrupt," Dante muttered and then focused on Mortimer and began, "I just wanted to ask if you have gloves."

"Gloves?" Mortimer asked with surprise. "Sure. There should be some—"

"Oh, sorry, not gloves," Dante said with a frown, realizing what he'd said. His mind must still have been on what he'd thought he heard Samantha say.

"He means condoms," Bricker said with amusement, apparently reading his mind where Mortimer obviously hadn't. Grinning, the young hunter said, "No unwrapped stags between Mary's legs, huh?"

"What?" Dante asked, his voice choked with shock.

"She wants you to cuff your carrot, before you share it?" Bricker suggested and when Dante just stared at him blankly, he added, "You have to sock that wanger before you bang her?"

"Bricker," Mortimer said with exasperation.

But Justin just added, "Got no protection? Can't use your erection?"

"The internet?" Lucian asked dryly.

Pausing, Justin Bricker grinned at the man and said, "Yeah. They have loads of sayings: hide old Harry, then take her cherry. Wrap that pickle, then slip her a tickle. If you can't shield your rocket, leave it in your pocket. Don't make a mistake; cover your snake. Cover your stump before you hump. Don't be a fool—"

"Truly, Justin," Lucian interrupted grimly. "The subject of your internet searches really worries me sometimes."

"What?" Bricker asked with surprise. "Why?"

"The fact that you have to even ask me that question also worries me," Lucian said dryly. "First cocks, now condoms. What is next?"

"Well, I did come across this site that has—"

"I do not want to know," Lucian interrupted shortly, and then glanced to Dante. "You said Mary was a psychologist before she retired?"

Dante nodded, surprised and a little confused by the question until Lucian said, "Then perhaps you could ask her to have a session or two with Bricker while she is here."

"Ha ha," Justin said dryly.

Lucian ignored him and added, "I shall pay for them out of my own pocket just to ensure he is well enough to be on the job . . . and carrying a weapon."

"I shall mention it to her," Dante said, amusement replacing his dismay.

"Hardy har, har," Justin said dryly. "I drag myself away from my hot and sexy Holly to help out around here, and this is the appreciation I get?"

"Mary is a new life mate," Mortimer pointed out as if Justin hadn't spoken. "It might be better to call Lissianna's husband, Greg. He is a psychologist, is he not?"

"Good thinking," Lucian decided, pulling out his phone. "I shall call him now. In the meantime, Justin, drive Dante to the nearest store that would carry condoms."

"Sure," he said, rolling his eyes. Leading the way to the door, he added, "I'll check the sense of humor aisle while I'm there and see if I can get you both one."

"Check the brain aisle as well," Lucian suggested. "I suspect you left yours there the last time you were shopping."

Justin paused abruptly with his hand on the door and turned to stare at Lucian with amazement. "Did you just make a joke?"

"No," Lucian said firmly.

"Yes, you did," Justin countered, grinning. "It wasn't a very good one, but you made a joke, Lucian. Holy shit, I never thought I'd see the day." Pulling the door open, he walked out into the hall, shaking his head, and crooned, "Lucian Argeneau, cracking jokes. Well, I never!"

Dante stared after the man and then glanced back to Lucian, his eyebrows rising.

"Go ahead," Lucian said on a sigh. "He is an idiot, but a good lad despite that."

"I'll take your word for it," Dante muttered and hurried out of the room after the other man.

Mary was out of bed and staring out the bedroom window when Dante returned from his quest for condoms.

"I have them," he said triumphantly, holding up the bag holding the items as he entered.

Mary glanced to the bag, but then asked, "Where are we?"

Dante had tossed the bag on the bed and was pulling off his T-shirt, but paused with it off his head but still on his arms at that question. "What?"

"Where are we?" she repeated more slowly. "Last I knew we were in Texas, but judging by the amount of snow out there, this isn't Texas. Where are we?"

"Oh." He finished taking off his shirt and tossed it over one of the chairs. He then crossed the room to join her at the window. Slipping his arms around her from behind, Dante pulled her back against his chest and peered out at the snowy back yard. It was night, but between the house's outdoor lights, the lights on the buildings behind the house, and his night vision, he was able to get a good look at the landscape. It was starting to warm a little as spring approached. There were patches of grass showing in spots, but it had been a hard winter and there was still a lot of snow out there.

Bending to press a kiss to the top of Mary's head, he explained, "We are at the Enforcer House in Toronto."

"Toronto?" she asked with amazement. "As in Ontario, Canada?" When he grunted a yes, she asked, "But how did we—?"

"We flew out an hour after the accident," Dante said

quietly. "We would have left sooner, but we had to pick up Bailey first."

"How on earth did you get me through customs and immigration without a passport or my even being conscious?" Mary asked, sounding stunned. "And what did they say about my injuries? I mean they must have noticed my head all bent out of shape."

"We have our own planes and do not go through customs and immigration," he said with amusement.

Mary turned slightly and tilted her head to ask, "How do you manage that?"

Dante just raised an eyebrow and waited.

"Oh," she murmured, after a moment. "Mind control and stuff."

Nodding, he smiled and then kissed the tip of her nose. "It comes in quite handy in certain situations."

"I guess," Mary agreed dryly and turned to peer out the window again before murmuring, "Toronto."

Something about the way she said the city's name caught his attention and Dante glanced down at the top of her head, wishing he could see her expression. He couldn't, however, so asked, "What are you thinking?"

"My daughter lives here," she said softly. "Her husband's company transferred him here four years ago and they moved. I've missed having her and the kids in Winnipeg. I don't get to see them as much."

"Oh," Dante said, suspecting what was coming.

"I can see her while we're here," Mary said and he could hear the smile in her voice at the thought, and then she added, "I haven't see her since Christmas.

Both of my kids and their families flew down to Texas for Christmas this year. I rented a house by the RV camp and we all stayed there for two weeks, enjoying the beach and visiting. It was lovely and I was thinking of detouring this way to visit them on the way home, but I—"

"Mary," he interrupted softly.

She paused and went still, and then her tone was wary when she said, "What?"

Dante suspected he'd given away something with his tone, perhaps pity or regret. He was feeling both right now. But it had to be said. "Mary, you cannot see your daughter."

Now she went stiff. "What do you mean? Of course I can."

Her tone was brusque and short. She was not going to take this easily, he thought unhappily, and withdrew his arms from around her to grasp her shoulders and turn her to face him. Meeting her gaze, he asked solemnly, "How will you explain the changes you have gone through? Your new youthful appearance? The new silver tint to your eye color?"

Mary glared at him resentfully, obviously not appreciating the question, but said, "Well, I'll just explain about immortals and—"

"You cannot tell her about us," he interrupted firmly. "Keeping our existence from the rest of world is a necessity. It is how we have survived so long as a people. If mortals knew we existed, fear alone would make them hunt us down and—"

"You told me," Mary interrupted almost accusingly.

"Yes, but you are my life mate," Dante pointed out solemnly. "I hoped to turn you. If the situation had arisen where you refused to be my life mate, I would have had to let Lucian wipe your mind of all memory of me and everything I told you."

"He can do that?" she asked with alarm.

"*We* can do that," Dante said gently. "Including you. You are one of us now, Mary."

She frowned slightly, and then shook her head. "Well, that's all right, and I can still tell her. I want to turn her. I want to turn her husband and children too, and my son and his—"

"You cannot," Dante interrupted and hated himself for having to do so. He was quite sure if their places were reversed, he would wish to do the same with his family. However, it just wasn't possible. "Mary, each of us is allowed only one turn. It is necessary," he added firmly. "If every turn, turned every loved one, we would soon outstrip mortals in number."

"So?" she snapped impatiently.

"So whom would we feed on?" Dante asked practically and saw the revulsion that immediately crossed her face. "I am sorry, but that is reality. Your reality now."

Mary swallowed and shook her head, but then said, "Fine. But I can turn one?"

"Each immortal can turn one individual in their life," he agreed quietly, already knowing where this was going. "They usually save it for their life mate."

"You're my life mate, though," she pointed out. "So I want to turn my daughter."

"It is your choice," he said mildly. "However, you have to gain her permission first, and she then would have to leave her husband and children behind."

"She can turn her husband," Mary said at once, and then added, "And he can use his one turn for his oldest daughter, who can use her turn on her sister, who can turn my son, her uncle, who can turn his wife, who can turn their son." She smiled triumphantly. "And then we can all be immortal."

"What if your daughter's husband is not her life mate?" he pointed out.

"They're married," she said with a laugh.

"That does not mean they are life mates," Dante said solemnly. "And if he is not, life together would be unbearable."

"They love each other and live together now," Mary pointed out. "They would be fine."

"They may be fine living together as mortals, but that would not be the case if they were immortals and not life mates," he assured her. "It is difficult to live with someone when you can hear their every thought."

"But if they were both immortal—"

"Then they would both hear every thought the other had about them," Dante said solemnly.

"You mean you guys can always read each other?" Mary asked with surprise. "It isn't just a new life mate thing?"

Dante hesitated. He'd really been looking forward to getting back here with the condoms and actually using them. However, that wasn't looking very likely if he had to explain— Sighing, he pushed those thoughts away. This was important to Mary. He *needed* to explain, "Immortals can read each other if they do not guard their thoughts. If they are guarding their thoughts, it is impossible to read immortals who are older than themselves, and harder, but not impossible to read the thoughts of immortals about their age or younger than themselves. We quickly learn to guard our thoughts, but it takes constant effort and can be exhausting, and immortals often end up avoiding spending time with each other because of this. Life then can become very lonely if they stay by themselves, or heartbreaking if they befriend mortals who age, sicken and die so quickly in comparison to us. It has led to immortals going rogue and doing things they should not," he added solemnly. "And that is why we have hunters, or Enforcers."

"That is also why life mates are so important to us," he continued without giving her a chance to interrupt. "A life mate is the one person, mortal or immortal, that we cannot read and who cannot read us. We can relax together and enjoy each other without the need to constantly guard our thoughts."

"If you turn your daughter and she turns her husband and they are not life mates, they would not long stay together. Worse yet, each of them would then be consigned to a life alone with no hope of ever turning a life mate should they meet one." Dante paused briefly to let that sink in and then added, "And just by the very fact of forcing your grandchildren to turn each other, each of them would lose their opportunity to ever turn a life mate. They would all be left to live a very long, very lonely life with no hope of respite except through death or going rogue."

Mary's shoulders dropped miserably. "Isn't there any way—?"

"No," he cut her off solemnly. "Each immortal can turn only one. And if you tell your family without the intention of turning them . . ." He paused, his mouth firming. "Well, it would be a wasted effort. Lucian would send a group of Enforcers to ensure their minds were wiped of the memory. And then he would have you locked up in the cells in that building you probably noticed at the back of the property until you could be judged by the council."

"Judged?" she asked weakly. "What would they do?"

Dante shrugged. "I do not know for certain. I suspect they would search your thoughts to see if you were likely to be a future threat to keeping our presence in the world a secret. If not, they might just keep you locked up for a while."

"But if they thought I was?" she asked with a frown.

"They might simply perform a three on one and wipe your family and past from your memory, or . . ."

"Or?" Mary prompted, when he paused.

"Or, they might terminate you," Dante admitted on a sigh, and then added, "I, of course, would try to stop them, would no doubt be killed in the effort, and we would both be dead."

Mary gaped at him at this prediction, and then they both glanced to the door as someone knocked on it.

Sighing, Dante released Mary and turned to cross the

room and answer it. His eyes widened in surprise, then narrowed warily when he saw Lucian in the hall. If the man read his mind and got wind of the discussion he'd interrupted—

"In his report, Russell mentioned that Mary lost her RV and all her possessions in the RV explosion," Lucian said abruptly.

"*Si*. She lost everything except the clothes she was wearing and they were badly damaged too," Dante admitted. "We were going to take her out to buy clothes, but then the kidnappers took her and . . ." He shrugged.

Lucian nodded. "Bastien will arrange for new ID and bank accounts for her. He'll put in a sum to cover everything she lost, but he needs to know what name to put on the ID and accounts, and what birth date Mary wants. She cannot use her original birth date or the name Winslow anymore," he pointed out.

"Right," Dante said with a frown. "I will have to talk to her about that."

Lucian nodded. "Do that. In the meantime, she will need clothes. We shall have to take her shopping. Would you prefer to do it first thing in the morning before retiring? Or in the afternoon after waking?"

"We?" Dante asked, his voice almost strangled with surprise. Lucian was not the sort to enjoy shopping for women's clothes, he was sure.

But Lucian nodded. "You and Mary, Russell, Francis and myself."

"Oh," he said weakly.

Lucian waited patiently, but when Dante just continued to stare at him, his mind in an uproar, he said, "Late afternoon it is then," and turned to walk away, leaving Dante staring after him.

Mary stared at Dante's back. She couldn't see who was at the door—Dante's wide back was blocking her view—but she didn't really care. She didn't even care enough to listen to what was being said and she no doubt could have heard with her super duper new hearing, but she couldn't be bothered. Her mind was spinning with all she'd lost.

She'd thought losing her husband last year had been a big blow, but losing her children and grandchildren, her entire remaining family and all her friends in one go? And if her being turned was the cause of her loss, then it had happened in basically the same area of Texas where she'd lost her husband last year, she realized, taking note of the irony.

But Dante had turned her to save her life, Mary reminded herself quietly. If he hadn't she would be dead, which would have lost her everything anyway, and in a more permanent way. But now she had her life, if a slightly different one that included the need for blood. And she had Dante. And she could still see her children and grandchildren from afar, and check their Facebook and twitter accounts to see how they were. She just could not actually speak to them or hold them in her arms again, comfort them when they suffered life's setbacks or losses, or encourage them when—

Turning sharply to the window, Mary dashed a sudden spate of tears from her eyes and took a deep breath. She was being a stupid, ungrateful old fool. She had been given a gift here that most would kill for. She had a young and healthy body again with no aches or pains, no failing sight, no pills for blood pressure or cholesterol.

She also had a strong, handsome man who she had mind-blowing sex with, literally, and who saw her as the holy grail of women. A man who wanted her for his life mate and had admitted just moments ago that he'd die for her.

And, she could have babies with him too with this new improved body, Mary reminded herself. But even that did not ease the pain of losing the children and grandchildren she already had, and she knew it never would. While she'd loved every dog she'd had in her life, none had replaced the one she'd had and lost before it.

But they had helped ease the pain a bit, Mary thought suddenly. Perhaps the distraction of a baby would help see her through not being able to see her children and grandchildren except through their Facebook posts.

The psychologist in Mary knew at once that that was a bad idea, that it wouldn't work to ease her loss, and in fact would simply add to her stress as new babies tended to do. But Mary was a woman first and didn't want to listen to the more reasonable and educated side of her brain. She suddenly just wanted a baby to hold in her arms, one that was born immortal and could not be taken away from her.

"Mary?" Dante said softly and she whirled to see that the door was closed and he was crossing the room to join her again.

Mary didn't even think, she just slipped the straps of her nightgown off her shoulders and let the gown drop to pool around her feet. "Let's make a baby."

Dante stopped walking and blinked. "What?"

Stepping out of the puddle of cloth, Mary moved to him and slipped her arms up around his shoulders to try to tug his head down for a kiss. When he resisted, a frown marring his perfect face, she grabbed his hand and dragged him the few steps to one of the chairs by the window and quickly stepped up on the seat so that she could reach his mouth.

"Mary," he said on a laugh, trying to avoid her lips when she tried to kiss him. "What—?"

"I want a baby," she said almost desperately. "Please, Dante."

"But, Mary, you said—" He paused and gasped when she gave up on trying to kiss him, and instead reached down to find and squeeze him through the thick cloth of his jeans. Shaking his head, he groaned helplessly, "But I got the condoms."

"We don't need them," she assured him, unsnapping his jeans with her free hand and then lowering the zipper. "I want a baby."

"But Mary, you—I—" His efforts to speak died abruptly as she got his jeans open, freeing his quickly growing erection. When she caught it in her hand and squeezed gently, he gave up arguing on a growl and covered her mouth with his own.

Breathing her relief into his mouth, Mary kissed him back and continued to caress him, her own body responding to the touch and telling her just how much pressure to apply, what speed felt best. It was a wonderful trick, allowing her to bring them both quickly to the brink. But when Mary realized she was about to push them both over the edge into orgasm with him not even in her, she quickly released him and broke their kiss.

Ignoring Dante's groan of disappointment, Mary urged him back a step, and got off the chair to stand on the floor in front of him. She then immediately turned and bent forward, bracing herself on the arms of the chair now with her behind nudging against his erection.

"Hurry Dante," she urged. "Give me a baby."

Dante clasped her hips and she waited, bracing herself for his thrust, but it never came. He just held her. Mary glanced over her shoulder, scowling when she saw the frown on his face. He was thinking when he should be doing.

"Dante," she said impatiently. "We can't make a baby that way."

His gaze shifted to her and then something like determination crossed his face, and he shifted his hands to grab her by the waist.

Relieved, Mary started to turn forward again, and then gasped in surprise when instead of entering her, he simply picked her up and set her to stand on the chair again, still with her back to him. She frowned and glanced around then. Dante was a lot taller than her and she supposed it would have been awkward for him with them both standing on the floor. Still, surely this put her up too high?

Mary had barely had the thought when he urged her feet further apart until they were on the very edges of the chair. She thought he was trying to arrange her so that she was at the right height for penetration, but he startled her by then squeezing his wide chest under and between her legs to sit in the chair facing her.

"What—?" she began with confusion, than gasped when he caught her butt cheeks in each hand and pulled her forward. Mary cried out with surprise and grabbed at the wall, then cried out again as his mouth was suddenly between her spread legs, his tongue thrusting where she'd wanted his erection.

"No!" Mary cried with a dismay that quickly turned to need. "Oh God, yes . . . no . . . yes . . . Oh Dante," she cried, bracing one hand on the wall behind the chair and tangling the other in his hair as he began to lick and suck at the nub of her excitement.

Apparently, the shared pleasure made it easy for him to know just exactly what to do to push them over that edge they'd been approaching before she'd stopped too. Dante didn't stop, though, he just pushed until they both rode over the falls and dropped into the dark waters waiting below.

Mary was slumped in Dante's lap on the chair, her legs on either side of his and her head on his shoulder, when she woke from their post-noncoital encounter. He was already awake, something she deduced from the fact that he was rubbing her back soothingly. Mary lay still for a moment, both enjoying the caress and avoiding having to face him. But it seemed she didn't fool him. Dante knew she was awake, which she deduced when his hands stilled and he spoke.

"Do you want to explain what just happened?"

Mary reluctantly sat up, but feigned ignorance. "It's usually referred to as oral sex. Although one of my patients said it's called having a box lunch now, or alternately a Bikini Burger or a Cherry Flip." She paused and grimaced before admitting, "He has a thing for looking up such words online and was always coming into his appointments with risqué lists of slang terms."

"Was his name Bricker?" Dante asked, his eyes narrowing.

"No," she answered, and frowned. "I can't tell you the name of my patients, Dante, even if they aren't my patients anymore. That would be unethic—"

"Never mind," Dante interrupted. "Of course it was not him. You are from Winnipeg and he has not even been there that I know of."

She tilted her head curiously at that, wondering who this Bricker was that he was talking about.

"Anyway," he said, "that's not what I meant when I asked you to explain. I do know it was oral sex, Mary," he added dryly. "I meant why the sudden desire for a baby when less than an hour ago you were determined we should not have one and *made me go out and find condoms*?"

Mary's mouth twitched with amusement at the complaint in his voice, and then she sighed and sat up a little straighter.

"I've changed my mind is all," she responded. "I want a baby now."

"Why?" he asked at once.

Mary shrugged and glanced unhappily away.

"They will not replace the children you already have," he said solemnly.

Her lower lip trembled and she bit it, and then lowered her head. "I know, but—"

"*Tesoro*," Dante interrupted. Catching her chin, he turned her to face him before saying, "I would be happy to give you a baby if you want."

"You will?" she asked uncertainly.

He nodded solemnly. "You are my life now. My future. My love. I will give you anything you want if it is within my power."

Mary stared at him, his words circling in her mind. The "my love" part really got her attention, but even it was not enough to distract her from her desire for a baby, and she asked plaintively, "Then why didn't you—?"

"Because I will not do so until I am sure it is what you truly want and—"

"It is," she interrupted impatiently.

"And," he continued grimly, "That this sudden desire is not merely an emotional response to the realization that you can no longer be an active part of the lives of the children you already have."

When she stared at him with frustration, Dante said gently, "It is not the right reason to bring a child into the world, Mary. And I do not ever want a child of mine thinking they are a substitute for your mortal children."

Mary flinched at the words and then closed her eyes on a sigh. "No. I don't either," she agreed sadly.

They were both silent for a minute, and then she slipped off of his lap to go collect her nightgown from the floor. As she bent to pick it up, Mary decided she needed a change of subject to get her mind off this sad topic and asked, "What does *tesoro* mean?"

"Treasure," Dante answered, standing to tuck himself away and do up his jeans.

"Really?" Mary asked, her expression softening.

"*Si*. It is most often used like *dear*," he murmured, reclaiming the chair. "But you *are* my treasure, Mary."

She could feel herself blushing, and glanced down to the nightgown she held. As she quickly pulled it over her head, Mary asked, "Whose nightgown is this?"

"Yours now," Dante said, watching her don the gown. When she poked her head through the neck and glanced to him in question, he explained, "They keep many things here for guests that might have to stay at the Enforcer House unexpectedly. There are pajamas, nightgowns, jeans and T-shirts . . ." He shrugged. "I picked that nightgown, but was not sure of your size, so you will have to pick the jeans and tops. I did get you a razor, hairbrush, toothpaste, and toothbrush from the storage room though."

"Thank you," Mary whispered, surprised by his thoughtfulness.

He shrugged and patted his leg. When she moved back to him, he drew her to sit sideways in his lap and then said solemnly, "The council has agreed to buy you a whole new wardrobe. They also intend to refund you the money for the RV and everything you lost. They will put it in a bank account for you and arrange ID for you just as soon as you tell them what name and birth date you wish them to use."

Mary eyed him uncertainly. "Can I not use my name?"

"You can use your first name and maybe your middle name if you have one. As for your last name . . ." He hesitated and then said, "Most try to avoid the name they are known as in their mortal life. Or they include it but alternate it."

"What do you mean?" she asked uncertainly. "Like Windy Mary or something instead of Mary Winslow?"

"No," he said with a laugh. "For instance, Francis was Francis Renart and Russell was Russell Argeneau-Jones. Argeneau was Russell's mother's maiden name. She kept it as part of her name when she married and took the surname Jones so that they were Argeneau-Jones. But we tend to have to change our names every ten years when we change identities and she and her husband alternated between Jones and Argeneau. Russell and Francis consider themselves Renart Argeneau Jones, but alternate between Renart, Jones and Argeneau on their ID when they have to change it."

"Oh," she said with a frown. "So I could be Mary Winslow Bonher."

"Boner?" Dante asked, his voice a bit choked.

"Bon-her," Mary said dryly and spelled it out before explaining, "It's my maiden name."

"Ah," he nodded. "Well, yes, of course you could use Bonher. As for Winslow . . ." Dante cleared his throat. "I thought perhaps Notte instead."

Mary stilled, her eyes meeting his.

"It will be Notte eventually," he said quietly. "When you are ready to make it so."

Flushing, she nodded and glanced down, then lifted her head right back up and asked, "What about my birthday? They want a different year, of course?"

He nodded. "Some keep their original day and month and just switch the year, but others change the day and month to the day they were turned."

"Hmmm," she murmured, thinking about that. Should she have a completely new birth date for a new life? Or should she settle for just a new birth year?

"You have a little time to think about it," Dante said reassuringly, his hand moving over her back.

"How little?" Mary asked.

"I would say you should decide by the time we go shopping tomorrow," he suggested. "Lucian will demand to know then."

"Lucian?" she asked with surprise. "He's going shopping with us?"

"*Si*, the council is paying for the clothes you lost, so he is accompanying us tomorrow to buy you a wardrobe suitable for a warm climate."

"Oh," Mary muttered, so dismayed at the thought of having to go shopping with Lucian that it took a moment for the rest of his words to sink in. When they did, she glanced to him sharply. "A warm climate?"

Dante nodded, and Mary just stared at him with bewilderment. It was still winter and cold. There was still snow on the ground, she thought, and then her eyes widened as a thought occurred to her. "Venezuela?"

He nodded again, a crooked smile spreading his lips.

"But I thought Lucian insisted you shouldn't go?" Mary asked.

"*Si*, but he has relented. He thinks that your presence will temper my nature and prevent me doing anything stupid," Dante said wryly and then admitted, "And he is right. I will not do anything to jeopardize my future with you." Lifting his hands, he cupped her face and said, "*Tu sei un dono del cielo. Con te voglio passare la ma vita.*"

Mary raised a hand to cover one of his and said softly, "I don't know what that means, but if it's your way of trying to get under my nightgown, it's working."

Dante chuckled at her candor and kissed her nose. "I said that you are a gift from the heavens." He pressed a light kiss to her lips then and added, "And with you I want to spend my life."

"Oh," Mary breathed. "Wow, you Italians sure know how to romance a gal."

Dante shook his head on a laugh and pressed his forehead to hers. "You, *amore mio*, are easy."

"Apparently I am," she agreed wryly, and then added seriously, "for you."

Dante paused, his expression becoming serious as well.

Mary cleared her throat and squeezed his hand, then suggested, "If we are going shopping in the morning, then we probably need to sleep soon. Perhaps you should show me what you bought."

His eyebrows rose in brief confusion, and then his eyes widened with excitement and he jumped quickly to his feet.

Mary immediately squawked in alarm, sure she was about to hit the floor, but he caught her against his chest and carried her swiftly to the bed. Setting her down to stand next to it, Dante turned to grab the brown bag he'd returned with earlier.

"You will not believe what I found," he said with excitement as he opened the bag. "I did not know they had so many varieties of condom. Do you know they come dotted, ribbed, studded and flavored? Truly, flavored," he assured her when Mary raised her eyebrows slightly.

"And then they have for her pleasure and his pleasure," Dante went on, upending the bag on the end of the bed next to Bailey. "Justin said those are shaped differently to pleasure him or her. Although there are some that say for his and her pleasure too, and then they had some with a lubricant that warms or goes cold or something."

Mary stared with amazement at the pile of boxes on the bed and gasped, "Dear God, Dante, how many did you buy?"

"One of every kind," he assured her.

"One *box* of each kind," she muttered, and then pointed out, "There are at least ten or twelve in each box, and at least a dozen boxes."

"*Si*, but we can pick up more when we go shopping tomorrow," he assured her.

Mary just gaped at him with amazement. How many condoms did he think they were going to need, for heaven's sake?

Apparently a lot, she decided, when Dante paused and frowned before asking, "Do you think it would be hard to find condoms in Venezuela? Perhaps I should see if they sell them in bulk somewhere so we may take enough for our stay."

"Would there be enough room on the plane for them?" Mary asked dryly.

Much to her amazement, Dante took her seriously and waved the matter away as he bent to look through the boxes of condoms. "Oh, that is not a problem. We can have them shipped down on a cargo plane."

"Dante," Mary said quietly.

"*Si?*" He asked absently.

"Stop playing with your condoms and kiss me."

Pausing, he dropped the boxes and straightened to catch her under the arms and lift her to stand on the bed beside the small hill of condoms. He didn't kiss her then, but caught her nightgown and began lifting it slowly upward as he murmured, "You want me."

"*Si*," she said simply, using his word and gasping when his fingers brushed against her skin as they moved upward.

"You find me irresistible."

"*Si*," she admitted, raising her arms as he lifted the nightgown off over her head. The moment her hands were free, Mary reached for his T-shirt and began to tug it upward.

After tossing the nightgown aside, Dante helped her

remove his shirt, then quickly shed his jeans as well before gesturing toward the pile of condom boxes. "Which one shall I wear for you first?"

Mary had never imagined a man would be so enthralled with condoms. Resisting the urge to roll her eyes, she bent down and grabbed the first box her hand touched and then held it out to him.

"Ohhhh, glow in the dark. Good choice," Dante said with excitement and suddenly rushed away.

Mary stared after him with amazement, then relaxed when she realized he was turning out the lights. So she could better appreciate his glow in the dark penis when he donned the condom, she supposed. The man was over a hundred years old, but give him a glow in the dark condom and he turned into a twelve-year-old. Honestly, she thought with exasperation, and then gasped in surprise when she was suddenly tackled to the bed.

"Be careful of Bailey," she squealed with dismay, reaching out to try to find the dog.

"I moved her after turning out the lights," Dante said reassuringly as he crawled up her body. "I suspect things are going to get interesting on the bed and did not wish her harmed."

"Oh," Mary breathed, and then, "Ohhh," as his hands began to move. Her last thought, before he stole her ability to think of anything but him, was that things were always interesting on the bed with Dante Notte . . . glow in the dark penis or not.

Seventeen

"**W**hat about this dress?" Francis asked, holding up a knee length dress in a deep crimson. "You might need something for dressy nights out if you can drag Dante out of bed long enough for him to take you out to dinner."

Mary eyed the dress and almost winced. The color was just too close to the color of bagged blood for her to want to wear it. It was bad enough she had to drink the stuff; she didn't want to dress herself in it. Fortunately, she didn't have to say as much. Francis must have read her mind because he suddenly lowered the hanger and grimaced.

"Yes, I can see that would not do then."

Mary smiled faintly and said, "I think I have enough, Francis."

"Thank God," Lucian said dryly.

Mary glanced over with amusement at the three

men all now rising from the chairs by the change room. Dante, Russell, and Lucian had sat there since entering this last store over an hour ago, all three of them keeping their opinions and comments to themselves as Francis helped her pick out clothes. Until now, that was.

"Not quite," Francis countered, and pointed out, "We have everything but lingerie."

Lucian groaned and sat down again. Russell did as well. Dante, however, moved closer to offer, "I will help with that."

"Oh, no you won't," Mary said at once on a laugh. "Lucian would end up dragging you out of the changing room again like he did at the last store."

This was the third store Francis had dragged them to since leaving the Enforcer House that morning. The first hadn't seemed to have much in the way of clothes suitable for warm weather. They'd left the second in a rush after Dante had decided to "help" her change and scandalized nearly everyone in the store with the moans, groans, gasps and cries he'd drawn from Mary as he'd helped himself to her rather than just "help" her undress in the tiny cubicle. If Lucian hadn't interrupted and dragged Dante out when he had, they'd probably just now be waking up from unconsciousness in a heap on the dressing room floor. Or in jail for indecent something or other.

When they'd entered this store, Lucian had insisted Dante sit with him and Russell and leave Francis alone to help her.

"Mary is right," Francis said at once, stepping between Dante and Mary. "You would be of no help at all. Go sit down."

She smiled faintly as disappointment immediately filled Dante's expression and he turned to reclaim his seat, and then turned to Francis. "Actually, while I appreciate all your help today, Francis, I don't think I want you helping me pick out intimate apparel either. It's kind of . . . well . . . intimate," she said dryly.

"He understands completely," Lucian said, standing up again. "We shall leave you to it and go have a beverage in the food court while you get what you need."

Dante looked surprised at the announcement and stood up with a frown. "I do not want to leave her by herself. What if something happens?"

"We are not in Texas," Russell pointed out reasonably. "She is perfectly safe here in Toronto, Dante."

"Russell's right," Lucian announced, and then turned to begin collecting the clothing Francis had been setting on the last chair as he spoke. "We will pay for all of this now so that you need not be hindered by trying to keep track of it all while you select your intimate apparel. Russell, Francis and Dante will then take it out to the car and join me in the food court for a beverage," he added, handing items to each man until all the clothing was gathered but he held none. "I shall leave my credit card with the cashier. Just have her ring up everything you want and collect my credit card when she is finished with it, and then join us in the food court."

Turning away then, Lucian headed for the front of the store. Russell and Francis immediately followed, but Dante paused to kiss her quickly on the forehead.

"Shout if you have any problem, anything at all. I will hear you and come running."

"I'll be fine," she said with amusement. "I have shopped before, Dante."

"I know, *Tesoro*. But you are my life. I worry."

"You're sweet," Mary murmured and leaned up to kiss his cheek. "Now go. I have scanty silky bits to buy to tempt you with."

As she expected, his dark eyes immediately began to glow silver and he moved toward her, growling under his throat.

Laughing, Mary ducked the hand he reached for her with and waved to the front of the store. "Go."

"Dante!" Lucian's voice rang out. "Get your ass up here. We need the clothes for the girl to ring up."

Sighing, Dante gave her a smoldering look, and then turned to carry his portion of her clothes to the front of the store.

Mary watched him go with amusement, and then headed to the intimate apparel section of the store. Without Francis there fussing, she was much quicker at picking things. Some white panties and bras, some flesh colored, a couple strapless, and then some sexy sets purely for Dante's appreciation. Mary picked up some fishnet stockings too, purely for the bedroom. She was not going to actually wear them out of the air-conditioned hotel room. It was too hot in Venezuela for that, she was sure.

Having grabbed everything she thought she might need, Mary headed for the front of the store, surprised to see that the men were just leaving with about a dozen bulging bags of her clothes. She almost picked up speed and called out to them, but then caught herself and slowed instead, making sure they were out of the store before she neared the front.

The cashier was very friendly and helpful when Mary set her purchases on the counter and mentioned that Lucian Argeneau had left his credit card for her. She immediately called a second woman to the front so that she could fold and bag each item as it was rung up. Mary was out of there so quickly she thought she would probably catch up to the men if she moved quickly enough, so she didn't.

Mary didn't want to catch up to the men. She wanted to do something she knew none of them would approve of, and didn't want interference. She glanced in the direction the men had headed as she slipped out of the store. Reassured that none of them were looking her way, she then headed in the opposite direction, in search of the nearest exit.

"I still think I should have stayed behind with Mary," Dante grumbled as they headed toward the exit nearest to the parking garage where they'd left the SUV.

"She will be fine, Dante," Lucian said grimly. "Let it—" He paused and sighed as music began to play on his person.

Dante raised his eyebrows, recognizing the tune as a song that had seemed to play quite frequently for a while. He thought it was called "Happy," but instead of singing "Because I'm happy," Lucian's back pocket was singing, "Because I'm tacky."

"It is Weird Al Yankovich, not Pharrell Williams," Francis told Dante as if that should explain everything.

"Leigh annoyed with you again?" Russell asked with amusement.

"Obviously," Lucian growled as he plucked his phone from his pocket.

"Lucian's wife, Leigh, puts rather interesting ring-tones on his phone when she is annoyed with him," Francis explained to Dante, his lips twitching with amusement as the phone crooned, "Because I'm Tacky, wear my belt with suspenders and sandals with my socks."

"I am guessing," Russell said when Lucian merely peered at the phone face without answering, "That her irritation is because you will not let her go to Venezuela with you?"

"Yes," he snapped. "Although to me her anger is completely unreasonable. She should be glad that I want her and the twins nowhere near the bastards who have been kidnapping immortals."

"Because I'm Tacky," the phone began again and he answered it impatiently and said, "I will call you right back, Derby."

He hung up so quickly. There was no way this Derby could have responded, and then he turned to the men and said, "Take the bags to the car. I have something to do. I will meet you in the food court."

Lucian didn't wait for agreement, but turned his back to them and began punching at his phone.

"Why does he not just change the ringtone?" Dante asked curiously as they watched Lucian press the phone to his ear as he walked away.

"Because he does not know how," Francis said with amusement.

"He knows how," Russell said with certainty.

"Really?" Francis asked with amazement.

"Oh, yeah," Russell assured him. "I showed him."

"But then why does he not change it?" Francis asked with disbelief.

"For the same reason I wear salmon colored T-shirts on occasion," Russell said dryly. "Because he loves his life mate."

Dante bit back a smile at Francis's expression at this news. The man looked like he was going to swoon.

"Come on," Russell said affectionately. "I am thirsty and the sooner we get all this stuff in the car, the sooner we can get to the food court and get something to drink."

They started moving again then, but after a couple of steps, Francis said, "I wonder what Lucian is up to?"

"What do you mean?" Dante asked absently as they negotiated the shoppers everywhere.

"Well, he had the two new guys, Derby and Hulkboy follow us into the city in an SUV. They followed us around the Eaton Center while we shopped."

"Are you sure?" Russell asked, slowing to glance around at his partner.

"Yes. I saw them loitering outside the stores we were in," Francis assured him and when Russell started to look around, he said, "Oh, they stayed by the store when we left Mary there."

Dante slowed now, glancing back the way they'd come.

"That explains why Lucian was not worried about Mary," Russell said quietly. "He has babysitters watching her."

"Yes, but why?" Dante asked grimly.

When both men remained silent, he started back the way they'd come.

"Dante, wait!" Russell called, hurrying after him, and when he didn't even slow, added, "At least give me the damned bags so Francis and I can put them in the car."

Dante did pause then, just long enough to pass over the bags he carried and mutter, "Thanks," before heading off again at almost a run. It didn't take him long to reach the store where they'd left Mary. Hurrying inside, he spotted the cashier who had checked them out and didn't even bother to ask questions, but simply slid into her mind to learn that Mary had already checked out.

Cursing, he whirled and rushed back out of the store, only to come to an abrupt halt in front of it as he realized he had no idea where to look for her.

Mary paused outside the bank, fussed nervously with her hair, and then took a deep breath and entered. It was a large open space with the tellers at a counter along the right side and a row of offices along the left. There was also a receptionist's counter directly in front of her and Mary approached it and smiled tentatively at the woman waiting there.

"Hello. Can I help you?" the receptionist asked, returning her smile.

"Yes, I was hoping to see one of your loan officers," Mary said nervously, and then added, "Jane Winslow Mullins." Her daughter, Janie, had kept her maiden name when she'd married, merely adding her husband's last name to it.

"Your name?" the receptionist asked.

Mary hesitated. She couldn't say Mary Winslow. While she wanted to talk to her daughter, she had to be careful about who knew what. Finally, she said, "Alice Bonher."

She had an Aunt named Alice. Bonher, of course was her maiden name, and the moment she said it, she worried she maybe shouldn't have.

"Do you have an appointment?" the receptionist asked as she wrote her name on a slip of paper.

Mary frowned. She hadn't considered that problem. Biting her lip, she glanced toward the offices along the wall, and then peered back at the woman. After a hesitation during which she considered trying some of the mind control business on the woman, Mary sighed and shook her head. She had no idea how to control minds, so there wasn't much use. "No. I don't."

"I'll see if she is available," the woman said politely, and started tapping numbers on her phone as she asked, "It's about a loan?"

"Yes," Mary lied and then simply waited, her gaze sliding over the offices again in the hopes of catching a glimpse of her daughter. She was almost hungry for the sight. Her little girl. A kaleidoscope of memories slid through her mind. Janie as a baby, a toddler, taking her first steps. She was a grown woman now, in her thirties, with two daughters and a husband, but she would always be Mary's baby.

"She has a few minutes."

Mary swung back to the receptionist at that announcement to see that she'd stood and was gesturing for her to follow as she moved out from behind the reception counter and headed for one of the offices. Mary followed quickly, incredibly nervous at the thought of seeing Jane . . . which was ridiculous. She was her mother.

"Here you are," The receptionist said, leading her into a small but tidy office. The girl handed the slip of paper to Jane and then left the room.

Mary noted that she'd left the door open and considered closing it, but then left it and turned to peer at her daughter. She was a pretty girl, her dark hair framing a round face with bright green eyes. They looked nothing alike, but that had never mattered to Mary.

Janie smiled at her politely and gestured to one of the two chairs in front of her desk, "Please, sit, Ms. . . ." She paused to glance down at the slip of paper the receptionist had given her and Mary's smile faded. Janie hadn't recognized her of course. But then she looked totally different, she reminded herself. Still, she'd hoped . . .

What? Mary asked herself dryly. You thought your daughter would recognize some twenty-five-year-old-looking gal as her sixty-two-year-old mom? Dream on. And what are you even doing here? Mary asked herself. She couldn't turn her daughter, couldn't explain about nanos and immortals and whatnot. What had she hoped to gain from coming here to see her?

"Alice Bonher."

Mary glanced up to see that Jane was reading the name from the slip of paper the receptionist had given her.

Jane smiled crookedly. "That was my mother's maiden name. Small world, huh?" she commented with a smile as she took her seat.

Mary tilted her head slightly. "That *was* your mother's maiden name?"

"Yes. She died last week when her RV crashed and exploded."

Mary blinked at the bald announcement, and then realizing she should respond, murmured, "I see."

But she didn't see at all. Well, she did see a bit. Obviously Lucian or one of his men had done some mind-control nonsense and made everyone believe that she'd died in the RV crash, which was handy and even sensible. What she didn't understand was how her daughter could talk about her death with so little emotion. There was no grief, no sense of loss at all. She'd used the same tone Mary would have used to say she'd visited friends last week.

She frowned over that and was starting to grow upset when it occurred to her to wonder if this too wasn't Lucian's work. Could they have done something to Janie to make her accept the death more readily?

Mary glanced to her daughter, and seeing her questioning look, cleared her throat, and asked, "Was the funeral nice?"

"Oh, there was no funeral. There was no body. She burned up in the fire. They couldn't even separate her ashes from the ashes of the RV." Jane sighed and then admitted, "We're considering buying a plot, putting up a tombstone and holding a funeral ceremony, but it will have to wait until I go to Winnipeg next month."

"Next month?" Mary asked with dismay.

"Well, there was no sense rushing off to have it right away. We don't have a body, and the ceremony is only for myself and my brother and our families."

"That's it?" Mary asked, appalled. "What about her friends? Surely they would want to attend?"

"Yes, but they all kind of abandoned her when Dad died. I think the other women were nervous of having a newly widowed woman around their husbands. Mom was a good-looking woman, young for her age and witty."

"Oh," Mary sat back and smiled slightly at the comment. She'd never really seen herself that way. It was nice to know her daughter did.

"It's probably better she died anyway."

Mary blinked and stared at her with horror. "What? Why?"

"Because Dad was her whole life. She was terribly lonely when he died. I'd hate to think of her sitting alone and miserable in some little apartment in Winnipeg with no friends or anything."

Since that had been the future she'd foreseen for herself, Mary shouldn't have been upset at her daughter's envisioning it that way too, but she was. Scowling, she said with irritation, "Maybe she would have made new friends, or found a boyfriend."

"No way," Jane said emphatically, and then grimaced and said, "I have a friend whose mother did that. Started dating and acting ridiculous after her husband died. She wears clothes much too young for her: tight jeans and low-cut blouses."

Mary glanced down at the jeans and T-shirt she'd chosen from the storage room. The jeans were a bit snug, and the neckline was a scoop. She tugged at the neckline to cover the bit of bra that was peaking over the top.

"And she's dating men ten and even twenty years younger than her. The woman's acting like a hormone riddled teenager instead of the grandmother she is."

Mary bit her lip, an image of Dante rising in her mind. He didn't look a day over twenty-five. And hormone riddled was probably a good description of how they had both been acting even before he'd turned her.

"She's even buying condoms and having sex with these men," Jane said with disgust. "At sixty! Can you imagine? I mean there comes a time when you just have to hang up your dancing shoes, you know?"

"Hmm." Mary muttered and wondered when her daughter had become so prudish. People over sixty had every right to have sex, for heaven's sake. Hell, at least they didn't have to worry about birth control . . . usually, she added grimly.

"My mom was much too sensible to go in for that nonsense."

Mary squirmed in her seat.

"Jane? The Dresdens are here for their appointment."

Mary jerked around in her seat to peer at the speaker, but the woman was already walking away. She stared after her silently, her mind suddenly racing as memories began flooding her thoughts.

"I'm sorry. I forgot about the Dresdens," Jane said with a frown, glancing at the clock. "We could book an appointment for later. I have an opening in an hour."

Mary stared at her silently, debating coming back later, but why bother? She couldn't tell her who she was. Jane wouldn't believe it. And she couldn't explain about nanos or immortals, and she couldn't turn her either. Really, she shouldn't have come here at all.

"No," she said finally, getting to her feet. "I think I've changed my mind."

"Oh," Jane frowned slightly, but stood as well. "If you're sure?"

"Yes," Mary said solemnly. "My condolences on your loss."

"Thank you," Jane murmured, but an odd look came over her face as she watched her slide out from between the desk and the chair, and Mary turned quickly away, afraid she actually might recognize her after all.

That anxiety plaguing her, Mary walked quickly out of her daughter's office and slam bang right into a wide chest.

"Sorry," Mary muttered, glancing up, then froze as she recognized Lucian Argeneau. Staring at him wide-eyed, she swallowed guiltily. "I didn't—"

"I know," Lucian said simply, then stepped to the side and gestured for her to lead the way. When she started walking, he immediately fell into step beside her.

"Thank you," he said as they walked toward the exit.

Mary paused and glanced at him with surprise, and then asked warily, "For what?"

Stepping in front of her, he bowed his head and said softly, "For not making me wipe your daughter's memory, and crush Dante's heart by having to kill you."

Mary stiffened, then pushed past him and strode out onto the sidewalk, aware that he was on her heels. Her mind was suddenly buzzing, first with questions, and then with answers. The Eaton Center was in downtown Toronto. The Enforcer House was outside Toronto. It had been a hell of a drive to get here, and she'd been surprised they'd bothered when there were so many malls closer to the house. Now she thought she under-stood.

"You picked the mall," she guessed grimly.

"Yes," Lucian admitted.

"You somehow knew where my daughter works and picked this mall because it was nearby."

"Yes."

"You did it deliberately, to test me," she said bitterly.

"Yes."

Mary stopped abruptly and scowled at him. "That was a cheap trick."

"Yes," he said again, completely unapologetic.

She glowered at him briefly, and then bowed her head and muttered, "I'm sorry I failed your test."

"You did not fail. You did not tell her," he pointed out.

Mary let her breath out on a sigh, and then lifted her head. Eyeing him curiously, she asked, "Would you really have killed me had I told her?"

"Yes."

Mary nodded slowly and then turned to start walking again, but after several steps she commented, "It must be hard."

"What?" he asked with mild interest, keeping pace with her.

"Being the asshole that gets stuck with the shit jobs to protect his people," she said solemnly and noted that he inclined his head as if to acknowledge that he was that asshole.

"Someone has to do it," he said simply.

"And that someone is you."

"Yes."

Mary merely nodded. There was really nothing else to do or say.

They entered the Eaton Center through the same doors she'd exited from earlier, and moved at a quick clip toward the food court. They were still a good distance away, though, when Mary heard someone call her name. Slowing, she glanced around, and then paused as she saw Dante rushing toward them.

"Are you all right?" he asked, taking her by the upper arms as he reached them. His gaze slid over her as if looking for gaping wounds.

Managing a smile, Mary nodded her head. "Yes, of course. I'm fine," she whispered, and then leaned up to kiss him gently on the cheek.

"Where were you?" Dante asked as she lowered back to stand flat on her feet again. "I checked the store where we left you, but you were not there and then I looked everywhere for you, but—"

"She got lost." Lucian interrupted him blandly.

"Oh." Dante stared at Lucian for a moment, and then shifted his gaze to Mary, and she knew he didn't believe Lucian, but all he said was, "I was worried."

"Yes, yes," Lucian said impatiently. "She was lost, you were worried, now she is found and all is well. Now, go on and kiss her so we can get out of this blasted mall."

Mary tipped her head up to Dante and grinned. "You heard the man. Kiss me."

Dante chuckled softly and then lowered his head to do just that. But it was no, hi-I'm-happy-to-see-you buss, it was a full on, God-I-am-SO-happy-to-see-you-and-just-wish-you-were-naked-and-spread-eagled-on-the-floor smackeroo.

"Lord save me from new life mates," Lucian muttered with disgust and then cursed as Weird Al Yankovich's "Tacky" began to play somewhere nearby. For some reason that made Dante laugh, Mary noted, as he broke their kiss. She peered at him with bewilderment for a moment, and then realizing that Lucian was moving away, called, "Lucian?"

Pausing, he swung back, a phone in his hand.

"What?" he asked tersely as "Tacky" continued to play.

"The man you want in Venezuela is Dr. Dressler," she announced, her response just as terse.

Dante went still beside her. "What?"

Mary turned back to him and grimaced apologetically. "I overheard someone mention the name Dresden while I was . . ." She hesitated, not really wanting to explain what she'd done right there in the shopping mall, then shook her head and said, "It doesn't matter. The point is hearing the name Dresden made me remember the name Dressler."

She wasn't surprised at their blank expressions and explained, "In the van, the men were talking about how pleased Dr. *Dressler* was going to be to have a new turn to experiment on." Mary turned back to Lucian to add, "So I'm guessing that this Dressler is who you should be looking for in Venezuela."

Lucian's mouth tightened. Punching numbers in his phone, he turned away, snapping, "Let's go."

"Rude man," Mary muttered, glowering after him.

"I love you."

Mary swung back to stare at Dante.

"What?" she asked weakly.

"I love you," he repeated, and then rushed on, "Mary, I know you will think it is too soon for me to say that, but it really is not. You are beautiful, and I do not mean in looks, although you are beautiful in that way too," Dante added quickly. "But the beauty I speak of is in here." He covered the general vicinity of her heart with his hand. "You have so much heart and you are so brave and strong and you do not take shit from anyone. You are my perfect woman, and I love you."

Mary opened her mouth to tell him that she loved him too, and blurted, "I went to see my daughter."

Dante raised his eyebrows, cleared his throat, and said, "I see."

Mary grimaced, knowing those weren't the words he wanted to hear, but she went on. "The bank where she works is very close by and when I realized that . . . I just had to see her," she said apologetically. "I wanted to tell her everything and I almost did, but . . ."

"But?" he queried quietly.

"But then her memory would be wiped and I can't turn her anyway, so I didn't."

Dante nodded, and then rested his forehead on hers and said, "When I saw you were alive and well, I knew you must not have said anything to your daughter, but thank you for telling me."

Mary pulled back to frown at him. "You knew?"

"I suspected," he corrected. "After Lucian disappeared and Francis mentioned that two of the new hunters had followed us into town and he'd seen them loitering outside the store . . ." His mouth tightened. "I recalled reading in one of the reports that your daughter worked at a bank near here and immediately rushed back to the store to find you, but—"

"There are reports on me?" Mary squawked, interrupting him.

"Yes," he admitted, but simply continued, "And when I got to the store and you were gone, I feared you had slipped away to see your daughter and that Lucian had followed. I was calling Mortimer to ask him for the name of the bank when I spotted you and Lucian entering the mall."

Hands tightening reflexively, he said, "I am sorry you could not say anything to your daughter, Mary. And I am sorry you have lost everything because of me."

"I haven't lost everything," Mary said quickly trying to ease his obvious guilt. She then grimaced, and said, "Well, okay, I've lost a lot, but it's not your fault, and I have gained a lot too."

"Still—" he began unhappily.

"Dante," she interrupted softly. "I was in my twilight years. I maybe would have lived another couple decades as a mortal, and that would have been probably in some one-bedroom apartment with my kids and grandkids too far away or just too busy to visit. I would have been the lonely old cat lady, who sat around watching jeopardy. Only with a dog," she added wryly, then smiled and said, "Now, I have a whole new life. I'm healthy and strong." She shook her head. "The strength is amazing. Every year that I aged I seemed to lose more strength and there were more tasks I couldn't perform. Now there is nothing I am not strong enough to do." Mary smiled. "You gave me my life back, Dante, and you have given me your love. You've given me everything," she said solemnly, and then smiled crookedly and said, "Besides, I can keep track of the kids and grandkids. They're all big on Facebook and that Twitter business. I'll be able to follow their lives. I'll just miss the yearly visits," she added wryly.

"God, woman, I do love you," Dante groaned, hugging her tight.

"It's a good thing, because you're stuck with me now," she informed him wryly, and then pulled back to peer at him solemnly, and added, "Because, although it's too early to say it, I love you too."

"Oh, Mary," he breathed and covered her mouth with his.

"Hey! Lovebirds?"

Mary and Dante broke apart and glanced around to see that Lucian had returned and was scowling at them.

"Move your asses," he growled. "We leave for Venezuela as soon as we get to the airport."

"I thought we weren't leaving until tomorrow?" Dante said with a frown.

"That was before we knew exactly who we were looking for. Now that we do, I want to get moving on this," Lucian snapped and turned away to head for the doors again.

"What about Bailey?" Mary asked with a frown as they started to follow Lucian.

"Mortimer said that she could stay at the house and they would watch her," he said reassuringly. "It is better she not be dragged around with her broken leg."

"Yes," Mary agreed, and then noting the worry on his face, she squeezed his hand reassuringly. "We're going to get Tomasso back."

He swallowed and then offered her a weak smile. "Yes, we will and it will be all thanks to you. A gift that is almost as good as the gift of your love," he assured her.

Mary suddenly wanted to kiss him again, but they were nearly running now to try to catch up to Lucian.

Later, she told herself as she smiled back at him. There was no rush. They had all the time in the world now. *She* had all the time in the world now . . . thanks to the strong, sexy, and sweet man running beside her. He might think her love was a gift, but she thought his was too, and Mary intended to enjoy every minute of it.

Lynsay Sands was born in Canada and is an award-winning author of over thirty books, which have made the Barnes & Noble and New York Times bestseller lists. She is best known for her Argeneau series, about a modern-day family of vampires.

Learn more about her and her novels at:
www.lynsaysands.net

Love  Funny and ❤ Romantic novels?

Be bitten by a vampire

Merit thought graduate school sucked – that is, until she met some real bloodsuckers. After being attacked by a rogue vampire Merit is rescued by Ethan 'Lord o' the Manor' Sullivan who decides the best way to save her life was to take it. Now she's traded her thesis for surviving the Chicago nightlife as she navigates feuding vampire houses and the impossibly charming Ethan.

Enjoyed Some Girls Bite?
Then sink your teeth into Merit's next adventure: Friday Night Bites

For more Urban Fantasy visit www.orionbooks.co.uk/urbanfantasy
for the latest news, updates and giveaways!

Love 👄 Sexy and ⚥ Romantic novels?

PREPARE TO BE SWEPT AWAY
BY A CHANGELING'S DESIRE . . .

Faith NightStar is tormented by a glimpse of the future, showing her aching need and exquisite pleasure. Jaguar Changeling Vaughn D'Angelo is tormented by his desire for a cold, mysterious Psy woman. But can Vaughn restrain his passion, and Faith come to terms with hers, before their love overwhelms her sanity?

Captivated by SLAVE TO SENSATION? Then be swept away by the rest of the series: VISIONS OF HEAT and CARESSED BY ICE

FOR MORE URBAN FANTASY VISIT www.orionbooks.co.uk/urbanfantasy
for the latest news, updates and giveaways!

Love ❤ Romantic and 👄 Sexy novels?

Snuggle up with a Vampire...

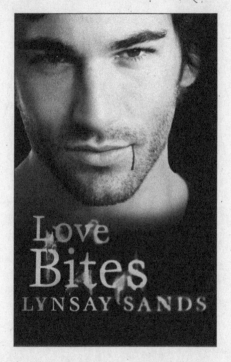

Etienne Argeneau can turn one human into a vampire in his lifetime – an honour his kind usually reserve for their life mates, to let their love live forever. But when Rachel Garrett, a beautiful coroner, saves his life at the cost of her own, Etienne has a choice to make. He can save her life in turn, and thus doom himself to an eternity alone, or he can watch his saviour die.

Have you fallen in love with **Love Bites?** Then why not continue the romance with: **Single White Vampire** and **Tall, Dark & Hungry**

For more Urban Fantasy visit www.orionbooks.co.uk/urbanfantasy for the latest news, updates and giveaways!

Love 💋 Sexy and ❤️ Romantic novels?

Get caught up in an Angel's Kiss . . .

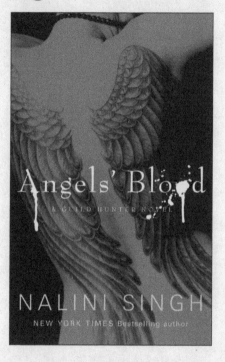

Vampire hunter Elena Deveraux knows she's the best – but she doesn't know if she's good enough for this job. Hired by the dangerously beautiful Archangel Raphael, a being so lethal that no mortal wants his attention, only one thing is clear – failure is not an option . . . even if the task she's been set is impossible. Because this time, it's not a wayward vamp she has to track. It's an archangel gone bad.

Enthralled by Angel's Blood?
Then get caught up in the rest of the series: Archangel's Kiss

For more Urban Fantasy visit www.orionbooks.co.uk/urbanfantasy
for the latest news, updates and giveaways!

Love  Funny and ◑ Romantic novels?
Then why not discover

IMMORTALITY'S BITE

IMMORTALITY BITES

Bitten & Smitten

Michelle Rowen

Blind dates can be murder – or at least that's how Sarah Dearly's turned out.
Her dates 'love bites' turn her into a vampire and make her a target for a zealous
group of vampire hunters. Lucky for her she's stumbled onto an unlikely saviour
– a suicidal vampire who just might have found his reason to live: her.

ENJOYED BITTEN AND SMITTEN? THEN STAKE OUT MORE IN THE SERIES:

FANGED & FABULOUS and LADY & THE VAMP

FOR MORE URBAN FANTASY VISIT www.orionbooks.co.uk/urbanfantasy
for the latest news, updates and giveaways!

ABOUT GOLLANCZ

Gollancz is the oldest SF publishing imprint in the world. Since being founded in 1927 Gollancz has continued to publish a focused selection of bestselling and award-winning authors. The front-list includes **Ben Aaronovitch**, **Joe Abercrombie**, **Charlaine Harris**, **Joanne Harris**, **Joe Hill**, **Alastair Reynolds**, **Patrick Rothfuss**, **Nalini Singh** and **Brandon Sanderson**.

As one of the largest Science Fiction and Fantasy imprints in the UK it is no surprise we have one of the most extensive backlists in the world. Find high quality SF on Gateway written by such authors as **Philip K. Dick**, **Ursula Le Guin**, **Connie Willis**, **Sir Arthur C. Clarke**, **Pat Cadigan**, **Michael Moorcock** and **George R.R. Martin**.

We also have a strand of publishing in translation, which includes French, Polish and Russian authors. Gollancz is home to more award-winning authors than any other imprint, with names including **Aliette de Bodard**, **M. John Harrison**, **Paul McAuley**, **Sarah Pinborough**, **Pierre Pevel**, **Justina Robson** and many more.

The SF Gateway
More than 3,000 classic, rare and previously out-of-print SF novels at your fingertips.
www.sfgateway.com

The Gollancz Blog
Bringing you news from our worlds to yours. Stories, interviews, articles and exclusive extracts just for you!
www.gollancz.co.uk

GOLLANCZ
LONDON

BRINGING NEWS
FROM OUR WORLDS
TO YOURS . . .

Want your news daily?

The Gollancz blog has instant updates
on the hottest SF and Fantasy books.

Prefer your updates monthly?

Sign up for our
in-depth newsletter.

www.gollancz.co.uk

Follow us 🐦 @gollancz

Find us ⨍ facebook.com/GollanczPublishing

Classic SF as you've never read it before.

Visit the SF Gateway to find out more!

www.sfgateway.com